# Blessed Assurance

*Inspirational Short Stories*
*Full of Hope and Strength for Life's Journey*

VICTORIA CHRISTOPHER MURRAY
JACQUELIN THOMAS
S. JAMES GUITARD
PATRICIA HALEY
TERRANCE JOHNSON
MAURICE GRAY

Literally Speaking Publishing House
Washington, DC
www.LiterallySpeaking.com

Literally Speaking Publishing House
2020 Pennsylvania Avenue, NW #406
Washington, DC 20006

© 2003, *Blessed Assurance*: Inspirational Short Stories
　　　Full of Hope and Strength for Life's Journey
© 2003, *Baby Blues* by Patricia Haley
© 2003, *Traveling Mercies* by Maurice Gray
© 2003, *A Sprig of Hope* by Jacquelin Thomas
© 2003, *Lust and Lies* by S. James Guitard
© 2003, *Sword of the Lord* by Terrance Johnson
© 2003, *The Best of Everything* by Victoria Christopher Murray

ISBN: 1-929642-12-1
LSPH hard cover printing 2003, Printed in the U.S.A.

# Author Biographical Information

**Maurice Gray** is the owner/operator of Write The Vision, Inc., formed in January 2000 to facilitate the publication of his first novel, *To Whom Much Is Given* (currently in its third printing). Maurice's second novel, *All Things Work Together*, is scheduled for release in May 2003.

**S. James Guitard** is the author of the ESSENCE Best-selling book, *Chocolate Thoughts*. He is a native of New York, who now resides in the Washington, D.C. area. He has devoted his professional career to improving the quality of education for poor and minority children as a college instructor, administrator, school teacher, Capitol Hill lobbyist, as well as an education policy specialist. *Mocha Love:* A Novel of Passion, Honesty, Deceit and Power is the second release of a series of books, plays, and movie scripts written by Guitard.

**Patricia Haley** lives in Pennsylvania with her husband, Jeffrey. With an engineering degree from Stanford Univ. and an M.B.A. from the Univ. of Chicago, readers are often surprised to hear that she is writing faith-based fiction, given her technical and business background. Patricia self-published her debut novel, *Nobody's Perfect,* in 1998 and sold nearly 20,000 copies, making many best sellers list, including #1 African-American paperback. Her newest titles are *No Regrets* (2002) and *Blind Faith* (2003).

**Terrance Clayton Johnson** is a freelance sports writer, publisher and author. In 1996 he completed his undergraduate studies at Chicago State University where he studied print journalism. He is the author of *Shades of Black*, *Eyes of Faith* and his latest release, *Baptism by Fire*.

**Victoria Christopher Murray** is the author of Essence best sellers, *Temptation* and *JOY*. She is a member of Delta Sigma Theta and a section editor with Black Issues Book Review. A native New Yorker, Victoria now lives in Los Angeles.

**Jacquelin Thomas** is the author of several books including *Singsation, The Prodigal Husband* and *A Change Is Gonna Come*. She has lived in southern California for eleven years with her husband and children but now makes her home in North Carolina. Jacquelin is currently at work on her next project.

# *Author Acknowledgements*

## S. James Guitard

Thank You, Jesus, for Your strength, power, mercy, grace and love.

To grandmother, Bernice J. Guitard; my mom and dad, Helena & Charles Paylor; my brothers and sisters: Shaun Reel, Andre Paylor, Tiomora Paylor, Lauren, Octavia, Olivia and Thia, I love you all.

To all of the authors: Victoria Christopher Murray, Jacquelin Thomas, Patricia Haley, Terrance Johnson, Maurice Gray, thank you for persevering and allowing God to use you in an anointed project. Each one of you has written a touching and moving story that testifies about the power, hope, strength, grace and mercy of our Lord and Savior Jesus Christ.

To all the readers of *Chocolate Thoughts*, *Mocha Love* and *Blessed Assurance* thank you so very much for taking the time to read and recommend my books to family, friends and colleagues. I'm very thankful and deeply appreciative. Your support makes a big difference. We are in this together. Your feedback is always welcomed and important to me. You can e-mail me at author@JamesGuitard.com. I look forward to hearing from you. Take care and God Bless.

To Maurice Calhoun of M&M Calhoun Enterprises, your website design for *Blessed Assurance* is a testimony of the myriad talents you possess in the areas of website development and management. It is also a testimony of your willingness to utilize your gifts for God.

"Have I not commanded you? Be strong and of good courage; do not be afraid, nor dismayed, for the LORD your God is with you wherever you go." Joshua 1:9

"The steps of a good man are ordered by the LORD, And He delights in his way. Though he fall, he shall not be utterly cast down; For the LORD upholds him with His hand." Psalm 37:23

To the Literally Speaking Publishing House staff – my deepest appreciation for all of your hard work and dedication. With each new publication, you are further establishing a level of excellence that very few will every reach, let alone imagine. Special thanks to Maurice Calhoun, Paul Robinson, Donald Burrell, Gregg Wragg, Paul Morgan, Anthony Harris, Lora Brown and Shaun Stevenson.

To Mychelle Morgan, Executive Editor, Jill Peddycord, Senior Editor, Jason Harley, Associate Editor, and Marie Carter, Contributing Editor at LSPH, there are not enough words that can be written or said to express my profound gratitude for all that you have meant to this project.

To Rod Dennis of Colabours Communications, the premiere graphic artist designer in the nation, I am extremely blessed that God saw fit to utilize the vast talents that you possess for the book jacket designs of *Chocolate Thoughts*, *Mocha Love* and now: *Blessed Assurance*. Your wisdom and vision capture the concepts we had discussed in ways other graphic designers can only dream about. You are unquestionably the best that there is in the industry.

To Catherine McAtee-Luick, Marcel Southern and everyone connected to *Blessed Assurance*, God Bless.

## Victoria Christopher Murray

There is not much to say—everyone knows their importance in my world. My parents know how blessed I feel to be their daughter. My daughter knows that she is the center. My sisters know my love for them. My in-laws (who have never figured out that I am not their blood relative) know that I have been given the best extended family. My friends—goodness, I have the best in the world. And all that I am, all that I have, has been given to me by my Lord and Savior, Jesus Christ.

I do have two special acknowledgements. First to my niece, Ciara Larisse Powell, God's miracle who has shown us the truth of God's blessed assurances. In you I see the goodness, mercy and promises of God. Ciara, you are my heart. To my grandmother, Zelda McCann Wilson who passed away days after I finished this story. Grandmother had me read sections to her as I was writing. I believe she knew she was going to be with the Lord soon and she wanted to connect with my writings one last time. Thank you, grandmother, for being such a fan. No one else read each of my books three times. I will miss you, but I thank God for the years we had together.

And special thank you to Frank Fontana, General Manager and Richard Petty, Executive Chef of Reign Restaurant in Beverly Hills for their support of this project.

### Maurice Gray

First, I thank my Lord and Savior Jesus Christ for this opportunity. I also want to thank the following: My parents Maurice, Sr. and Joan Gray and my sister Regina Gray for listening to me while I wrestled with writing this story and for helping me brainstorm when my creativity was running dry. Victoria Christopher Murray, for her encouragement and editorial feedback down the home stretch. All of my fellow authors in this project we did it! And finally, Literally Speaking, for taking this project on.

### Terrance Clayton Johnson

First and foremost I give thanx to God the Father, Son and Holy Spirit. Lord, You are my all and all. Thanx to my mother, Daisy Johnson, my Pastor, Dr. Donald L. Parson, and my Proverb 31 bride Leah; big ups to my siblings Albreta, Spring, Travis Jr., Darnell, Lyonel, Bertram, Trent, Tracie and Denise; much love to my FBX siblings Patricia (big Sis), James G, Big Mo, Victoria, Jacqueline, Marni, and of course Audrey, Jeffrey and Mark the Hammer. Much love for ya.

### Jacquelin Thomas

I would like to give honor to God, who is the head of my life. I am so thankful for His love and grace.

I would be remiss if I didn't acknowledge my loving husband and best friend, Bernard. You are the delight of my life and I am so thankful that you are in my life. Achieving the dream of a lifetime wouldn't mean a thing if I didn't have you to share it with. You complete me.

### Patricia Haley

Thanks to my loving husband, Jeffrey Glass, for your inspiration, ideas, and encouragement. Rena Burks, 'my sister', I can't leave you out. I needed a title and in ten minutes you had three. That's how you are, always there for me and I love you. To my 'little sister' Frances Walker, thanks for your perspective. Audrey D. Williams, much praise for helping me to coordinate the initial East-coast faith based tour. May God bless your efforts as you continue to walk in faith on His word. Finally, thank you to the LSPH publishing team and my fellow authors -- Victoria (my sister in Delta Sigma Theta and in Christ), Terrance, James, Maurice, and Jacquelin. Who knew that our tour would lead to something as incredible as the creation of *Blessed Assurance*. I am grateful to the Lord for allowing us to see this project to fruition. I pray that each story will glorify God and bless His holy name.

# *Blessed Assurance*

*Inspirational Short Stories*
*Full of Hope and Strength for Life's Journey*

## CONTENTS PAGE

# Baby Blues

## By
## Patricia Haley

S arah didn't notice the busboy overfilling her glass of water and scurrying to wipe the spillage before it reached the edge of the table and possibly her lap. "I know this is an enormous and, perhaps, bizarre request, but I couldn't come to anyone else but you." Sarah pulled her chair in as snug as she could and leaned across the table to grab Gayle's hand. "I want you to have my husband's baby."

Gayle choked on the iced tea she was drinking. Her back stiffened, eyes dilated and bewilderment danced across her face without resistance.

"I'm not crazy," Sarah assured her friend. "My husband never talks about having children anymore, but I'm sure he wants to father a child with his own genes."

"What about Lotus? He's like a son to you and Carl," Gayle reminded Sarah.

"We love our nephew, true enough, but I'd like for Carl to have a child of his own."

"Sarah, I don't understand. Why don't you have your

own husband's baby?"

"Now you know I'm too old to be trying to have a baby. There's no substitute for natural." Gayle looked away. Sarah sensed her discomfort and gently squeezed the hand that she was still holding in an effort to regain Gayle's attention. "...And that's okay with me. I have a wonderful relationship with my husband. He is my soul mate, and we have accomplished more in our twenty years of marriage than most couples can only dream of doing in a hundred. This baby is my gift to him, and you're the only one I'd trust to carry this out."

Gayle and Sarah had been friends for more than a decade. Ever since Sarah joined the aerobics class that Gayle used to teach, an instant bond had formed between the two women. Gayle had even worked as an assistant to Sarah for nearly seven years before making the decision last year to enroll in nursing school as a thirty-fifth birthday gift to herself.

Carl was nearly sixty, but undoubtedly a catch. The thought of having a baby with her best friend's husband, a man with class, finesse, money and appealing genes, was almost too much to grasp. It made her lightheaded. She considered pinching herself to make sure the blood was flowing and oxygen was still getting to her brain. "Sarah, you have to admit, it's not everyday a request like this comes along. Are you sure, absolutely sure, this is what you want?"

"Positive. Carl's happiness means so much to me that I'm willing to put aside any uneasiness I might have about not being the mother of his child and let it happen with someone else." She squeezed Gayle's hand in acknowledgment. "Besides, it's not like I'm asking him to have some adulterous relationship with a stranger for his own pleasure and then a baby pops up. That's why it has to be you, Gayle. You're the only one who can be intimate with my husband without having any on going romantic interest in him. You're the only woman I trust with Carl."

"What about Carl?"

Sarah laughed and took a sip of the flavored iced tea sitting in front of her. "Oh Carl, you know he would never be interested in any other woman but me. I'm definitely not worried about him falling for anybody." Sarah winked, wearing a smile of confidence, and patted the back of Gayle's hand, which was lying flat on the table.

Thoughts were swirling. Gayle couldn't get her words and emotions to line up. What was Sarah saying, that Carl couldn't find her attractive and become smitten? Other men had. Carl was near perfect, but even he was made of flesh and hormones.

"I meant, how does he feel about being with me?"

"Well, that's kind of a little problem," Sarah admitted.

"What, with me?"

"No, more so with the concept. I haven't told him yet."

"Sarah, you haven't told him, but you're already asking me?"

"Don't worry. I know my husband. I'll talk him into it. All I need is for you to agree."

"I'm not sure what to say."

"Just say yes and make two old people happy by giving them something they can't attain on their own."

"I... I don't know."

"Please, I'm begging you to do this for me and for Carl."

Gayle had to force her emotions to remain under control. She wanted to leap forward and scream, yes! Yes, I'll do it, but such an unbridled display of enthusiasm might give Sarah a glimpse of the direction her heart was heading. In case this entire fantasy turned out to be real, she needed to take it slow and not blow the only chance she'd ever get for happiness with a good man. She decided that reserved, but calculated, was how she had to respond.

"Okay, I'll do this, if you're sure."

"Thank you, Gayle, thank you." Sarah stretched back across the corner of the small table to embrace Gayle. "I love you, and you won't be sorry. I promise." She jumped up from her seat and fumbled to get her purse strap freed from the back of the chair. "We can work out the details later. Right now I have to get home and put the final touches on my anniversary celebration. You have made me so happy, and Carl will be, too." Sarah grabbed the bill. "Feel free to stay and finish your lunch." She kissed Gayle on the cheek and told her, "Thank you for being our friend," and hurried out of the restaurant.

Gayle remained in her seat, stunned. What had she agreed to do? The Abrahams were a couple she respected and admired, perhaps envied a little. She chewed on the implications for a bit longer and finally relaxed in her chair. Why not have a taste of what they shared? She felt young, vibrant, and ready. Carl could be the father of her children, and whatever else naturally came with it.

## Chapter 2

Balloons and streamers filled the banquet room of the Hyatt. Life was good. Sarah couldn't believe twenty years had already passed since she married Carl, right after her thirtieth birthday. International travel, the comforts of a mansion, a circle of loved ones, leadership in the church, good health and a successful business framed their lives. No need to ask for any more, but, selfish or not, she did want more for Carl. He deserved this special gift, and she was the only one who could make it happen. Carl made sure their marriage was grounded in prayer, and it was good, but some tasks could be handled without reinforcements from Heaven. She grabbed her husband's hand as they stood before the crowd at the podium preparing to express a few words of gratitude in celebration of their anniversary.

"I have the wife of my dreams. God is good, real good," Carl was quick to say and sealed it with a strong embrace and kiss.

Gayle watched from the back of the room, fidgeting and hanging on Carl's every word. This would be the performance of her life. She had to act normal and show no unusual interest in Carl, despite the raging fire of affection scorching inside.

The crowd applauded and encouraged Sarah to make a speech. She pulled in tight to Carl and drew the microphone close.

"I have a wonderful husband. I am looking forward to

19

spending at least another fifty years with him." She looked into his eyes and passionately laid her hand on his chest. "All I have to do now is get him to retire," she said, stirring laughter from the crowd.

The evening continued, and a good time blanketed the room making it easy for anyone in the place to walk away feeling fulfilled.

One of Carl's CEO buddies from another company offered his congratulations. "So, what's this business about retiring, Carl? I didn't know you were giving it any consideration?"

"I'm ready to retire, but there's nobody to take over my company. Whatever God has in store He hasn't revealed."

"What about your nephew? I thought you were grooming him for an executive position."

"Who? Lotus? Are you kidding? It would require a miracle to get him ready to run the business on his own. He claims to be finding himself. At the rate he's going, I wouldn't be able to retire until I'm a hundred years old and would probably have reservations even then."

"That's how it goes sometimes. Your children don't always have an interest in taking over the business you've spent years building. This generation of youth is a whole new breed."

"You're telling me," Carl affirmed, shaking his head.

"I guess your desire to golf year-round isn't on the horizon yet, buddy." He patted Carl on the back. "You'll have to stay in the game, ducking and dodging hostile takeovers like the rest of us, and you're just the one to do it.

Congratulations, my friend—continued success."

The men shook hands.

"Thanks for the encouragement. It carries a great deal of weight coming from you." Carl had joked with his colleague about hostile takeovers but deep down never worried about such an event. God had prophesied, established and multiplied the business. There was no need to worry about the livelihood of the company when God Almighty had backed it. Carl looked around the room feeling blessed to have so many people impact his and Sarah's lives. God had promised him so many things in his youth, and almost everything, except for one, had come to pass.

## Chapter 3

The evening had been more spectacular than Sarah had hoped. She sat in her bedroom reflecting on the abundance of love and support that had filled the banquet hall. Carl unsnapped the buttons on his tuxedo and began disrobing. "I don't know what to do about our company. God gave this business to me, and I can't understand why He hasn't made provisions for us to be able to hand it down to anyone."

Sarah looked up at Carl through her vanity mirror but didn't offer any advice.

"I am so disappointed with that nephew of ours," he admitted to Sarah.

"Face it, Carl, we spoiled him."

"What's wrong with wanting to give your child a good

life? So we made sure he had a few comforts in life. Big deal. There is no justification for his irresponsibility. We raised him in a godly home, but you'd never know it by the way he's living. All he does is hop back and forth between Los Angeles and New York dabbling into all kinds of shameful activities."

Sarah let the thought of Carl fathering his own child bounce around in her spirit, ignoring any opposition. She wasn't sure where the original notion had come from, but this was probably the most suitable time to verbalize the idea to her unsuspecting husband. She wrestled with the idea in her head one last time before letting it lunge forward with the force of a tidal wave. "What about having a child?"

Carl stopped and jerked his head around so rapidly that he had to rub his neck to ease the ping of pain. "What!"

"Let's have a baby. I know we haven't talked about it in years, but why not?"

"I'm a little surprised to hear you talk about having a child. For the past seven years you've consistently said you're too old. If I didn't know you better, I'd think the bubbles from the sparkling cider tingled your brain cells and sent you to a temporary place of euphoria." Carl walked over to Sarah's table and kissed her on the neck.

"I'm serious, Carl. Now is the time for us to add a baby to the family."

Carl knew his wife well and could detect by the tone in her voice that she was serious. In their idyllic years together, he'd never denied her even the smallest of requests. Outside of serving God, his next task, which he held in high regard, was to please Sarah and make life wonderful for her every day that he could. If she wanted a baby, there wasn't much to think about in making his decision. "If that's what you want, I'm with you."

Sarah fumbled with the perfume bottle on her vanity table. "Carl," she spoke softly without looking up to meet his eyes, "I just turned fifty. You know I'm too old to have a baby."

Carl threw his hands up in the air and let out a wail of merriment. "So why are we having this conversation about a baby if you can't have one?"

"Because...," she began to say, but paused long enough to mount the courage to spill it out, "I want you to have a baby with Gayle."

"What!" Carl laughed until his stomach shook. "Gayle!" He continued undressing. "You are funny. You almost had me there. Gayle," he said again, continuing with the humor.

"Carl," she said, turning away from the mirror and connecting with her husband's eyes, "I'm serious. I want you to have a baby with Gayle."

"You can't be serious. Have you lost your mind?"

"Think about it, we need an heir and Lotus isn't it. What other options do we have?"

"What about adoption, or something else, anything except what you're suggesting. My goodness, Sarah, Gayle is your friend. I can't have a child with her. You're my wife, the only woman I plan to see naked, let alone touch intimately. There is no way. I'd rather be childless than sleep with your friend, our friend for that matter." He stood in the middle of his walk-in closet, leaning on a shelf and shaking his head. "Don't you remember the prophecy I got from Rev. Daniels at our wedding?"

"Of course I do, but that was so long ago. Let's face it, Carl. What Rev. Daniels told you hasn't manifested, and it isn't going to at this rate. We need to be realistic and take matters into our own hands instead of waiting around for some angel to deliver a baby on our doorstep."

"Well, if God wants us to have children, we'll have them. If not, my life is complete just the way it is, with you."

"Rev. Daniels said that your offspring would be too many to number. He didn't say mine, he said yours."

"I'm not listening to this craziness. I don't know what's gotten into you, but the answer is no."

Sarah went to her husband and hugged him while letting the tears ease up and over the ridge of her eyelids. She nestled into his arms. "Carl, I love you and I love what we have, but you deserve a child. I would love to have given you one, but we both know I'm too old to bear a child. Gayle is the only woman I trust to be alone with you. It's not the most ideal solution. It's the only solution. When we're eighty years old, your son would be approaching a point in life where he could take over the business. Imagine the pride we'd both have in that moment."

Carl couldn't deny the satisfaction he tasted with the mere notion of having a child, maybe a son, and an heir to take over the company he had labored to develop. He didn't have complete peace about it, but Sarah loved him, and if she was willing to make such a tremendous sacrifice for his happiness, the least he could do was to give his support in return. He squeezed his wife tightly and reflected on the prophecy he'd received in the past. Maybe this was the way his offspring was intended to come, from the womb of another woman. It seemed a bit odd, but pleasing Sarah was more important to him than some twenty-year-old word of prophecy.

"I'll do it."

## Chapter 4

Attending the party last night had been difficult, but Gayle felt she'd pulled off the charade with neither Carl nor Sarah the wiser. Gayle was sitting on pins and needles, awaiting Sarah's call. It was like a miracle, more than she could ever have dared to dream. Carl could be hers. If he decided to participate in the arrangement, her world would be flipped upside down. Her mind went traveling through the mansion, on exotic vacations, with Carl and the baby, of course. She sailed down the boulevard, dipping in and out of classy boutiques. A dab of good sense crept into her head. This was nonsense, wishful thinking. Carl was an intelligent, successful businessman. He wouldn't dare go for a surrogate relationship. Gayle shook herself back into the clutches of reality and prepared a cup of tea.

By eight-thirty, the phone was ringing. Gayle knew it was Sarah and braced herself for whatever news was heading her way.

"He has agreed," Sarah excitedly shared with Gayle.

Gayle was shocked but happy, anxious but composed. She didn't know how to respond—with a thanks, a congratulations, a yahoo, or what? For now, the less said the better. Letting Sarah do the talking would be the best approach for handling a potentially sensitive matter.

"Gayle, I can't tell you how grateful I am to you for doing this. Not everyone could be such a dear friend."

"I'm not clear about the logistics. How are we going to work this?" Gayle asked.

"You know, I haven't really given it any thought. We know you can't conceive in our house or yours."

"Maybe we should go away for the weekend," Gayle suggested.

Sarah took Gayle's input under advisement and found favor with it. "Going away with Carl is a good idea. Gayle, I know I've told you this repeatedly, but you are a true lifesaver. You are special to us, and no one else in the world is more suited to do this with Carl than you."

Gayle agreed with Sarah's sentiments. She was the only woman worthy of carrying Carl's child.

"Don't worry about anything. I will make all of the arrangements," Sarah assured. "I will try to make this as comfortable as possible for you. You'll have a nice suite at the Ritz Carlton. I'll arrange for a personal chef and private butler, that way you won't have to leave the room. I'm thinking the privacy will help you be able to concentrate on the task at hand and conceive immediately, because I know you don't want to waste two weekends cramped in some room with Carl." Sarah giggled at the thought of poor Gayle having to be sequestered in a hotel room with her husband for an entire weekend. She knew it wasn't right to subject Gayle to so much isolated time with him, a man that didn't find her intimately appealing. On top of the awkwardness, they had to somehow manage to conceive a child. It was preposterous but had to be done. Sarah contemplated praying for the conception but felt a bit out of sorts about getting God involved in such an unconventional situation. She decided it would be better to wing it with her own abilities.

## Chapter 5

Sarah had diligently contacted the travel agent to make the air, hotel and limousine reservations earlier in the week. All was set, and the day to drop them off at the airport was finally here. She was overwhelmed with excitement and anticipation.

Carl and Gayle said goodbye to Sarah without much uneasiness.

Long after Carl and Gayle had cleared security, Sarah was standing on the balls of her feet with her arm extended into the air, waving in the direction she saw them vanish into. She skipped back to the parking garage, knowing this would be the weekend, the magical moment when Carl would become a father and she a mother.

The flight landed on time, and the two travelers maneuvered to the ground transportation for their ride. Carl sat on one side of the limousine peering out the smoke-colored window with Gayle braced against the door on the other side. The distance between she and Carl seemed like a continent apart. She wanted to utilize every second in his presence to work her magic. No time to waste. "The weather is beautiful. What a great day to be out, don't you think?"

"Uh, huh."

"Boy I'm hungry. I hope the hotel has something good on the menu. Have you ever stayed at this Ritz?" she asked him.

"No."

Come on now, Gayle thought. He was going to have to do better than this. Sure, he was nervous and maybe a bit apprehensive, but no fear. She knew how to break down the strongest resistance. It had been some years since she'd used her old tactics and was admittedly rusty, but charming a man right out of his shoes was like riding a bike. It wasn't something she had completely lost when several years ago she committed to attending church regularly.

The rest of the ride to the Ritz Carlton didn't foster much more conversation. The limo pulled into the circle drive of the hotel, and Carl got out before the chauffeur could reach his door. He stood at the back of the car and let the driver assist Gayle.

Opening the door was a basic courtesy Carl extended to any woman, but he held back this once, feeling a bit reserved about how to act with Gayle.

The penthouse was ready, and the hotel manager escorted them personally up the private elevator to give them a guided tour of the unit as well as to review the long list of amenities. The bellhop was waiting by the door with their luggage.

When the wooden double doors leading into the penthouse were opened, Gayle's mouth flew open. The skyline was visible through the floor-to-ceiling windows. Fresh cut bouquets, like the ones seen in lobbies, were everywhere. Without checking out every room, from what she could see, the suite was two to three times the size of her entire apartment. Such grandeur wouldn't take much getting used to. If she could stretch this out for several months, it would be an absolute wonder.

"You can set my garment bag in one of the smaller bedrooms," Carl instructed the bellhop while handing him a tip. "Her suitcases can be put in the master suite."

The bellhop moved as directed with the luggage.

"We have a maid, a chef and a personal assistant reserved exclusively for you. Would you like for me to summons them immediately?" the hotel manager asked.

"No, I don't believe we'll need anyone right now, except for the chef. We'll call if we need the maid."

"Very well, Mr. Abraham. If you need anything, sir, please don't hesitate to phone me personally." He handed Carl his business card. "We will make sure your stay with us is most enjoyable."

"I'm sure it will be fine." Carl slid the card into his pocket and pulled out a tip and discretely handed it to the hotel manager.

"Jean Pierre is the chef that we have especially selected for you. I will send him in immediately. Enjoy your stay, sir and ma'am."

Gayle wasn't expecting such lavish accommodations. She'd stayed in nice hotels many times, particularly when she was a personal assistant to Sarah and traveled with her. The penthouse went far beyond her typical two-room suite. This was a house, their house, Carl and hers, the one where their new family and life would begin. "I'll be back, Carl. I'm going to change into something more comfortable."

All aspects of the event had to be perfect. Once he felt the connection, no telling what doors might open down the road for her and the baby's father. This was a delicate matter, requiring time to manifest. She needed ample time to work on Carl and get to know him in a personal way. After all, they were having a child together. She wanted the baby. She continued to block out any thoughts of morality or spirituality. Right or wrong was irrelevant. After all, she didn't go looking for Carl. He was sent to her.

She unpacked her lingerie and protection, which would be the secret weapon she needed to create adequate time for the two of them to gel. There was no reason to rush Carl through the process. He deserved the opportunity to enjoy every second Sarah had planned for them, and maybe a few extras.

\*      \*      \*

Friday night wouldn't budge, and Sarah couldn't sit still. She wanted to know how it was going. Was it over? Did it work? She picked up the phone a countless number of times, but convinced herself that the distraction would only prolong the project.

The weekend sauntered by, and it was finally time to rush to the airport and find out.

## *Chapter 6*

Sarah felt strange lying next to Carl on Sunday night. Gayle would be having the baby, but she wanted to be included, from beginning to end. He slept comfortably while she laid in the dark wondering about the details of the past few days but letting the quiet squeak by without asking her husband any questions. She wanted to know what, how and when events took place over the past two days. Then again, did she?

Sarah rolled over and the clock displayed two-forty-five. She pulled the sheet up to her neck and closed her eyes, not sure if it was to block out her creeping emotions or attempt to fall asleep. Didn't matter to her which one it was. Either would be a welcomed guest.

Friday afternoon, Sarah met Gayle at their usual restaurant. Gayle had used a home pregnancy test, and the results hadn't been favorable. The two women agreed it would be best to have the doctor do one. Gayle had gotten the doctor's results earlier in the morning, and she was meeting Sarah to share the news.

Gayle picked up the menu and flipped through the first few pages.

Sarah put her hand on top of the menu and pushed it to the table. "Don't even try it."

"What!" Gayle responded.

"Don't keep me in suspense. Tell me, are we pregnant?"

Gayle took a swallow of water from the glass sitting in

front of her. Sarah sat on the edge of her seat with eyes wide open and fixed on her friend. Gayle shook her head to say no. Sarah's shoulders and head drooped, and she didn't respond immediately to the news.

Gayle reached over to rub her hand. "Don't worry. We can try again. I know how much this means to you. The doctor said I'm ovulating right now. This is the best time to try."

"When? You mean now, like this weekend?"

"Might as well go ahead and get it over with," Gayle said.

Sarah squinted her eyes, pursed her lips, bobbing her head up and down. If this conception was going to take place, Gayle was right. They needed to go ahead and get it over. It was just that Sarah hadn't considered the possibility of the process having to take more than one try. In all of her planning, how could she have missed such a major component?

"Are you sure you don't mind giving up another one of your weekends for us?"

"It's the least I could do for you and Carl. I want to do this for you."

"Okay then, let me get home and make the arrangements. I assume you want to leave tomorrow morning since this is short notice?"

Gayle blurted out, "No, tonight," before she could catch herself.

Sarah arched one eyebrow and stirred the straw rapidly in her glass of seltzer water. "My, you seem eager?"

"Not eager, more like determined to make this happen

so Carl can have the gift that you want for him." She wanted to kick herself but maintained a straight face with Sarah. It was vital that she not reveal how much being with Carl meant and just how much she wanted his baby. If Sarah sensed any hint of her true feelings, the rendezvous would be over and possibly her relationship with both of them. This was a once-in-a-lifetime opportunity, and it couldn't be blown on a mere slip of the tongue. Damage control was necessary. "Sarah, you are such an incredible wife to do this for your husband. Carl is so blessed to have a soul mate in you."

Sarah accepted the compliment and let it light up her countenance. "I better get out of here if you intend on leaving tonight. There is so much to do. I have to make arrangements and pack for Carl." Sarah took a quick gulp from the mostly full glass of water. "Oh my goodness, I have to get going." Sarah got up, kissed Gayle on the cheek and did her goodbye before jetting towards the exit.

Gayle took a sigh of relief. That was a close call. This wasn't going to be easy, neither the getting pregnant part nor stretching the number of weekends out long enough to allow Carl a chance to get to know her personally, intimately, in ways he'd never been exposed to as a friend. She had initially hoped for months, but longevity was in question based on a glimpse of Sarah's earlier reaction. Since Sarah left before they had ordered lunch, Gayle poked with the lemon floating in her water glass. What should she do, use birth control one more time and try to squeeze in at least one more weekend or take her chances without it? She had to get another weekend, especially since next week was her true ovulation period. It was bound to happen then, but she needed time to bond with Carl in ways that Sarah couldn't. His wife might be his soul mate, but Gayle felt secure being his soon-to-be baby's mother, and that had to carry some weight. She felt calm and raised her hand to beckon the waitress. She would eat and then run home to pack the final touches. Thank goodness she followed her first mind and got her hair and nails done this morning in anticipation of going away again with Carl. Most of her suitcase was already packed. This time she wasn't taking nearly as many outfits as she had on the last trip. Impressing with her wardrobe wasn't the focus.

## Chapter 7

Sarah dusted the china cabinet and polished every piece of silverware in the house, which wasn't necessary with their full-time staff of servants on duty. The conception had to work this time. Her steadfast position on making it happen was wavering. It had been a great idea several weeks ago, but now that the deed was being done, the thought of another woman having her husband's first and only child wasn't settling well. The nausea in her soul threatened to erupt. She wiped harder, swifter, but without enough force to block out her worries. Regardless of whether she should or should not have started Gayle and Carl's ball rolling down the baby-making hill together, the final result would be a child. That's what she had to remember—the sole reason this craziness got started in the first place. On the bright side, Gayle was ovulating and Sarah had to believe it would work this time. All she had to do was hold on for another twelve hours and that would be the end of it. Life could get back to normal for the Abraham household and for Gayle. Sarah would rehearse the goal over and over, hoping the repetition would somehow make it more palatable and easier to digest.

## Chapter 8

Sarah was spending a small fortune on home pregnancy tests for Gayle. Two weekends spent in seclusion and all they had to show for it was a garbage can full of negative test results. In spite of her best intentions and elaborate planning, Sarah felt defeated. She had attempted to orchestrate the creation of a child and had ended up barren. "I don't know what I was thinking. I guess this was foolish from the beginning. Gayle, you're supposed to be my friend."

"I am," Gayle eagerly announced, wondering if Sarah had picked up on some of the vibes of interest she'd been shooting Carl's way.

"Then why didn't you stop me from doing something so stupid, and on top of it all, to drag the love of my life and my dear friend into a tangled web." Sarah didn't try to conceal her sadness. "I'm so sorry. Can you ever forgive me?" She pulled a tissue from her purse and wiped her watery eyes.

"Sarah, you don't have to apologize to me. I think you're an incredible woman." She leaned in to console

Sarah. "I don't know anybody else who would go as far as you have to make sure their husband has a child. Don't be so hard on yourself. It wasn't a bad idea, not at all. We've gone this far, let's try one more time and then call it quits."

"I couldn't ask you to do this again."

"I want to do this for you. If you're willing to go this far for your husband, who am I not to support my dear friend and go along with the program."

"Are you sure?"

"I'm positive. I'm just happy that I can help. It's going to work out, don't worry. We can do this. You'll see."

"Okay, if you're willing to give it one more try, I will make the arrangements."

Gayle was relieved inside. She had managed to dodge a major missile. Two more seconds and Sarah would have sunk any hopes she had of warming up to Carl and having his baby. This weekend would have to work. It was clear that Sarah couldn't endure much more time beyond the upcoming forty-eight hours. Since she had lied last week by telling Sarah that she was ovulating when in actuality it was this weekend, closing the deal would be easy. By Sunday evening, Carl Abraham could start picking out the bassinet and getting the nursery ready. His baby would be on its way.

## Chapter 9

Time crawled by, and the forty-eight hours that Carl was gone felt like years. Sarah opted to pick him up from the airport herself instead of waiting for the car service to bring him home. Like the other two weekends, he got in, gave her a generous hug and smooch without mentioning a word about what had transpired. Sarah had let it go the other times. When they got home and retired to the sitting room, she couldn't hold back any longer.

"Aren't you going to tell me about what happened over the weekend?"

"What is there to tell you? I did what you asked me to do. That's it," Carl said without lowering the newspaper he was reading.

"It's a little more to it than that, Carl. You spent the weekend with another woman who's probably pregnant with your child. Surely there's something you can tell me."

"See, Sarah, I was afraid of this." Now he put the paper down.

"What?"

"You getting upset about my being with Gayle. I knew this didn't sit right with my spirit from the beginning."

"I'm not upset. I just want you to share the details with me. I don't want to be left out of what you and Gayle have going on."

"Going on! We don't have anything going on. Don't forget, Gayle and I were together only because of you."

"Do you have feelings for her now?"

"Feelings for Gayle? Don't be absurd!" He took time to let the raging winds of tension die down. "Sarah, please, don't do this. It's awkward enough without you embellishing the situation."

"Can you blame me? You're going to have a child with our friend."

Carl scratched his head and stood silent, afraid to engage in a conversation that was destined to end badly.

"Be honest with me. Were you attracted to her at all?"

"Sarah, why are you doing this?"

"Answer me," she yelled.

"No, I wasn't."

"How can you say that? If you weren't attracted to her, then how could she get pregnant?"

Carl plopped down on the seat next to Sarah and rested his forehead in the cradle between his thumb and index finger, contemplating how he'd gotten into this mess. If only he'd followed his initial inclination and resisted his wife's request.

"Sarah, you have to believe me when I tell you that I don't have any interest or intimate love for Gayle. She is our friend and maybe the mother of our child, the one you want more than either of us. That's the beginning and the end of the story about Gayle and the past three weekends. I didn't feel good about any of it. If you must know, each time I felt like I was committing adultery. Do you know how that makes me feel? Me, a man of God, having a child with someone other than my wife because I didn't have enough faith to believe that God could fulfill a twenty-year-old covenant?" He put his arm around his wife who didn't put up a struggle. "Let's not get ahead of ourselves. It didn't work the first two times. It probably didn't work this time either. We've learned our lesson about tampering with God's business, and now we can put all of this behind us and start fresh tomorrow. Okay, darling?" he said kissing her forehead.

She agreed, and they decided to turn in early and be rested for their fresh start.

## Chapter 10

Gayle was in tune with her body. It didn't take a doctor's exam to confirm what she already knew. She was definitely pregnant and savoring every moment with satisfaction. Carl was the first person she wanted to tell but acknowledged that she had to go through his wife, at least for now. There was so much to do. She needed to call Sarah and then begin preparing for the nursery, a new wardrobe and a new place, something much larger where little Carl could run around. What if it was a girl? Oh well, either a boy or girl would be fine so long as Carl was the father and she the mother.

In recent weeks, Sarah felt like she should buy stock in the restaurant on the corner of Egypt and Euphrates. She had met Gayle there no less than five times in the past month. So much had changed in such a short while. The schoolgirl energy she'd exuded with Gayle prior to the anniversary party was a distant memory. Gayle was technically still her friend, but it was different. The trust and admiration she'd had for her just four weeks ago was converting into something more like envy. Wherever the relationship went from here wasn't clear, but it wouldn't go back to what it once was. Sarah was prepared to hear, for the third time, that Gayle wasn't pregnant. This was the final discussion on the topic. No more weekends away with her husband. It didn't matter if ovulation was scrolled across Gayle's forehead and a sign reading "*prime time for conceiving*" oozed out her toes. The mission had failed and needed to be aborted.

"Don't tell me, the test came back negative again," Sarah said, kicking off the conversation.

"Actually no. It came back positive."

Sarah sat still, totally stunned and unsure if she'd heard Gayle correctly. "What did you say?"

"I'm pregnant! Can you believe it? I'm going to have Carl's baby. I should say, we're going to have a baby."

"I don't know what to say..., except congratulations." Sarah maintained a plastered grin, careful not to reveal her mixed emotions. "This is good news." She'd gotten exactly what she'd wanted, a child for her husband. So, why didn't it feel good? "I'm excited," she lied.

"So am I," Gayle said. "What about Carl?"

"What about him?"

"You think I should call and tell him the good news?"

"No, let me do that. You know how unpredictable husbands can be. Oops, I'm talking to you like you're married. I'm sorry, silly me."

Gayle growled inside. Sarah knew she wanted to be married some day. They'd talked about it enough times in the past for such a comment to never see the light of day. It was all right, though. She was single, but the way it looked from her view, some changes would be coming. Sarah might be wearing Carl's diamond ring, but she was carrying his baby. Let Sarah keep talking down to her. Carl was sure to put a stop to it seeing that she was the one carrying his little bundle of joy and needed to be protected from that wife of his. From now on, it wasn't about what Sarah wanted. Many decisions would need to be made with Carl directly. It wasn't like they were strangers who required Sarah to referee their every conversation. They had managed to communicate over the past three weekends without her and had obviously made some type of connection and with more to come.

"I just realized that we've never discussed the custody details," Sarah brought up.

"What custody details?"

"I know we're friends, but since Carl will have full custody and I will be adopting the child, we should have all of this done legally. I'm sure we'll all live at least another fifty years, but in case something happens to any of us, we would want the child protected. Don't you agree?"

"I never said Carl would have full custody of this baby!"

Sarah sat straight up and spoke firmly. "What did you expect, for us to share custody with you?"

"I never really thought about it, but I guess so. I never considered giving the child to the two of you, not completely."

"What do you mean? From the very beginning, I asked you to have a baby with my husband, for us."

"No, you asked me to have a baby with your husband. That was it. I always expected to raise this child with the father."

"You've got to be kidding. You think I would encourage you to sleep with my husband so you could end up with his baby and be in our lives on a regular basis?

Come on now, you know me better than that."

Gayle leaned back in the chair with her arms folded.

Sarah cackled. "And what kind of an arrangement did you think we'd have? Were you going to move into our home and sleep a few doors down from Carl, in case your maternal instinct kicked in and you wanted to single-handedly expand the Abraham family?" She continued cackling.

"To tell the truth, I haven't given much thought to where I'd be sleeping. Wherever it is, I hope it's as nice as the comfortable bed that I just spent the past three weekends in."

Sarah was mortified.

Gayle jumped to her feet. "Please excuse me. I have so much to learn and so much preparation to make for my new baby. You can't imagine how wonderful it feels to be pregnant. Stay as long as you like. And don't worry about the bill this time," she said snatching it off the table. "I'll take care of it. Toodles."

Sarah remained speechless. What in the world had she done? How would she tell Carl that Gayle was pregnant and planning to keep the baby? Just when she thought the farce was over, it was gaining momentum. She sure could use some guidance from the Lord, but she couldn't bring herself to approach God with such catastrophic nonsense. She would hide from Him a while longer, just until matters settled down. She had to face Carl in the meantime.

# *Baby Blues*

## *Chapter 11*

If Sarah was happy, Carl was too. For the ten months since Chris was born, happiness seemed to zoom past the house each day without so much as ducking in for a quick visit. Life with Sarah was all he needed. Adding a baby to the mix had been okay with him because that's what his wife had wanted, but he didn't know what to do to ease the tension between Sarah and Gayle. A significant part of him was thrilled to have a son, but the joy was suffocated by Sarah's anguish. If only he'd stood up and said no from the beginning to what he felt would turn out to be a disaster. Instead, he conceived a child with a woman other than the wife that God had blessed him with. To make matters worse, he had tainted the covenant God had made with him about having children. Was anything too hard for God? He was a man known for walking in faith when it came to his professional life. Faith was generic. He knew it, but why hadn't he exercised that same faith in waiting for a child?

"We were only gone a few hours and there are already five messages from Gayle." She slammed her purse on top of the kitchen counter. "I can't take much more of this. She calls every time we turn around. We can't keep running over there every time Chris cries. I can't take it."

"What if I bring him over here for a few days. Would that be better?"

"You can't bring him without bringing her because she's breast-feeding a child who's almost a year old."

"Isn't there some kind of way she could send enough milk for us to keep him just for a few days?"

Sarah could see the concern in Carl's eyes. Regardless of the conditions under which he was conceived, Carl loved Chris and enjoyed spending time with him. Loving her husband enough to love his son, without revealing her contempt for his mother, would take some work. She couldn't make any guarantees but would at least try to calm the waters for Carl's sake.

"Why don't you ask her about storing up some extra milk. She'll listen to you before she'll hear one word I have to say."

"I'm not sure that I have much more favor with her than you do."

"Oh, trust me, your wishes go a long ways with her. Think about what we went through with the name."

Carl cringed reliving the ordeal.

"If you hadn't been so insistent, she would have named him Junior just because she knew that I didn't want it."

"The name didn't matter to me, but I understood and respected how you felt. I will always care about your feelings and put you first, even if it means having limited time with my son."

Hearing the cracking in Carl's voice generated a sense of guilt in Sarah's soul, but her flesh didn't care. The less of Chris around the better if it meant being subjected to the stifling presence of his mother.

## Chapter 12

Time passed and before long Chris was toddling around. Gayle made sure that he spent larger and larger

44

chunks of time with his father. She cherished the affection Carl had for his son and used every ounce of it to stay welded into his life. The three-bedroom house, new car and generous monthly allowance weren't all she expected out of the deal. Carl hadn't given in to her advances yet. Chris wouldn't be leaving home for another fifteen years. There was plenty in store for Mr. Carl Abraham.

"Owwie," came from the direction of the mass of toys piled in the middle of the family room.

"Be careful, Chris. Mommy and Daddy don't want you to hurt yourself." She got off the couch and went to pamper him. She tickled him until he giggled uncontrollably. "Look at that, Chris. I can't believe you still have new teeth coming in the back. We'd better call your dad. We might need the dentist to check you out just to make sure everything is okay." She sat her son on the floor. "Sit here, baby, until Mommy calls Daddy. I love you, sweetie." She gave him a kiss and picked up the cordless phone sitting on top of the entertainment center to call her baby's daddy. Sarah would probably be there to run interference. She wished Carl would just give her his cell phone number, but so far, he hadn't budged. Gayle knew Sarah was behind his reluctance, but it was fine. Eventually she'd get through to Carl and he'd be over anyway. It was just a matter of time.

\*     \*     \*

After the phone call, Sarah was out of sorts. "I am so sick of Gayle calling this house every time she gets a whim.

First it was the pregnancy. Now it's been three years since Chris was born. Will she ever stop? You're going to have to tell her no sometimes instead of always being the perfect dad."

"I don't think Chris should suffer because of the situation we adults have created. He's an innocent child, and I am his father. I am accountable for him."

"Well, if she can't take care of him without requiring your constant input, then maybe she shouldn't have him." Sarah stopped abruptly with a pondering looking on her face. "You know, that might be just the answer we're looking for."

"What?"

"We should get custody of your son."

"You considered filing for custody when she was pregnant, but you changed your mind. Why would you want to do it now?"

"I don't know what I was thinking back then, but now I keep telling myself that he is just as much yours as he is hers. It was never our intent to leave him with her from the beginning. She was having the baby for us, that is until you let her get this crazy notion that you have some remote interest in her."

"Me! How did I do that?"

"You had to show some interest in order for her to get pregnant."

"I can't believe we're going over this again. Did you forget that this entire concept was your idea? I went along with it to make you happy."

"This wasn't for me. I knew you wanted a child, and

this is how you repay me for making such an unthinkable sacrifice, by shutting me out of your son's life?"

"Sarah, you know I'm not shutting you out. What do you want me to do?"

"I want you to go to court and get custody of our son."

"I don't want to drag you through a drawn out legal battle." Wrong and right were so clouded now that he couldn't figure out what to do. "Is there some other way for us to work this out among ourselves?"

"No, there isn't. Chris must be under our care. I can't live with him any other way. This is the only way for us to get back to a normal life. It has to be this way, Carl. We don't have a choice."

"Okay, I will call Tom tomorrow and get the legal matters underway."

Sarah gave a sigh of relief. "This really is for the best. You'll see."

"Heaven knows, I truly hope you're right."

The couple embraced standing in the center of the kitchen.

"How should we handle Gayle? You think we should tell her first?" Sarah asked.

"I don't think we should say anything. She won't be happy about our wanting custody. We need a strong plan before approaching her. Let's just wait for direction from Tom. He'll know what to do." Carl had gone as far as he could go. He was sinking into deep waters and only God could provide the lifeline that he needed. It was time to repent for any wrongdoing that he was both aware of and ignorant to regarding the entire sordid mess. Before turning in for bed, he decided to seek guidance and pray that God would order his footsteps back to a state of peace. *I need to hear from God,* is the last thought he had before heading to their bedroom for the evening.

## Chapter 13

Normally Carl hated having to leave home for business trips. With all of the commotion surrounding Chris, a break from the home front was a pleasure. He buckled into his seat in first class and held his head down while rolling his thumbs.

The flight attendant came to take their lunch orders before the plane took off.

"Nothing for me," Carl told her. "I don't feel like eating."

The petite older woman sitting next to him told the attendant, "The chicken for me, please."

The attendant moved on, and Carl remained restless in his seat.

The lady was looking out the window. "Sho' ain't no way somebody can look out there amongst all those clouds and not know there's a God," she said to Carl.

"Pardon?"

"It ain't no way ya can't know it's a God in Heaven when ya sees all that He's created."

"That's right, there is definitely a God. Even when we don't listen to Him, He exists."

"Oh now, that sounds like a confession," she teased him.

"Well, I guess in a sense you could say that it is."

"Sounds like ya know the Lord?"

"I know Him, but I've done something totally outside of His will, and now I'm paying the price for my disobedience."

"Well, I'ze can't say much. I'ze done made a heap of mistakes in my life and done a heap of wrong, specially before I'ze got to know the Lord the way I'ze know Him now. But you know," the lady paused to ask, "what's your name?"

"Oh, forgive me for being so rude. It's Carl, Carl Abraham."

"Carl Abraham, I'm Emma Walker, but most people just call me Big Mama, others Mother Walker."

"It's a pleasure to meet you Mother Walker."

"Like I'ze was saying, we all done fell short of the glory of God, but thank the Lord for His mercy and His grace to help us keep a going."

"It's sad when you know the Lord and have seen His promises manifested in your life, and then when something doesn't happen exactly how or when you want it to, we're so quick to pursue other means of trying to make it happen. I'm amazed at how easily I allowed myself to be lured outside of God's will into a state of confusion."

"Ya only a man, a human being, made of flesh and bones. The Word says there's nothing good in the flesh. Some of my biggest mistakes turned out to be my biggest testimonies, and they led me to the biggest miracles in my life. I'ze can honestly say that every time I've done the wrong thing, it helped me to grow stronger in the Lord. Ya can't beat on yourself. If it's something ya done wrong that ya know about, ask God to forgive ya and move on. Don't let the enemy keep running that thing around in your head. If God forgives ya, then you're forgiven, but then I'ze don't need to tell you that because I'm believing it's something ya already knows deep down in ya spirit. Ya already know that He can make a wrong situation right."

"I don't know why I feel so comfortable talking with you, but this is exactly what I needed to hear."

"See there, that's how our God is. Ya know it's no accident that He put us in these here seats together. If it was up to me, I'ze would have been somewhere in the back where the tickets don't cost so much, but Neal is always getting my ticket up here. He's like a grandson to me. So, this is where I'ze have to sit, but I'ze don't mind. Wherever God has me is where I'll be." She made eye contact with Carl. "I'ze can see that ya got too much God in ya to walk around here with ya head hanging down. Ain't no call for that. God is still on the throne, and He wants you to hold on to the word that He promised you in the beginning."

"I'm a little confused by the prophecy that I was originally given. I was told that I would have a child, but my wife is too old. Maybe it's supposed to come from another woman. I'm just not sure."

"Mr. Abraham, if something don't quite sit right with ya spirit, then it's probably not right. God don't need no other woman to keep His word with ya. I'ze hear Him saying this child that He promised to ya is coming from your wife. I'ze don't know how, but it's going to happen if

God says so."

"My wife won't believe me when I tell her that she's going to have a baby. She'll probably laugh in my face."

"I'ze believe the word God is giving to you this day is that nothing is too hard for Him. Trust in Him that created ya." She softly rubbed the back of his hand that was resting on the center console. "I'ze hoping all this will do ya some good."

"Yes, Mother Walker, it has." He eased back in his chair and stretched his legs out under the seat. He rang the call button, and when the flight attendant arrived, he said, "Looks like I'll be having lunch after all."

## Chapter 14

The onslaught of filing motions, preparing responses, petitioning for summary judgments about this issue and that issue had kept the Abrahams and their attorney tied up in the legal system for over a year. The day had finally come. The case was scheduled on the court docket, and Sarah and Carl were eager to get this step behind them and get back to the life they once knew and enjoyed.

"All rise, court is in session. The Honorable Judge Hayes will be presiding. The matter before the court is a custody hearing between Carl and Sarah Abraham vs. Gayle Anise Hagar."

The newly appointed judge took his seat, and the rest of the courtroom followed. Judge Hayes took a short period to review the documents. He noted the host of reporters in the courtroom and said, "It's nice to see that so many citizens are interested in the welfare of this child. If you're here for any other reason, I'm going to ask you to leave now. I will not tolerate any disruptions or circus acts in my courtroom. Be forewarned, if you deem it necessary, I will have no qualms about citing you with contempt of court, which will land you with jail time and a fine."

The entire back row on both sides of the room emptied out, leaving only the interested parties remaining.

Judge Hayes resumed his review of the documents. "With that said, let's get back to the matter of this hearing. This looks to be a very unusual set of circumstances surrounding this case. Before we get the hearing underway, I want to ensure that both parties have made every effort to work out a suitable arrangement outside of court."

Both attorneys responded by admitting that they'd tried but nothing could be worked out without legal intervention. Hearing that no resolution could be reached prior to court, Judge Hayes allowed the hearing to commence.

Grueling testimony ensued, and Carl felt like the hostility in the room was thick enough to be cut with a knife. In several instances, Gayle broke down on the stand, requiring five-minute recesses. He gave his testimony, barely able to speak above his shame. He could only imagine what the judge was thinking. He wanted to be truthful and tell what was necessary without having to go into superfluous details, particularly with the media parked outside the door and impatiently waiting to get a story about his personal affairs into the local news. Many advantages and blessings came with owning a major corporation in the area. This public display of his family life wasn't one of them. The negative attention beaming on his family was bad enough, but what really hurt was how compromised his testimony had become. Who would ever listen to him again when it came to matters of spirituality, the biggest sinner in the house?

Gayle and Carl had given testimony, and it was Sarah's turn. She stood to her feet and approached the testimony box. The room began to swirl, and before she could catch herself, air swooped under her feet and the next clear image she had was Carl standing over her. "What happened?"

"You passed out."

"Passed out!" She patted her arms as if there were invisible needles hanging from places she couldn't see. "Where are we?"

"In the emergency room, sweetheart, but I'm sure it's nothing serious. The doctor drew a blood sample, and he'll have the results back any minute."

"Really, I didn't even feel it. How long have I been out?"

"Less than an hour. I know it's from the stress associated with the custody hearing." Carl broke down and cried. "Sarah, I owe you such an apology. How did I let this happen to us?"

"Carl, no, you can't take responsibility for this. Having the baby with Gayle was my idea from the beginning. Obviously, I didn't think it all the way through. I'm sorry for putting you in this situation."

"No matter what you did or said, I am the head of our house. I'm accountable to God for you. He entrusted you to me as my wife. I'm not sure what to do, but I will fix this. You won't spend another day in any hospital because of my reckless and short-sighted behavior." He kissed the back of his wife's hand. "I love you and adore you. Every promise God has made has come to fruition, the company, our marriage, our health, and in a weird way, even having a child. My life is fulfilled, and when we leave here, my goal is to get back to making you happy."

The attending physician entered the small examination room with an expression that was hard for Carl to read. If there was anything wrong with Sarah, he wanted to know first so he could shoulder most of the shock and spoon-feed it to his wife. "Okay doctor, you're going to tell us that my wife is exhausted and needs plenty of fluids, rest and relaxation, of which I am fully prepared to make happen the moment you release her." Carl caressed her hand again to ease any rising anxiety.

"R and R would be exactly what you need, Sarah," the doctor agreed.

"How long do you think she needs to recover? I want to make sure she follows your instructions to the letter."

The doctor smiled and responded with, "How about, let's say, seven or eight months."

"Why so long?" Sarah asked, wanting clarification.

"You're pregnant, Mrs. Abraham. You're going to have a baby."

Sarah's hand went limp in Carl's. "There must be some mistake."

"No mistake, Mrs. Abraham. We ran the test three times to make sure the results were accurate."

"Oh my goodness," she shrilled drawing her hands to cover her wide-open mouth.

"We never expected to have a baby at this age in our lives. I can't believe it." Carl got up and wrapped his arms and body around his wife, his soul mate and the soon-to-be mother of his legitimate heir.

"Consider it a miracle," the doctor said as he gave his final comments and left the room for Sarah to get dressed.

Carl and Sarah sat still in the room, connecting without saying a word. The word God had spoken to him about having a child with Sarah immediately bombarded his thoughts. It had come to pass. No one could have believed God would grant a baby to a couple approaching their retirement years. He had a hard time believing it, and he was someone who had known the Lord for years. In spite of the shortcut he and Sarah had concocted to fulfill the promise, God had kept His word in His own time.

## Chapter 15

Initially Sarah gave resistance but soon had to succumb to Carl's unwavering appeal that she stay off her feet and away from any stress. The medical world put his wife in the high-risk category since she was over fifty and having her first child. Labels were of no consequence to him. If God could enable her to get pregnant, then He was also able to keep their baby until the delivery.

After Sarah became pregnant, Carl instantly put the court case on hold. No other pressures could creep into their home. He had to put a stop to the calls as well. He made it clear to Gayle that he loved Chris and would always be his father and his provider, but Sarah came first, before anyone in his life.

Gayle tossed the ball back and forth with her rambunctious four-year-old son on the sidewalk. She was thankful for the joy and fulfillment he brought into her existence. The plan to have his father be an integral part of their world was in jeopardy, but not totally at a loss. Sarah's pregnancy had thrown the program off course, but Gayle was sure she could get Carl back on the right track. After all, Chris was his first born, his eldest and for the moment, his only child. Even if Sarah had a hundred children, they would never take the place of Carl's first. She continued playing ball with Chris while contemplating her next move, realizing that time was short. She only had another couple of months, at best, before Sarah delivered and set the court hearing back in motion. Whatever her plan was, it had to work, otherwise she might lose her son, a baby that she wasn't willing to give up, with or without having his father in the picture.

Gayle sat on the floor with her soul exposed. She had avoided the inevitable long enough. It was finally time to do what she had avoided at all cost. She needed to ask God for help. She had done some stupid things in her youth but never anything this outrageous or reckless. Double doses of guilt, confusion, shame and loneliness swirled around, plucking at her every so often but not fully penetrating. Looking at Chris made it all right. If God could make a way for her to keep full custody of her son, she was willing to do whatever she had to do. She would figure out what, if anything, she could do to save her son. Nothing else mattered, not her upgraded lifestyle, not Carl. Whatever she needed to take care of her son, God would have to provide.

## Chapter 16

The miracles kept coming. The doctor had prepared Sarah for a Cesarean. As God would have it, she delivered naturally to the amazement of the entire medical team. A healthy baby boy was the fruit of her nine-month pregnancy with most of it spent bedridden.

Carl sat in Sarah's room beaming with pride. He held his son a little while before gently placing him back in the hospital bassinet.

Sarah gazed at the two most important males in her life and felt an overwhelming sense of conviction. She hadn't given much credence to the prophecy that Carl had heard on the plane a few years ago about them having a baby together. She remembered laughing out loud when he first told her about it. If she'd had just a teeny bit of faith and had waited on God to fulfill the original prophecy that Rev. Daniels had told them when they got married, they wouldn't be in such a mess with Gayle, someone who was once a cherished friend.

"I can't believe you're holding our son," she told Carl.

"Isn't it a miracle? I should have never doubted God's word. He's been so faithful in every other area. It shouldn't have come as any surprise that He was going to bless us with a child like He'd said."

Sarah fiddled with the seam of the bed sheet. "We

made a mess of things, didn't we?"

"Not you, I did. God put the promise on my heart, and I disobeyed Him."

"But it was my suggestion. I asked you to have a child with Gayle."

"Sarah, no one made me follow through. Regardless of the reason, I committed the act, and I hold myself fully accountable."

"So what are we going to do now?"

"I still want to do what will make you comfortable. We can go back to court whenever you feel up to it," he told her.

Sarah sat quietly, organizing her thoughts. "I don't want to go back to court."

Carl perked up, hoping he had heard her correctly. Fighting for full custody of his son never sat right with him, but he was willing to go along with it for Sarah. "Did you say that you don't want to go back to court?"

"Yes, I did. It's too agonizing."

Carl was relieved. His prayer was being answered. "Would you prefer for us to have joint custody?"

"Actually, I'd prefer for Gayle not to be around us at all."

"I know, but it's kind of hard to do since she doesn't seem interested in letting us have custody. Unfortunately, it looks like she'll be in the picture until Chris becomes an adult."

"Not necessarily."

"What does that mean? Do you have an idea that could help us solve this problem? If so, let me hear it because I'm open."

"Have Gayle leave."

"Oh, you know she won't leave Chris."

"I know."

Carl wasn't following Sarah's logic.

"Have her leave with Chris."

"What do you mean by 'leave with Chris?' "

Sarah knew this wouldn't be easy for Carl. He loved Chris without question, but having the child's mother in their lives would only make a bad situation progressively worse. Gayle had to go, even if it meant taking with her a son that meant so much to Carl. "I can't think of any other way to put distance between us and Gayle. You know if she stays around she'll want constant contact with you, and I won't stand for it."

"Whatever contact I have with her is strictly for my son."

"We know that, but Gayle probably sees it as a chance to make more out of it. We can't trust her. She's going to be a problem for us, and I want her gone."

Carl's heart grieved. He wanted to cry out at the mere thought of Chris not growing up in his presence but held back. He had exercised poor judgment by getting involved with Gayle in the beginning, but Chris wasn't a mistake. Only God could grant life, and Chris was a blessing. Carl had repented for his disobedience and was sure God had forgiven him. He also acknowledged that some situations, even though forgiven, had consequences. Perhaps this was one of those situations. He ached thinking about Chris leaving, but what could he do. Sarah's happiness and comfort came before his. "We can ask her to leave, but there's no guarantee that she'll go."

Sarah hated seeing her husband so brokenhearted but was determined to hold fast to her position. "Regardless of what I think about her, I admit that she is a good mother and she loves her son. If we agree to drop the lawsuit and let her have full custody, with a guarantee that we'll never seek custody in the future, I think she might listen to reason. We'll probably have to give her a modest settlement to get rid of her."

Carl scratched his head with his eyes closed. His love was for God, but pleasing Sarah was forever guiding him. If only there was some other way, but he had no other suggestions which would be acceptable to Sarah. Whatever the future held, he wanted to be by her side, and that was all the push he needed to swing the pendulum in the direction she wanted to go. He might as well prepare for the separation, in his mind first and then in his heart. He knew his son was as good as gone. "I'll present the arrangement to her and see what she says."

"Don't take no for an answer, Carl. I realize this is going to hurt you, and I am so sorry, sweetheart, but it has to be this way. Have Tom draw the papers up before you go see Gayle. That way she won't have time to change her mind after you leave."

"I'll give him a call as soon as I leave here. Just so we're on the same page, what do you think about giving her ten thousand dollars?"

"Sure, that sounds reasonable. She's getting your son. That ought to be enough. She's lucky to be getting any money at all."

"I'll also have Tom put provisions in the settlement that will allow Chris and Junior to split the ownership of the business down the road, after you and I pass away."

"Absolutely not. Junior is your only legitimate heir. I do not want any contact with Gayle after they leave, never."

Carl waited for Sarah to share her heart. He couldn't voice any opposition. God had said from the beginning that he would be blessed with a child. It was later confirmed that he would have an heir through Sarah. This was the child God had promised would carry the family name forward for generations to come. That's what he had to continue telling himself in order to do the unthinkable act of turning his back on a child he loved and adored. No need fretting. He would seek God for guidance and speak with Gayle by morning. By this time tomorrow evening, he would have this deed behind him and experiencing, once again, the peace that came with being in God's will. In spite of the bumpy road he had traveled, the day had finally come when he would be taking their son home.  Junior would be the seed of a long line of Abrahams to come, just like God had promised, and nothing felt better.

### *Many Years Later*

"The ongoing legal battle is heating up between the heirs of the late Carl Abraham, Sr., the business mogul. Two families claim to be the rightful heir of the family fortune and the thousands of acres of prime real estate in this area. Although a legal will was prepared by Mr. Abraham and witnessed before his death, its validity is being contested. Based on inside information, it looks like this battle may go on for some time since neither side seems willing to concede. We will keep you informed in the days ahead on this developing story. On to local news...."

# Traveling Mercies

## By
## Maurice Gray

How can I be sure I'm going to Heaven when I die?"

Joshua "J.C." Carpenter smiled inwardly. Hardly a day went by when his friend and fellow church member didn't initiate a deep conversation. Even in church, Barry Sterling was ever the attorney, asking question after question. J.C. suspected that this time, as was often the case, Barry was more interested in showing his spiritual depth than in increasing his spiritual knowledge. As a lay preacher, J.C. was often the one Barry came to with his questions and comments. Despite his lack of formal religious training, J.C. was known far and wide to be a man of quiet demeanor and great spiritual knowledge.

"Tell me this, Barry. What is the greatest commandment?"

Barry smiled and from memory not only gave all Ten Commandments of the Old Testament but also the greatest commandment, proving J.C.'s assumption about Barry's motives correct. "The greatest commandment says 'You shall love the Lord your God with all your heart, with all your soul, and with all your mind.' This is the first and great commandment. And the second is: 'You shall love your neighbor as yourself.' On these two commandments hang all the Law and the Prophets.''

J.C. smiled back at him. "Good. Accept Jesus Christ as Lord and Savior, and that's how you'll get to Heaven."

Barry frowned, a sure sign that he wasn't through being deep just yet. "But, I have a question. Does that mean I have to be nice to the guy next door even when his dogs mess on my lawn?"

J.C. laughed. "Afraid so. But your neighbor isn't just the person who lives next door. Your neighbor is anyone you might encounter."

Barry looked puzzled. "What do you mean?"

J.C. smiled and gestured to a pew near the back of the now-empty sanctuary. "Let me tell you a story."

*     *     *

Matthew Hayes couldn't remember anything, including where he was, how he'd gotten there and the name of the exotic woman who was standing over him.

"You're awake. Good, I was starting to worry."

Fragments of memory flashed through his head. Matt saw fists descending on him mercilessly from all sides, but he couldn't remember who those fists belonged to. He did know that he had been moved recently; instead of bleeding on a cold, hard pavement, he had awakened in a hospital bed, looking up at a woman.

Very shapely, very fine, Matt thought. Who *is* she?

Matt studied her closely; the woman seemed to be part African-American, part Hispanic and, if her cheekbones and long, straight black hair were any indication, part Native American as well. She wore a bright red midriff-revealing T-shirt with matching Capri pants; the outfit emphasized every one of her formidable curves.

The woman seemed amused at the attention Matt was giving her. He focused all his energy into vocalizing his next thought. "Where...?"

The woman smiled. "Relax. You're in Christiana Hospital. I brought you here earlier tonight."

"Hosthpital? Why?"

The woman was clearly trying not to laugh at his impaired speech (due to a fat lip). "Shh, don't try to talk. The short version is, you got in a fight, you lost, and I brought you to the emergency room for treatment. I'll give you more details later, but right now you need to sleep."

She scribbled a phone number on a piece of paper and put it on his night table. "I'll be back later. Call if you need anything."

She turned and left the room. Matt couldn't resist admiring her rear view through the eye that wasn't swollen shut. He then drifted off to sleep, still trying to remember just who this woman was and why she would help him like this.

\*       \*       \*

*"Excuse you!"*

*The slightly bigger man stopped in his tracks, letting his two companions enter the Marriott Travel Plaza and turned to face Matt, who was coming out and not pleased to note the condition of his car.*

*"You got something to say, brother?"*

*Matt was livid. He'd been driving for hours and was not in the mood for anyone trifling. The brisk March weather did nothing to cool his temper.*

*"Matter of fact, yeah. How you just gonna throw your door open, hit my brand new Lexus and try to walk away like you didn't do it?"*

*The bigger man did his best to look bored. "If you ain't park so close, there wouldn't be no problems."*

*Matt rose up to his full six foot two, only an inch shorter than his opponent. "You mean if you knew how to park that rusty hoopty you driving…."*

*The other man stepped closer, looking grim. "Don't make me put my foot in your butt."*

*Matt was less than intimidated. "If you fight like you park, I got no problems."*

*Without warning, the bigger man lunged at Matt, catching him off guard. Matt braced himself, absorbed the impact and then used both of his arms to break the man's powerful grip and push him away. The bigger man was thrown backwards, colliding violently with his own car (an old Lincoln). He lunged again, but this time Matt was ready. Timing it perfectly, he grabbed the man's left hand with his left and pulled him into a punch in the mouth from the right. Before the man could react, Matt was all over him. Five punches later, the man was semiconscious, and Matt finished by slamming the bigger man into his own car a second time. This time, the man bounced off and fell to the ground face first, barely moving.*

*"Watch that car door next time, punk."*

*He barely had time to finish gloating before the back of his head exploded with pain and the world around him blurred.*

\*     \*     \*

"Huuuh!"

Matt jerked awake. He didn't recognize his surroundings and started to panic before remembering where he was. His right arm was hooked up to an IV; some unidentified medication was working its way into his system and burning slightly at the point of entry. Whatever it was, it felt pretty relaxing.

Light was beginning to stream in around the closed blinds. Matt vaguely remembered a female nurse drawing blood from him while it was still dark, but he had no clue when that was, or what time it was currently.

Most of Matt's body was perfectly content to stay in bed, but his kidneys felt otherwise. Looking over the side of the bed, he noticed that his IV was on a wheeled unit and could move with him as he walked. He gathered his strength and slid first one leg and then the other from under the covers. So far, so good, he thought.

Matt didn't realize the extent of his injuries until he tried to put weight on his right knee, which promptly collapsed under him. He reached backwards, barely catching the rail of his bed with his right hand before he and his IV unit collapsed in a heap. Matt tried to use his left hand to help pull himself up, but pain shot through his arm like fire at the attempt. He hooked his other arm through the bed railing and painfully held himself in position until he could gather more strength to right himself.

"Are you all right?"

The nurse who'd drawn his blood earlier appeared at his side, looking concerned as she helped him back into bed. "Your alarm went off at the nurse's station. You shouldn't be trying to stand."

Matt tried to laugh off his embarrassment at being found in such a state. "Tell it to my bladder."

The nurse chuckled. "Okay, I understand. You can tell your bladder that your dislocated kneecap has to stay in bed if it hopes to heal properly. I'll get you a bedpan."

Ten minutes later, Matt was resettled under the covers with memories starting to flow as he lay still. The doctor entered the room right after the nurse finished attending him and explained more about his condition before leaving Matt alone to ponder his situation.

Kidney infection, he thought. Guess somebody hit or kicked me in the back enough times to cause a problem. Badly bruised left arm, dislocated kneecap, bruised ribs, mild concussion and enough bumps and bruises to make me look like Mike Tyson's sparring partner. And the doctor says I need to take it easy once I get out.

I'm starting to remember more of what happened, but I wish I could remember everything, Matt thought. It has to be an interesting story.

"Good morning, Matthew. Or do you go by Matt?"

Matt looked up, startled to realize that someone had entered the room while he was thinking. Not just someone, he thought; it's her again. How does she know my name?

This morning the woman had on low rider jeans and a hot pink T-shirt, tied off to display her belly button. She smiled as she answered Matt's unspoken question. "You told me your name last night. Guess you were pretty out of it, though; I'm not surprised you don't remember."

Matt chuckled. "Oh, yeah. Matt's fine. You helped me out?"

The woman focused clear blue eyes on Matt and looked him up and down, unnerving him slightly. "Yeah, that was me. You had a rough time of it."

"You don't know the half of it."

Matt was stunned to realize that he didn't know the half of it either. He knew he'd been in a fight, but some of the details were still hazy. The only thing he knew for sure was that either during or after the partially remembered fight, somebody robbed him. He cursed under his breath, and then followed it with a mental apology to God. "Can I ask you a crazy sounding question?"

She looked Matt in the eye. "Go ahead."

"Who are you?"

She smiled. "Samaria Lewis. I was at that rest stop last night when you got jumped. The guys who did it were pulling off in two cars when I saw you."

Crap, Matt thought, they *did* take my car!

"I take it from the look on your face that one of those

cars was yours."

Matt's face looked as if it had turned to stone. "If it was a brand new silver Lexus, then yes, it was."

Samaria smiled. "Look at you. Too stubborn to die or even be too badly hurt when you clearly should have. You must be a Taurus."

Matt sighed. He knew a lot of people caught up in astrology, some more deeply than others. Sister Sawyer at church was among the worst. She could shout and praise the Lord with the best of them, but most of the church knew that she wouldn't even go to the bathroom without reading her horoscope first to make sure it was the right time.

Maybe we'll get the chance to talk about this, he thought. I don't know if she professes to be a Christian or not, but that astrology garbage is just more deception.

Then again, if that tight outfit is any example, I'm guessing she hasn't seen the inside of a church in a few years.

Matt heard Samaria saying something, but a sudden and powerful burst of weariness prevented him from answering. He awoke half an hour later, alone in the room. Looking around, he found a note on the night table.

> *Call if you need anything. I'll be back*
> *later this afternoon.*
> *Samaria*

Curious as to why Samaria was still hanging around, Matt carefully assumed a corpselike position and went back to sleep, dreaming of the previous night before he even realized it.

\*       \*       \*

*"Hey! Your brother's fighting some dude out there!"*

*A few moments earlier, the two companions of the man parked next to Matt had reached the door with their purchases. They were emerging with assorted Roy Rogers burgers, fries, drinks and desserts when they saw the altercation in the parking lot.*

*"Dag, he sure is, and dude's kicking Tony's behind."*

\*       \*       \*

*Reverend Jason Thatcher exited the rest stop, steeling for the drive that remained. Okay, he thought, only half an hour more. You've made five and a half hours already. This is just the homestretch. Hang in there, Thatcher.*

*He yawned as he headed for his car, happy at the prospect of finally returning home to Wilmington, Delaware. The revival services he'd preached in Raleigh, North Carolina, had been exhausting, and all he wanted to do was go to bed and stay there. He was definitely regretting having driven there himself instead of taking the train or even flying in.*

*A commotion directly in front of Reverend Thatcher seemed to be taking up a lot of the parking lot. As he made his way forward, he noticed a crowd forming and heard the sounds of a fight. Great, he thought. Now I'll never be able to get to my car.*

The crowd parted enough for Reverend Thatcher to see two black men, each over six feet tall, slugging it out. The slightly smaller of them slammed the other into a car, and when his opponent stayed down, celebrated his victory.

*Looks like it's over,* Reverend Thatcher thought. *Good.*

Just then, two more black men shouldered their way past the reverend and ran towards the fight area. Before Reverend Thatcher could respond to being thrust out of the way, the bigger of the two men tore into the man who'd just won the fight.

*     *     *

Tom and Torrence put their food down beside the door and bolted towards the fight, shoving assorted bystanders aside in their haste to help Tony. Torrence, the smaller of the two, hesitated slightly, but Tom dove into the fray without hesitating, punching Matt in the back of the head. Matt tried to stand and fight, but that one punch nearly knocked him cold. Matt staggered backwards, trying not to pass out.

"Best back up off my brother."

Matt braced his hands against his car and mule-kicked backwards with his right leg, managing to connect with Tom's groin. Tom doubled over in pain, giving Matt the chance to turn and press the attack. Not seeing the third man, Matt lashed out at Tom, managing to land a solid left to his jaw.

*I ain't stupid,* Matt thought. *Better get outta here*

*before both of them jump on me.*

A lance of pain shot through his shoulder and raced through his left arm, effectively paralyzing it. Matt turned to face this new attack and promptly took a second hard blow, this time to the chest. It knocked the wind out of him.

Matt turned to see a third man, noticeably shorter and skinnier than the other two. Tony and Tom's friend Torrence was brandishing the Club (taken off his steering wheel) as a weapon. Matt knew he had no chance now.

As if to punctuate the hopelessness of the situation, Tony slowly got to his feet, shook his head as if to clear it and smiled at the change in his fortunes.

"How you like me now, Holyfield? All of a sudden you ain't looking so tough. And I sure don't hear you talking no more trash."

Shaking off the pain from his beating, Tony joined Tom and Torrence in going upside Matt's head (and various other body parts). Matt was unconscious in less than a minute.

\*       \*       \*

"Hey, there's a fight outside!"

Soon-to-be recording artist Ernestine Rush came out of the Ladies' Room and noticed various patrons of the rest stop running outside and assembling on the sidewalk.

What's going on out there, she thought? She looked around for the members of her band, Barak. Spotting her drummer Kareem, she made her way gingerly through the crowd, managing to get to his side. "What's going on?"

The six foot five Kareem peered over the crowd. "Fight. Looks like two guys going at it because one guy parked too close to the other guy's car or something."

The fight seemed to end, and Kareem sighed with relief. "Come on, Ernie. We've got a schedule to keep. I see most of the others over there, near the van. Let's start edging our way out of here."

Kareem put a protective arm around Ernestine and shielded her with his body as they pushed through the crowd, sliding towards the fight scene to get to their van. Ernestine sighed with relief; large, unruly crowds tended to be detrimental to the health of people her size (five foot one).

"Whoa!"

Ernestine and Kareem had just reached the other Barak members when the crowd reacted to something. Ernestine noticed her keyboardist's eyes widen with surprise.

"Joe, what happened?"

He pointed towards the renewed battle. "The first guy beat the second guy down, and then two more guys jumped in it. Looks like they're friends of the guy who got his butt beat, 'cause they're beating the first guy like he stole something."

\*     \*     \*

With the fight over, Torrence tossed the Club back into Tony's car. "Man, we can't take you nowhere without you starting stuff! You lucky we didn't let him kick your butt *some more!"*

Tony glared down at Matt's unconscious form. *"Shut up, man. He was the one out here starting stuff!"*

*"Uh huh. And that lady over there calling the cops on her cell phone is about to finish it."*

Tony looked where Tom was pointing, cursed and then quickly went through Matt's pockets. Tom looked appalled. *"Man, what you doing?"*

*"Dude was talking smack about my car, I'm taking his!"*

His right eye rapidly swelling shut, Tony removed Matt's car keys, wallet and leather jacket before jumping into Matt's Lexus. Tom and Torrence hesitated, and then, not wanting to be left to take the blame, grabbed their food and jumped into Tony's Lincoln. They drove off in both cars, leaving Matt to bleed in the parking lot.

\*     \*     \*

Ernestine couldn't see over the crowd, but judging by the sounds of lopsided combat drifting her way, she was glad she couldn't. Just then, tires screeched and two cars fled the scene. One man lay at the scene of the fight, unmoving and apparently unconscious.

Joe strained on tiptoe to see what was going on. *"I think they stole that brother's car."*

Kareem was also straining to peer over the crowd. *"I think they robbed him, too; looked like one of them was bending over him after the fight ended. Hard to tell from here, though."*

*The van driver, David, the bass player, honked the horn. "Come on! We have a schedule to keep!"*

*Theresa, one of the backup singers, hesitated. "Shouldn't we try to help the guy or something?"*

*Some of the crowd lingered, also wondering what to do. Kareem pointed in their direction. "He's got some help. We have a recording session at ten o'clock tomorrow morning. Actually since it's after midnight, make that this morning. We're currently in Delaware. We still have nearly an hour more to go before we get to Philadelphia. If we want to salvage a decent amount of sleep once we finally get to the hotel, we need to leave now."*

*Ernestine had the same question as Theresa, but she relented and allowed Kareem and the others to escort her in a path around the prone body of the fight victim and towards the van. She pulled a cell phone from her purse and made a quick call to their hotel in Philadelphia. Reassured that their room reservations were still in effect, they got back on the road.*

\*     \*     \*

*My God, that was brutal! Reverend Thatcher thought. Wonder what it was all about?*

*Thoughts of stepping in, of trying to help the wounded man, of mediating the disagreement and of helping in general flashed through the minister's head. Seeing the assailants leave sent a wave of relief through him.*

*I probably would have gotten beaten up, too, he thought. Surely someone in that crowd will call 911 and get that man some medical attention. I need to get back home to my family and stop trying to save the world.*

*Shaking his head in disgust, Reverend Thatcher took a wide path around the fight scene, found his car, climbed in and took off for home, completing his journey in twenty minutes flat. His yearning was to collapse into bed the minute he got home and not to get out until he was fully rested. His Saturday schedule was empty, and he was looking forward to a good rest followed by quality time with his wife and children. However, it didn't work as planned. Instead of comatose sleep, he got fitful slumber sprinkled liberally with visions of the violence he'd witnessed earlier.*

*He didn't remember every image from his assorted dreams, but one stood out above the others. The man he saw, the one who took such a horrendous beating, was in his face. He was pointing an accusing finger and kept repeating one phrase over and over:*

*"Why didn't you help me, Man of God?"*

*Reverend Thatcher woke up from that one in a cold sweat. He sat up so forcefully it awakened his wife, Sheila. After apologizing for waking her, he promised to explain later what alarmed him so badly and tried again to get a good rest.*

\*     \*     \*

Matt woke up, feeling somewhat refreshed after having slept for seven hours. Just as before, he'd dreamed of the previous night's events, but this particular vision puzzled him. He kept his eyes closed for a moment longer as he thought things over.

I was seeing folks who weren't anywhere near me last night, he thought, and hearing conversations that there's no way I could have heard. Those guys must have hit me harder than I thought.

He was still pondering this when he opened his eyes and saw Samaria sitting there.

"How are you feeling, Matt?"

Matt winced; the effort of inclining the bed upwards to talk to her hurt, but hearing Samaria's voice was soothing. "Like I got hit by a bus."

"I saw what happened. You're not far off."

Matt smiled faintly. "It hurts to breathe. Bruised ribs, they tell me."

"Are you all the way awake now?"

Matt looked puzzled. "Why do you ask?"

"Well, when I came in, you were mumbling to yourself and your eyes were sort of open. I thought you were awake, especially when you said, 'What happened?' I was telling you what I saw when you woke up for real."

Matt chuckled to himself. Explains where all those details came from, he thought.

Samaria looked him up and down as he lay in the bed. "I'm glad the hospital admitted you as fast as they did. They tried to put you off when I first brought you in."

"Why?"

"There was a big accident on I-95 right around the time we got here. It was a seven-car pileup, and a lot of folks were injured. They wanted to hold off on examining you until they took care of all those folks."

Matt blinked in surprise. "Why didn't they?"

Matt could hear the pride in Samaria's voice. "Because I insisted they look at you right away. I told them you'd been jumped by three guys, that they kicked you a few times while you were down and that if you had internal injuries and they didn't realize it, they'd be open to a huge lawsuit."

Matt laughed, and then stopped as fire shot through his ribcage. "And I'm sure they thought that you might be the one filing said lawsuit."

Samaria blushed. "I might have implied that you were my boyfriend."

Matt smiled, suppressing another laugh. "Did you imply that you're a lawyer, too?"

She chuckled. "No, but once they realized that I do have some medical knowledge, they backed down and admitted you rather quickly."

They fell silent for a moment. Matt looked Samaria up and down. She does love her tight clothes, he thought.

"I'm curious. What brought you to that travel plaza last night?"

Matt said, "I was on my way back home to North Carolina. My sister lives in Bristol, Connecticut, and I was there visiting her, her husband and my nephew."

Samaria smiled. "And you got to the rest stop just in time for your beat-down."

Matt chuckled. "Guess so. Wish this had been one of those times when I was running late."

They both laughed. Just then, Matt's doctor came in to

check his injuries. Samaria excused herself so that the doctor could work and went in search of caffeine.

\*　　　\*　　　\*

"We are screwed!"

Tony looked menacingly at Torrence. "Fool, what are you talking about?"

Torrence stood up to his full five feet four inches and glared daggers at Tony. "I'm talking about the fact that you stole some dude's wallet, leather jacket and Lexus in front of about a hundred witnesses, after you started a fight with him and forced us to help you beat the snot out of him. Did you think maybe nobody would notice?"

Tony ran his hand over his shaved head. "You see any cops coming to get us? Looks to me like we got away."

Torrence slammed his hand on the table hard enough to make Tony jump. "That's not the point! The point is, none of that mess had to happen! Beating a brother down is one thing, but you done robbed him too! You must want to see Gander Hill Prison from the inside."

"Ain't like I planned it! He the one talking all that smack and trying to act like I wrecked his car. I ain't hardly touch it. Punk. Coming off like he was gonna try and sue a brother for damages or some crap like that."

Tom came in from the kitchen, a can of Coke in his hand. "Fool, you ain't got no money! How's anybody gonna sue you when you fifty cent short of having a quarter? You just got mad because he got a Lexus and you got a raggedy piece of crap Lincoln older then your momma."

Tony laughed. "Last time I looked, I had a Lincoln and a Lexus."

"How you gonna drive it, fool? You know that brother done called the cops about his car being stolen by now. You do so much as start it up and the cops be all over you."

Tony glared at his brother. "I ain't gonna be no more fools, Tom."

Torrence rolled his eyes. "Dude's got a point, Tone. You can't *ever* drive that car. Shoot, we can't even leave this *house*. You know that dude got the cops looking for us by now."

Tony laughed again. "Ain't nobody gonna find us here. If they looking, they be looking at my crib or my parents' or even yours. They ain't gonna just wake up and go, 'Oh, let's go by Torrence's aunt's crib; they be hiding there.'"

Torrence glared at Tony again. "You're lucky my aunt and uncle asked me to house-sit while they're in Florida. Otherwise, we'd have to skip town over this mess."

Tom drained the rest of his Coke. "Yeah, man, we need to be glad his aunt and uncle are scared somebody's gonna break in and rob them again."

Tony laughed. "Man, anybody breaks in here, we'll kick his butt same way we beat that punk down last night!"

Tom glared at Tony. "We? Please, Torrence and I whupped that dude. All *you* did was start the whole mess and make us bail your butt out after he put his foot up in you!"

Tony gave Tom the finger and issued some more idle

threats, but deep down, he was thankful.

We can chill here for now, he thought. By the time his aunt and uncle get back, the heat should be off.

*     *     *

Samaria slowly walked back from the soda machine, sipping a Mountain Dew as she thought things over.

Why am I still in this state, she thought. When I left Houston, my goal was not to stay anywhere for more than a night. I was gonna keep going until I hit New York, or at least New Jersey. I should be back on the road by now.

It's because of him, she thought. I couldn't just keep walking. Not after those other folks just left him for dead. And church folks to boot! They should have been the first ones to pick him up off the asphalt instead of passing on by. Bunch of phonies.

Her decision made, she quickened her pace back towards Matt's room.

*     *     *

I never knew two days could be this long, Matt thought. After forty-eight hours of hospital food, blood tests and time spent watching Demerol drip from IV bags into his veins, Matt was being released.

I still don't know where to go, though, he thought, sitting on the edge of his bed. They stole my wallet with all my cash and credit cards in it, which means I can't even check into a hotel. And my bag was in the car, which means I don't have any clothes except what I got on.

He looked at his watch. Four o'clock, Matt thought. Three hours later than when they said they were releasing me. Well, it's not like I have anywhere to go. God, show me what to do. I don't have any family nearby. I don't want to call Elaine to come all the way from Connecticut to get me, and I don't have any money for a hotel.

Just then, a knock sounded at the door. "Are you decent?"

Matt smiled at the familiar voice. "Yup. Come on in."

Samaria reentered the room and chuckled to see Matt dressed in the same clothes he was wearing when the fight happened: black jeans and a red sweatshirt, both of which had sufficient rips and tears to testify that their wearer had been through something.

"That outfit's seen better days, huh?"

Matt laughed, protecting his sore ribs as he did. "Yeah, guess so."

Samaria snickered and then cocked her head to one side, as if checking him out. "I see they're releasing you soon. What are your plans?"

Matt shrugged his shoulders. "Good question. I suppose I should get over to the police station first. I called when I woke up yesterday and filed a report, but I need to follow up and see if they've found any leads. After that, I need to figure out my next move."

He tried to stand up, but his knee buckled, and he sat back down on the bed hard. Samaria shook her head. "That knee isn't in any kind of shape for you to be driving. Your left arm either, for that matter. Do you have someplace to stay around here until you heal up a little more?"

Matt started to reassure her that he was okay, but decided to tell the truth instead. "Actually I don't. I was going to grab a cab and check into a hotel for a few days, but then I remembered they stole my wallet."

Samaria looked concerned.

"You don't have any friends or family in the area?"

Matt shook his head no. "My only close family still living is my sister Elaine. I called to let her know I was here, but I didn't want her trying to come down from Connecticut. She's been sick herself, and she needs to stay home and recover. Her husband Ray would come if I asked him to, but I'd rather he stay and take care of her. She doesn't need to be running around after their two-year-old son when she's not that far removed from a serious bout with pneumonia."

"Well, let me know where you need to go. I can give you a ride to wherever."

Just then, the doctor came with Matt's release papers. Forms were signed, a wheelchair was brought, and an orderly wheeled Matt to the elevator.

Samaria followed them, lost in thought. An idea was forming in her mind; given her limited finances and the major decisions she had to make, it was ridiculous for her to even think about getting any more involved, but she couldn't help herself.

She went and got her car and brought it around to the front entrance. The orderly helped Matt get into the car. Samaria slid in behind the wheel and prepared to leave the parking lot.

"Have you decided where you want me to take you yet?"

Matt sighed. "No. I guess the police station will have to do. I suppose they can help me from there in finding someplace to stay.

"You can stay with me."

Matt's head snapped up. "What?"

Samaria struggled to maintain a neutral expression as they pulled out of the parking lot. "I checked into the Embassy Suites the other night. I've been on the road since I left Texas four days ago, and I need a day or two to rest before I get back on the road. I don't know anyone around here, and frankly, I could use someone to talk to."

Matt's mind whirled at this unexpected offer. We're both single, he thought. It's not right for us to spend time together like that in close quarters. But I don't have anywhere else to stay or anyone else I can call.

A line from the movie "An Officer and a Gentleman" ran through Matt's head: "I got nowhere else to go! I got nothing!"

Apparently sensing Matt's discomfort, Samaria spoke up again. "Don't worry, it's a suite. There's plenty of room for us both without getting too close, if you know what I mean."

"I'd be completely freeloading. I mean, I don't have any money, and I don't think there's a branch of my bank here in Delaware for me to get any."

Samaria smiled. "Did I say anything about you paying your way? If it makes you feel better, your payment would be keeping me company and making me feel safer at night."

Matt shrugged in resignation. "Well Samaria, you've made me an offer I can't refuse."

Samaria sighed. "But, there's something you should know before you decide."

Matt looked expectant. Samaria took a deep breath, inexplicably dreading her next sentence. "I'm a prostitute."

\*     \*     \*

"Okay, hold up! What in the world was that?"

Ernestine Rush sighed wearily and removed her headphones. She and the rest of Barak had been futilely trying to record her first single, Living Sacrifice, all afternoon.

The devil is all up in here, she thought. We haven't gotten one thing accomplished.

Obadiah Saunders, music minister of Greater Mount Sinai Christian Church and producer of this debut CD, was furious at what he perceived as a lack of effort on the part of the group.

"Barak' means 'Praise!' Let me tell you all this: If that's the best praise you can offer, God isn't interested!"

Already tired, the members of Barak said nothing, knowing the truth in Obadiah's statement.

"Deborah and Theresa, you are backup singers. That means you back Ernestine up, not drown her out! I know you have those powerful soprano voices working, but try to hold it down! Kareem, would you like to play the same rhythm that the rest of the group is working with instead of randomly beating that drum to death? I think that would make things run a bit more smoothly!"

Obadiah ranted and raved for another three minutes, adjusting a microphone here and giving more scathing advice there until he was satisfied. "Okay, let's take it from the chorus. Ernie, you lead in."

Obadiah signaled his technicians to start over, and then cued the musicians. As they started a lively gospel beat, Ernestine took a deep breath and started to sing.

*(Lord let my life) Lord, let my life be a living*
*sacrifice (living sacrifice)*
*(Let Your Spirit) Let Your Spirit show throughout*
*my life (throughout my life)*
*Through trials and temptations*
*Stay here by my side (right here by my side)*
*Let my life be a living sacrifice.*

Just as they began to repeat the chorus, a sudden flash erupted from Joe's keyboard. Simultaneously, one of the microphones chose that moment to shut down as well.

Obadiah signaled everyone to stop again and called the group together. "Clearly the devil is working against us. He knows that Ernestine and Barak will bless some lives, and he can't stand to see that happen. We need to agree in prayer, to come against him and let him know we won't stand for it."

Barak murmured their agreement. They formed a prayer circle, and Grady Barnes (one of the backup singers) led them. His resonant bass voice rang out as he rebuked the devil and implored God to be with them as they sought to lift up His name in song.

Normally, Ernestine loved her group's prayer time, but this time didn't feel right. It felt as though someone had sealed off the ceiling with concrete and that no matter how fervently they prayed, their prayers couldn't pass through.

*     *     *

Matt did a double take. Samaria regarded him stoically.

"I could have said I'm in the entertainment industry or that I'm a 'social worker,' but I've been around too much to play word games. Besides, you can tell from my clothes that I don't exactly work for the government."

Matt smiled grimly. "Hope you're not in this for the money. I had some, but those three thugs stole it all."

Samaria glared daggers at him. "Not too judgmental, huh?"

Matt closed his eyes, wishing he could take back his statement. "Sorry, that was uncalled for. You've done nothing but help me; I really appreciate that. I apologize for being snide."

Samaria waved dismissively. "No problem. I wasn't surprised; you Christians are nothing, if not consistent."

Matt raised his eyebrows questioningly, unconsciously fingering the small golden cross around his neck (the one thing the thugs didn't take).

"Let me explain what I mean. You talk a good game, and some of you really mean it, but when all is said and done, you're all about number one. And when you have an attitude like that, you tend to treat other folks like number two, if you get my meaning."

Matt struggled to sit up straight. "All Christians aren't like that. There are some folks who actually do walk the walk instead of just talking the talk."

Samaria maintained a stony expression. "Mmm hmm. And there are others who clearly don't. There was a time I was doing three pastors and two priests every week, not to mention a whole lot of members of their congregations. They might have been in church on Sunday morning, but they were with me on Saturday night. And those folks who walked right by you? Your own kind."

Matt looked at her, eyebrows raised.

"Oh yes, my brother. After you got beat down, there were lots of folks standing there, and nobody but me helped your butt. I saw a preacher with his collar on walk about twenty feet in a wide circle to keep from getting too close. Guess he didn't want your blood on his shoes. And then I saw a whole bunch of folks, men and women alike, get on this bus with crosses and 'Praise the Lord' painted all over it. They were a gospel choir, I think. Guess they were too busy getting ready to sing to pick you up off the parking lot. Maybe all you Christians aren't like that, but the ones I always see are."

Samaria fell silent again, leaving Matt with his thoughts. *She's right*, he thought. *Christians sure aren't perfect.*

*But she's a prostitute*, he thought. *I can't shack up with a prostitute; they'll run me out of church if anyone was to* find out!

*"Judge not that ye be not judged."*

The words landed feather-light in Matt's spirit, startling him and shocking him out of his negative train of thought. Okay God, he thought, I get it.

"So, is it much further to your hotel?"

\*        \*        \*

Reverend Thatcher sat brooding in his home office, wondering what to do. For two straight Sundays, he'd preached perhaps the worst sermons of his six-year-old preaching career, and deep in his heart, he knew exactly why. His wife had noticed that he wasn't at his best and tried to get him to tell her what was wrong, but for once, he wouldn't tell her what was on his mind. Instead of trying further to draw him out, she took their three children to visit her mother, but only with his promise that they would talk this out upon her return later that afternoon.

"God," he prayed aloud, "I know I missed a chance to minister that night, but what can I do to correct it now?"

His gaze fell on the Sunday paper. His routine was to read the paper cover to cover after returning home from services, but in this case, he'd somehow managed to avoid reading the local section from the previous Sunday. He thought it had been tossed out with the other old papers, but somehow it remained here on the floor of his study. Maybe this will help clear my head, he thought.

After reading the day's paper end to end, he picked up the Local section from the previous week. He skimmed through it and was about to put it aside when an article at the bottom of the first page caught his eye.

### Man Carjacked At Rest Stop

*An out-of-state visitor was carjacked Friday night by three men following a disagreement.*

*The victim, Matthew Hayes of Durham, NC, said that he got into an altercation with one of the men after the man allegedly hit Hayes' car door with his. They argued and a fight broke out, at which time the second man's two friends joined the fight. After overpowering Hayes, they apparently took his leather jacket, his wallet and car keys. Witnesses say that the first man involved in the fight drove off in Hayes' silver Lexus while the others left the scene in a gray Lincoln Continental. None of the witnesses was able to give a clear description of the three assailants; anyone with information is encouraged to contact the New Castle County Police as soon as possible.*

Reverend Thatcher sighed. Okay, God, he thought, you don't have to post a billboard.

\*      \*      \*

"By the way, you can relax. I'm out of the life for good. I know you were wondering, but you don't have to worry about me conducting any business in the room we'll be staying in."

Matt fought back a smile. "You said you're from

93

Texas."

Samaria expertly wove in and out of traffic, handling her green Toyota Tercel as if it were a sleek sports car. "Well, I'm actually from Louisiana, but I wound up in Texas eventually. My mom was a blond-haired, blue-eyed Hispanic, if you can believe that, and my dad was black. Well, that's what my mom told me, and it's clearly some black in me. Anyway, my childhood sucked. I left home at eighteen and found myself working the streets at nineteen."

My God, Matt thought, that's awful!

Samaria continued without awaiting a response. "I was in the life for maybe three years now, but I finally decided enough was enough. I waited until Crazy Craig—my pimp—was asleep, slipped him a little something to make sure he wasn't going to wake up before I left, and then I cleaned him out. I took four thousand dollars—money I earned and never saw any of—and I also took my car back. I had the Tercel when I started with him, but he hardly ever let me drive it."

Matt was stunned silent as Samaria wove her tale. "I just started driving. My plan was to get out of town and not look back. I figured once I got far enough away, I'd settle down somewhere and reinvent myself. No more selling it to whoever has an itch to scratch, no more getting slapped around by some pimp. I'm starting fresh."

She looked at him and smiled wanly. "I didn't think I'd be spending any of my money on anyone but me, but looks like we're stuck with each other until we both can get it together." She pulled into a shopping center. "And if that's the case, we'll need a few things."

\*     \*     \*

Ernestine Rush had had a long day.

It seemed that nothing went right. She'd gone to church in a good mood, praying that there wouldn't be a second straight day as disastrous as Saturday's attempt to record the single. They'd had to abort their efforts once they discovered that both the keyboard and the sound system were basically fried.

However, it seemed like Saturday's aura of mishaps spilled over into their Sunday worship service. The organist was late, half the choir had attitudes, and the soloist for one of the songs they wanted to minister that day was home with the flu. As choir director, Ernestine had to pull things together the best she could, which meant everything from soothing ruffled egos to switching from the song they had planned to one that she led. After singing all day yesterday, leading a song today was the last thing Ernestine wanted to do. The congregation seemed to get a blessing from it, but she and the choir felt like they'd run a marathon by the time the pastor got up to preach.

Ministering in song isn't usually this tough for us, she thought. It seemed like we had to fight the devil hand-to-hand for every note. Something's wrong, she thought, and I'm not sure what.

Just then, the phone rang. "Hello?"

"Ernie, it's me."

Ernestine relaxed to hear Kareem on the other end.

"Is it me or did today feel less like a labor of love and more like hard labor?"

Ernestine sighed with relief. "Kareem, you just put my thoughts into words. It was rough today, and I can't figure out why."

"I think I can."

He read the story to her from last week's Local section about Matt Hayes.

"We saw that, Ernie. We saw almost the whole thing, and we walked away. We left that man bleeding in the parking lot because we wanted to keep our schedule. No, because I wanted us to keep our schedule."

Ernestine took a deep breath. He's right, she thought. I agreed to that without putting up a fuss. God can't be pleased with us right now.

"Kareem, let's pray. And after that, let's call the others."

\*        \*        \*

"Hey, wake up!"

Matt blinked awake to see Samaria standing beside his bed, an amused expression on her face.

"You were snoring like a champion; I'm glad I needed to wake you up—you might have scared the neighbors."

Matt laughed and gingerly put his feet on the floor. He carefully got up, trying not to put much weight on his bad knee.

"The knee didn't buckle; that's a good sign."

Samaria took the opportunity to look Matt over and check his bandages. "Well, Matt, your bruised left arm is a lot better. The knee seems to be improving, too, but you still should stay off it as much as you can. You're healing nicely. Of course you're still walking like Fred Sanford...."

Matt laughed. "Gimme a break! I got triple-banked not that long ago. It's not like I can run the marathon or anything."

Samaria looked at him with a barely suppressed giggle. "'Triple-banked?' Just how old are you?"

Matt feigned anger. "Old? Come on now. I may have a year or two on you, but I'm not the only one in this room who remembers Run DMC and Kurtis Blow!"

They laughed. "And since we're on the subject, just what is the cool way to say I got my butt kicked?"

Samaria smiled. "I believe it would be to say that you got 'housed.'"

"'Housed,' is it? Well whatever you call it, it sure hurt while they were doing it!"

Samaria cracked up. "Okay, I see your point."

Matt reached for the phone to see if there were any leads in his case. He hung up after a few minutes, smiling.

"Samaria, would you mind giving me a ride to the police station?"

Half an hour later, Matt and Samaria returned to the hotel. Matt had his travel bag hanging over one shoulder by its strap. A borrowed cane occupied one hand, but with the other, Matt unconsciously caressed the bag like it was his most treasured possession.

"Should I leave you two alone?"

Matt didn't need to look at Samaria to know that she was smiling her familiar smile. "Laugh all you want; it feels good to have my drawers back!"

Samaria laughed. "Yeah, I guess it is kinda bad not to have any clothes at all with you."

Matt dropped the bag beside the couch and sat down heavily, favoring his right knee. "Glad they didn't see anything in there they wanted to keep. Apparently they just threw it out the car while they were rolling. The police found it beside the road about three miles away from the travel plaza."

Samaria pointed to a white plastic covered tag on one side of the bag. "Good thing you marked your territory."

Matt laughed. "I use this bag a lot when I travel, and the airport has lost my luggage more times than I care to remember. After the second time, I marked this bad boy in a hurry!"

He reached a hand out in Samaria's direction. "If you and this cane can help me stand up, I think I'll take advantage of this blessing and go change my clothes!"

Matt came out of the bathroom dressed in a Carolina Panthers sweatshirt and jeans. "I feel like a new man."

Samaria smiled. "Well, you certainly look like one. I'm glad they found your bag; I thought I was going to have to take you back to that K-Mart and hook you up with another outfit or two."

Matt hobbled over to the couch and sat down. "You really would have, wouldn't you?"

"Yup. Any excuse to shop."

Matt laughed and took a deep breath. "Feels kind of weird not being in church."

Samaria smiled. "Old habits die hard, huh?"

"Sure do. My parents had me in church from the

womb. I knew from an early age that every living creature in our house best have its behind dressed and ready for the eleven o'clock service. I think they even had the dog baptized."

Samaria laughed until tears flowed. "You are crazy!"

Matt chuckled. "I've been accused of worse. I haven't missed a Sunday at church in about three years, and that was when I had a nasty case of flu."

"Ahh, I'm harboring a church boy! Better throw you out before you get to preaching."

"I take it you're not a church girl."

Samaria smiled. "Well, church and I have an agreement; I don't bother church and church don't bother me. God knows where to find me if He wants me; not that I think He cares to look."

She laughed, but Matt couldn't find any humor in her statement. It always concerned him when he heard someone so convinced that God didn't care about them.

Samaria noticed Matthew flexing his leg, and frowned. "Let me see that knee."

Matt obliged, rolling up his pant leg gingerly. Samaria knelt in front of him and began to probe cautiously. "It's still more swollen than I'd like. Let me put some more ice on that."

Samaria went to the ice bucket she'd filled earlier and replenished one of the ice packs they'd picked up from K-Mart. He flinched as Samaria applied the ice pack to his knee.

"I know about the other injuries, but how did this one happen?"

Matthew grimaced as the cold hit his joints. "This is from the third guy who jumped in the fight. He was about a foot shorter than I am. Apparently he didn't feel confident enough to take a swing at me, so the little weasel kneecapped me with the Club. He wanted to make me fall so they could kick my butt more efficiently. It worked."

He fell silent for a moment as he gathered his thoughts. "That little creep got me in the ribs and tore up my arm, too. Amazing how he did more damage than those other two guys my own size did."

Samaria looked somber. "If you had the chance, would you beat the crap out of them in return?"

Matt pondered that for a second. "I would surely want to, but I hope God would give me the ability to resist that temptation. Bad enough I provoked that fight in the first place. God's not pleased with me for that, and I know he wouldn't approve of me going after those guys."

Samaria looked puzzled. "But doesn't the Bible say 'An eye for an eye, a tooth for a tooth?'"

Matt perked up. Hmm, he thought. She knows some Bible, but she doesn't believe God cares about her. Interesting.

"Sure does. But, if everybody did that, we'd all be blind and toothless."

Samaria laughed until tears flowed. Matt gingerly reached into his travel bag for his Bible. He turned to Exodus 21:24, the scripture she was referring to. He then explained that this was part of the law of Moses.

"Jesus came to fulfill the law, which means that we don't have to follow all those fifty million rules and regulations any more. The basics still apply; that's the Ten Commandments."

Samaria smiled. "You mean all the 'Thou shalt nots?'"

Samaria's smile infected Matt. "Yep, that would be them."

"Isn't the first one, 'Thou shalt not do anything that might be remotely fun?'"

Matt laughed like a lunatic. "Yeah, I guess it does seem like that." He leafed through the Bible again. "Now this is the one I needed to have followed that night." He turned to Matthew 5:38-39. "You have heard that it was said, 'Eye for eye and tooth for tooth.' But I tell you, do not resist an evil person. If someone strikes you on the right cheek, turn to him the other also." He paused. "That's one of the things I still need to turn over to God: my nasty temper. I shouldn't have provoked that guy. I definitely needed to turn the other cheek."

Samaria smiled. "Maybe not. They probably would've kicked you in that one, too!"

Matthew looked at her a moment and then roared with laughter.

\*     \*     \*

Samaria idly flipped channels on the TV set. In the other room, Matt was sound asleep on the bed, ice pack securely tied to his knee.

What am I doing, she thought. What possessed me to let that man stay with me? For all I know, he could be a serial killer or something, and I gave him a free pass to come in and work me over. He might be hurt now, but what happens when he recovers some more?

Images of Matt turning on her and taking her remaining money and whatever else he cared to help himself to whirled through her head. But, as quickly as she entertained those thoughts, she dismissed them.

He's not like that, she thought. He's had plenty of chances to rob me, but he hasn't. And he's looked, but hasn't tried to touch. If he weren't hurt, I'd swear he was gay.

I need to be honest here, she thought. I wouldn't have done this for just any man, even one injured as badly as he was. This is about Isaiah.

Samaria tried to suppress tears at the thought of her younger brother, the only male in her life who never did her wrong. It's not fair, she thought. With all the thugs and dealers and child molesters out there, why did my brother have to die?

Tears rolled down Samaria's cheeks as she gave in to the wave of sadness.

*    *    *

Ernestine Rush had been pacing around her apartment and praying since she got home from work.

God, she prayed silently, thank You for giving me and Barak another chance. We didn't do Your work, but You're still willing to forgive us.

The conversation she had first with Kareem and then with the other members of Barak replayed in her mind.

After they prayed, Kareem and Ernestine called the other members. Since everyone had three-way calling, they were able to assemble the entire group on what Grady jokingly called Ghetto Conference Call (which they used often when they couldn't meet in person). They talked about having left Matt instead of helping him, they repented of their selfishness, and then the ones who saw what had happened compared notes. Between Kareem and Joe, they saw enough to describe at least two of the three men who beat Matt into the pavement, and the two men made a commitment to go immediately to the police station and share what they knew.

Thank You for straightening us out, God, she prayed. Lord, for the sake of that man, Matthew Hayes, please reveal those men who attacked him. Restore everything they took from him, and if he doesn't know You, please send someone to Him who can tell him how good You are.

The phone rang, interrupting her praying. "Hello?"

"Hey, Ernie, it's me."

She smiled. "Kareem? You sound out of breath."

"I am. We just got in from the police station, and there was a call from Obadiah. They fixed the equipment, and he's asking if we can come in tonight and make up for the time we lost on Saturday."

Ernestine smiled. "Have you talked to the others?"

"Sure have. They're all down. Obadiah said we can come anytime tonight. I told the others to come around seven."

Ernestine looked at her watch, six-fifteen. "Good. I'm going to head over now. See you later!"

Smiling and still praying, Ernestine grabbed her purse and keys and left her apartment.

*       *       *

Matt woke up when he heard the sound of a key in the door. Startled, he slipped out of bed and hobbled towards the front of the suite. Samaria was there, putting two KFC bags and a two-liter bottle of Coke on the table.

"Man, I must have been out cold. I didn't even realize you'd gone out."

Samaria smiled. "You've been knocked out most of the day. I figured you'd be hungry when you woke up. I know I sure am."

Matt laughed. "And you figured—correctly I might add—that I wouldn't say no to a nice piece of chicken."

They dug into the food with gusto. After they finished eating, Samaria reached for another bag and pulled out the News Journal she'd picked up in her travels.

"Listen to my horoscope for today. 'You will cross paths with a tall, dark stranger.'" She chuckled and offered him the paper. "That one sure came true. How about yours? Does it mean anything to you?"

Matt didn't want to break their pleasant coziness, but he couldn't help himself. Enough is enough, Matt thought.

He took the paper from her without reading the horoscope section. "Why do you believe that stuff?"

Samaria looked puzzled. "Because it makes sense. A lot of it fits."

"So you do believe that there is a power higher than

yourself."

Samaria looked annoyed. "I suppose so."

"You're letting what you think the stars can tell you about life dictate what you do and don't do. By giving credibility to this Taurus, Virgo, Capricorn stuff, you're basically worshipping those stars."

Samaria rolled her eyes. We were having such a nice time, she thought. Where did all this come from? "Is there a point to this?"

Matt smiled. Got her, he thought.

"Yes. God *created* the stars; also the sun, the moon, the planets and everything that lives. There's no need to seek answers from His creations when you can get them straight from the Creator."

Just then Matt yawned. He tried to stifle it, but failed, amusing Samaria.

"Wow. Your preaching is putting you to sleep, too."

Matt started to reply and surprised both of them by chuckling. Before they realized it, both of them were consumed by an uncontrollable fit of laughter. Matt tried to stop in deference to his sore ribs, but he couldn't contain it.

Samaria recovered first. "Seriously, though, thanks for sharing that. You have a way of making a sister think. And right now, I think you need to get some sleep. I know it's only like nine-thirty, but the healing process takes a lot of energy; don't be surprised you're so tired. You'll be feeling this way until you heal more."

Matt chuckled. "Sure this is my injuries talking? Come on now, after a good meal, what's the first thing you want to do?"

They chimed in together. "Sleep!"

Samaria laughed. "Okay, maybe it's not your injuries; you're just trifling! Either way, you need some sleep, and I'm not going to keep you from it. Go on and get in bed if you need to. I ain't mad atcha."

Chuckling, Matt limped towards the bedroom he was starting to consider his.

\*     \*     \*

Reverend Thatcher had enjoyed a good night's sleep for the first time since walking away from the injured man at the travel plaza. He'd made a statement to the police yesterday, and it felt good to be doing the right thing.

*Lord,* he prayed silently, *thank You for the push to do the right thing. Now if it's in Your will, can they catch those guys who robbed that brother?*

He continued in prayer for another half hour, interceding for the man whose life he now felt somewhat responsible for.

\*     \*     \*

"Hello?"

Ernestine Rush wasn't surprised to hear her bass backup singer Grady Barnes on the other end of the phone. Hey Grady, you won't believe this, but I was just about to call you."

His deep, rumbling chuckle resounded through the phone. "I believe it all right. I feel a burden to pray for somebody, and unless I miss my guess, you feel it, too."

Ernestine smiled; Grady was the de facto spiritual leader of Barak; a prayer warrior without peer, he was often the one to initiate the "Ghetto Conference Call" so that they could pray as a group.

"I do. That man from the rest stop, Matthew Hayes, has been in my spirit all day long. Can we get the others on the line? I feel like he needs our prayers right about now."

Grady smiled. "Consider it done."

\*     \*     \*

Matt jerked awake. A blood-curdling scream had awakened him, and a second one jolted him into action. Grabbing the cane Samaria had bought him, he limped towards her part of the suite as fast as he could. Samaria lay in her bed, screaming and thrashing. Matt touched her shoulder and shook her.

"Samaria, wake up! You're having a nightmare. Wake up!"

Her eyes popped open. She looked around in pure panic; when she saw Matt standing over her, she recoiled as if dodging a blow. He stepped back, hands raised in a conciliatory gesture. His act of submission seemed to calm her, and her screaming stopped.

"Are...are you okay?"

Samaria waved him off, threw the covers off and bolted for the bathroom. Matt heard the unmistakable sound of retching. She returned to the room a few minutes later, looking surprisingly vulnerable. She had on an oversized T-shirt and sweatpants, and for the first time since Matt met her, looked her age. She sat on the edge of the bed.

"Samaria, do you want me to leave you alone?"

Samaria shook her head no, and he sat down in the chair facing her bed.

"I had a nightmare."

Matt waited for further explanation.

"It's the same nightmare I've been having since I started working the streets; about my brother."

Matt felt a burst of dawning comprehension. "What happened to him?"

"Isaiah and I were close growing up. Our dad ran out right after Isaiah was born, and Mom wasn't always there. She loved us, but most of the time she was either working one of her two or three jobs to support us or she was too depressed to function."

Matt remained silent, listening intently. *Help me, Lord,* he prayed silently. *Samaria is carrying a world of hurt, and she's trying to figure You out. Help me to help her see You clearly.*

"I'm older by three years, but Isaiah was always more mature. Mom always told Isaiah that he was the man of the house from the time he could walk, and he really took it seriously. He always wanted to protect us, to do right by us. He got a job the minute he could get a work permit and delivered papers before that to help bring in money. The neighborhood drug dealers knew we were poor, but Isaiah never even considered that, even when we were at our poorest. It's like he always knew right from wrong."

Matt nodded. "Sounds to me like a man after God's own heart."

Samaria threw her hands up in exasperation. "Exactly! That's a great way to describe him. So why did he have to die so y-young?"

Samaria caught herself before tears could flow. Matt could feel the depths of her anguish.

"What happened?"

"He was coming home from working a late shift at McDonald's and saw these two guys trying to drag some girl off with them. She was on the small side, and these guys were about your size. Well, Isaiah jumped in to help."

Samaria's voice broke, and Matt waited for her to compose herself and continue if she felt up to it. She took another deep breath.

"They beat him to death, Matt. They beat Isaiah like a slave and left him in the street like road kill. He was alive when the police found him, but not conscious, and he died in the hospital. Those thugs either hit him in the head while they were beating him or kicked him in it after they knocked him down."

"Did they catch the guys who did it?"

Samaria nodded. "The girl he rescued got away while they were beating Isaiah and called the cops. They caught those two before they could get two blocks. I'm glad they're locked up, and I'm glad that the girl survived. I just can't understand why thugs like those are still alive and my brother isn't. Wasn't he good enough for God? Why did he have to die?"

A scripture floated into Matt's mind, and without

thinking, he relayed it to Samaria. "Greater love hath no man than this, that a man lay down his life for his friends."

Samaria looked at him in surprise. "What did you say?"

"'Greater love hath no man than this, that a man lay down his life for his friends.' It's from the book of John, fifteenth chapter, thirteenth verse. And it pretty much describes the level of what you did for me."

Samaria's eyes widened. Matt took her hands gently in his. "I know it's hard to take in, but your brother didn't die for no good reason. He chose to give himself up for that girl. You've seen those WWJD bracelets and bumper stickers? Well, WWJD stands for What Would Jesus Do? In that case, your brother did just what Jesus would have done. He stood in the gap between that girl and those men the devil sent to abuse and kill her, and he did it out of love. He died so that she wouldn't have to. And that's what Jesus did for all of us."

Samaria started to reply, but broke down, weeping uncontrollably. Matt held her close as she poured out her grief she'd been holding all this time.

\*     \*     \*

Tony walked briskly through the aisles of the Super Fresh, head down, not looking at his fellow shoppers. The weight of his shopping basket was starting to affect his right arm, still sore from the fight.

Thought I'd go crazy if I had to stay in that house, he thought. Ain't nobody looking for us. It's been more than two weeks; it's over with. Trying to keep me in that house like a slave boy.

The hood of his gray sweatshirt was starting to bother him. He snatched it off his head and took a deep breath; feeling less constricted, he continued his shopping.

*          *          *

Shopping, Reverend Thatcher thought, is God's way for wives to punish their insensitive husbands.

He laughed to himself as he recalled his wife's comments that he'd been in la-la land all weekend, and that maybe he needed some fresh air to clear his head. He was outside with his car keys and a mammoth shopping list in his hand before he knew what hit him.

As usual, he'd chosen the wobbliest cart available, which made it difficult to consult the list and successfully steer at the same time. He'd already had to apologize to one lady whose cart he'd accidentally run into and had nearly been hit by a cart being navigated by a child who was far too small and weak to do a good job of it.

Just a few more items, he thought. Penance done, forgiveness from wife prayerfully accomplished.

He found the last items on the list and headed for the nearest checkout lane, settling into one not far from the express lines.

I don't think I've *ever* had less than twelve items, Reverend Thatcher thought, chuckling to himself. Guess once you have kids, quick shopping trips go out the window.

A commotion to his left attracted his attention. Three of the five shoppers in the express lane were not so politely informing a young black man in a gray-hooded sweatshirt that he had considerably more than twelve items in his cart and that they would greatly appreciate his moving to a more appropriate checkout lane.

What is going on, Reverend Thatcher thought? Seems like everywhere I go lately, there's violence or a threat of violence.

Just then, the young man angrily swept his purchases back into his basket and stormed out of the line, hurling curses and a stiff middle finger at the ones who'd challenged him. As he turned, Reverend Thatcher got a clear view of his face. His eyes widened with surprise and recognition, and despite a strong sense of self-preservation, he found himself unable to stop staring.

"What are you looking at, old man?"

The young man stomped to the end of the line in the next lane over. Reverend Thatcher forced himself to stop staring.

Second chances, Reverend Thatcher thought. Well God, I won't fail you again.

He set his basket on the counter, praying that his cell phone was still in his car where he thought he left it.

*        *        *

"A'right y'all, we got more groceries!"

Tony entered Torrence's aunt's house, all smiles. He felt light from his first outing since they went into hiding the previous Saturday.

"Fool, where you been? What is your problem?"

Tony smiled; he'd barely gotten in the door before Tom was on his case. "I ain't got no problems now, dawg. I finally got out this house and didn't have to look at y'alls ugly mugs for a few hours."

He took the bags into the kitchen. Tom followed him, turning red with anger. "Yeah, and while you was out living the good life, you probably let half the state see *your* ugly mug and get a chance to call the cops."

Tony laughed. "Man, go look in the mirror. Ain't nothing funnier than a yellow man like you turning red."

Torrence came up and smacked Tony in the back of his head. "Don't you take anything serious? We *told* your dumb behind to stay inside until we were sure the heat was off. It's bad enough I went out a few times, but you're the main one they looking for! And you go sneaking out the house like you ain't wanted for nothing."

"Y'all been watching too many movies. I had my hood on most of the time while I was out, and even when I had it off, it ain't like it's folks out there combing the streets looking for the dudes who jacked that brother for his Lexus last week. Ain't like I drove it to the store!"

Tom was livid. "No fool, you drove your same raggedy piece of crap you *always* drive, and that everyone and they momma knows is yours!"

Torrence sat down heavily on the couch. This is getting ugly, he thought. What if somebody recognized Tony while he was out?

Just then, a knock sounded at the door.

*       *       *

"Well, I guess this is goodbye."

Samaria was dressed for the road. She had on a new pair of jeans and yet another pink shirt, but this ensemble wasn't as tight or as provocative as her previous attire. With her duffel bag slung jauntily over her shoulder, she looked like someone going off to college or headed out on vacation.

Matt gave her a quick hug. "Samaria, thank you so much for all you've done for me. You were there when people I should be able to count on weren't, and I am eternally grateful."

Samaria blushed. "You're welcome. You know, I still don't know why I put myself out there for you. I mean, in my line of work—my old line of work, that is—I know what danger is. For all I knew, you could have been faking so I'd get close enough to rob or whatever."

Matt chuckled. "Yeah, I pay those guys to follow me around and beat the crap out of me whenever a fine woman comes around. Works every time."

She glared at him. "All right, wise guy, don't make me regret saving you. I'd give you back to those guys if they weren't already locked up."

They both laughed. Samaria had driven Matt to the police station earlier in the day so that they could identify three suspects who had been arrested the night before. Matt and Samaria both fingered them as the ones, and under interrogation, they quickly confessed. They even went so far as to tell where they'd hidden the Lexus and the jacket. (They'd spent the one hundred dollars they took from Matt's wallet.)

"Samaria, don't ever think you're a nobody. What you did for me proves that you are somebody, that you have character you haven't even scratched the surface of. And believe it or not, God does care about you."

He wrote his home address and phone number on a piece of paper from the notepad on the table and gave it to her. "I don't care where you are or what you're going through. If you need anything, whether it's something material or just a shoulder to cry on, you can count on me."

Samaria winked at him. "How about if I show up on your doorstep? Bet that'd do wonders for your reputation in your church."

Matt laughed. "Let 'em talk. You've shown me the true meaning of the old saying 'Don't judge a book by its cover.'"

She checked his bandages one last time. "I paid for the room already. Thanks for the conversation and all; it's been real. You got me thinking maybe I was wrong. Maybe all Christians aren't phonies."

With a peck on the cheek and a hug, Samaria walked out, leaving a stunned Matt standing there. It took him five minutes to realize that she'd slipped a note into his pocket.

*It was interesting getting to know you. Thanks for being a
special man.
Samaria*

*P.S. You'll need something for gas and tolls to get you back to North Carolina. Drive safely!*

Matt blinked in astonishment. Taped to the very bottom of the note and folded into the tiniest possible square was a hundred dollar bill.

*       *       *

Barry struggled to regain his speech. "Wow! That was a great story!"

J.C. smiled. "Tell me, out of all the people in that story, which acted like a neighbor to the man who was carjacked?"

Barry shrugged his shoulders. "The one who helped him out."

J.C. put a hand on Barry's shoulder. "Next chance you get, make sure you do the same."

# A
# Sprig
# of
# Hope

# By
# Jacquelin Thomas

# A Sprig of Hope

The time had come ...

He was going to have his way with her. Spencer lay in his bed waiting for Dianna to arrive. She was only eighteen years old, yet she fired his blood in a way no other woman had, and he wanted her for himself. Her delicate beauty haunted him night and day, making her his one obsession.

Spencer could not go a day without thinking of Dianna and the way she made him feel. The lilting sound of her voice; the way she held her head whenever she was contemplating something—just the very sound of her laughter set his heart to a rapid beat. He had never loved anyone as much as he loved her. It was so much that Spencer found himself without an appetite.

He heard the sound of the front door opening, and Spencer broke into a sly smile. His eyes traveled to the clock sitting on the bedside table, and noting the time, he knew distinctly that it was Dianna. She usually arrived home from her last class around this time of day.

Spencer listened closely for the sound of Dianna climbing the curving staircase. After a few minutes, he heard her just outside his room. Closing his eyes, he pretended to be asleep.

Dianna strolled into the room to check on Spencer. She smiled when he opened his eyes. "Daddy told me you were sick this morning before I left for school. Are you feeling any better?"

His mouth turned downward, and Spencer shook his head. "I don't know what's come over me. It just hit me all of a sudden."

Dianna was in her freshman year at the university and dreamed of becoming a doctor one day. She placed a hand to his forehead. "It's flu season. You don't eat well, and you work too many long hours. I wouldn't be surprised if you've come down with it." Removing her hand, she asked, "Can I fix you something to eat? We still have some of my famous chicken soup left. I know how much you love it."

Spencer managed a weak smile. "Thank you, Dianna." He could hardly breathe whenever she was around. His heart skipped a beat as he lay there soaking up her beauty like a sponge.

She moved closer to the bed and made sure Spencer was covered. "I don't want you to catch a chill. You get some rest while I warm up the soup."

The light floral scent Dianna always wore tickled his nostrils and warmth spread to his loins. Spencer resisted the urge to run his fingers through her short, wispy curls. He didn't want to move too fast. He didn't want to risk frightening her.

As soon as Dianna left the room, Spencer sat up in bed and removed his shirt. He knew that she loved him. Soon she would know the depth of his love for her. His anticipation grew with each passing second.

When Dianna returned, she found a half-naked Spencer sitting on the side of the bed. The fact that he was only wearing boxers didn't bother her—he was her big brother. Although they had different mothers, Dianna had grown up with Spencer, and they were very close.

"What are you doing up?" she questioned. "I just told you to lay down and get some rest."

He pointed toward the steaming bowl of soup in her hands. "I think it would be much better to eat sitting up."

"Oh." Dianna held out the bowl to Spencer. "Be careful now," she warned. "It's hot."

"Why don't you feed it to me?" he suggested.

"You're certainly milking this illness for all it's worth," Dianna teased. She sat down beside him. "I'm only doing this because you're sick." Both her brothers were big babies whenever they were sick.

Spencer pretended to be hurt by her words. "What? You don't love me?"

Dianna laughed. "You know I love you, Spencer. Now stop being such a spoiled brat and eat. You need your strength."

He loved to hear her laugh. The sound of her laughter warmed his heart. Spencer eyed her face lovingly before his eyes traveled downward to her breasts.

Dianna followed his eyes and asked, "Is there something on me? What are you looking at?"

"No, there's nothing on you. Not yet anyway." Spencer reached out and took the bowl from her hands. He sat it down on the nightstand.

Puzzled, Dianna stated, "I thought you wanted me to feed you."

In response, Spencer grabbed her arm, pulling her closer to him. Dianna had a petite frame and weighed little more than one hundred five pounds. She would not present a strong challenge. "I want you to feed me, but not the way you're thinking."

Confused and a little fearful, Dianna tried to snatch her arm away. "What are you doing, Spencer?"

Spencer saw the fear in Dianna's eyes but refused to be swayed by it. He pressed on. "I want you, Dianna. You are always on my mind...."

She shook her head as her eyes filled with tears. "You're scaring me."

"There is nothing to be afraid of—just let me love you." Spencer pulled her closer to him. "I have to have you, Dianna. You make me crazy." He covered her mouth with his own.

Dianna struggled against him. "This is wrong, Spencer. You're my brother. Don't do this," she pleaded with him. "Please don't do this...."

## Chapter 2

Wrapped in damp sheets, Dianna shuddered and her eyes filled with tears. "How could you do this horrible thing to me?"

Her question was met with a long silence. In her pain, Dianna clawed at the sheet and began to sob louder. Her mind was clouded with disbelief and grief.

Spencer glanced over at his sister, his eyes filled with disgust. "Get dressed," he ordered. "And when you're done, get out of my room."

The cold contempt in his voice took Dianna by surprise. She couldn't believe that Spencer had raped her and now was throwing her out as if she had done something wrong.

*I'm the victim*, she thought miserably.

"Shut up your crying."

Spencer looked as if he were about to hit her. Dianna cowered beside him for a moment. He didn't lay a hand on her, though—just put his hands to his face.

Humiliated and afraid, she climbed out of bed and dressed as quickly as she could.

Just as Dianna slipped on her right shoe, Spencer knocked the bowl of soup off the nightstand. "I said get out of here, tramp," he yelled.

Picking up her other shoe, Dianna rushed from the house for fear that Spencer might actually try to harm her again. She could hardly drive because she was crying so hard.

Normally she enjoyed the short drive to Taylor's place— the picturesque view of historic homes and colorful flowers nestled around huge oaks and towering magnolia trees along the way. Dianna loved living in Savannah, Georgia. She'd loved her life, until today.

She made it to her younger brother's townhouse and

parked in the driveway.

Shame flowed through her. Dianna fought the urge to vomit and leaned back against the seat of her car. She placed a trembling hand to her mouth. *Dear Lord, what did I do wrong?*

She sat there for a while longer trying to pull herself together before going into the house. When she felt strong enough, Dianna got out and made it up the steps to the front door. Taylor answered the door almost immediately.

"Hey sis." He reached out to embrace her, but Dianna took a step backward. He studied her face for a moment. "You've been crying. What's wrong?"

Dianna stood with her arms folded across her chest, rubbing her arms. She didn't know what to say. How could she begin to explain what had occurred between her and Spencer?

"Dianna, come inside." Taylor reached out again to take her by the hand, but she moved away. Stepping around him, she entered the townhouse.

Taylor closed the door behind his sister. They stood in the foyer eyeing one another warily. Finally he spoke. "What happened to you?"

"I ... I was r-raped," Dianna managed. Her eyes filled with tears of shame.

"What?" Rage filtered through him, causing his body to twitch. "When did th—." He stopped short and took several deep breaths. "Do you know who did this to you?"

"Spencer did it," she quickly interjected. Dianna had to say it before she lost her courage. "My own brother did this horrible thing to me."

Taylor shook his head in disbelief. "I ..." His head hurt from the anger he felt. Surely, he hadn't heard Dianna correctly. "*Spencer raped you?*"

Dianna could only nod.

He guided her into the living room. "Sit down, Dianna. I'm going to make you some tea."

She did as she was told. While Taylor was in the kitchen, Dianna tried to sort out her feelings. She was devastated and so disappointed in Spencer. How could he ruin her life this way? Why hadn't she seen it coming? There had been times in her life when she'd felt something wasn't quite right with her oldest brother—times he seemed a bit overly affectionate, and there was the way he would look at her sometimes.

Taylor's entrance interrupted her silent musings. He handed her a cup of herb tea.

She took a sip, then another. Soon Dianna could feel a slow warmth inching its way through her body.

"I'm so sorry, Dianna."

"How can I ever face Daddy?"

"This is not your fault, sis. Spencer is sick in the head. He has to be to have done such a thing."

"Taylor, I don't know what to do. Should I go to the police?"

He shook his head. "Honey, I know this is going to sound horrible, but I really don't think we should involve outsiders. This is a family matter and should be treated as such. Dad and I will take care of Spencer—just leave everything up to us."

Dianna knew that Taylor was right. Their father was a

U.S. Congressman with ambitions to become the Governor of Georgia one day. The media would have a field day if they ever found out that Spencer had raped her. She knew their father was grooming him to follow in his political footsteps.

"Don't get me wrong. I think Spencer should pay big time. We just don't want the press to get a hold of something like this." Taylor paused for a second before asking, "Do you think you need to see a doctor? I know someone in Charleston. We could leave tonight."

Dianna shook her head. "No, I don't want to see anyone, Taylor. I just want to take a shower."

"You can do that here. Go on upstairs."

"I don't want to go back home. Can I please stay here with you? I just can't go back to that house right now."

"You can stay here as long as you like, honey. And you don't have to worry. Spencer will not be allowed to come here. I'll make sure you're safe."

"Do you mind going over to the house to get me some clothes?"

"I'll get them."

Dianna gave him a sad smile. "Thank you, Taylor."

He stroked her cheek; she tried not to flinch. Dianna rose to her feet. "What will you tell Daddy?"

"The truth."

Dianna stared out the picture window, trying to blot out the sick memory. She could still feel Spencer's hands on her body. Her mind flashed back to his once handsome face twisted in hatred as he glared at her afterwards.

When Dianna heard Taylor call her name, she glanced

over her shoulder. He gestured for her to join him. She left the window and walked over toward her brother.

Leaning against the column that separated his living room from the dining room, Taylor requested, "Keep this just between family, okay? Don't tell anyone what happened. No one."

She nodded in agreement. "It's enough that I have to live with the shame of what Spencer did—I don't want to make this public. I could never survive that."

Taylor stood there, his eyes filled with venom.

Dianna cast her gaze to the floor so that he wouldn't see her tears as she grieved for her lost virginity. All these years of waiting for her wedding night.... She placed a fist to her mouth to keep from sobbing out loud. The fact that it had been Spencer who robbed her of the precious gift made her all the more woeful. *How could my own brother do such a vile thing to me?*

She thought about Marc Baines and how close they were becoming. *He would never want me now*, she thought sadly. They had discussed the importance of remaining chaste until marriage.

Dianna placed a trembling hand to her stomach as a terrifying thought occurred. *Dear Lord, please don't let me become pregnant.* What would she do then? Her anxiety level was so high that she could hear her heartbeat thundering loudly. Earlier that day, Dianna's worst fear had been passing her physics exam, but now the threat of having conceived a child with Spencer loomed dangerously before her. She prayed fervently that God would spare her further humiliation.

Taylor's voice cut into her thoughts.

"I'm sorry. What did you say?"

"I asked if you'd like some more tea?"

She shook her head no. When Dianna finished her tea, she sat the cup on the coffee table and headed up to the guest bathroom on the second level. Taylor was getting ready to drive over to her father's house to pack some clothes for her. She was grateful to have some time alone.

Dianna locked the bathroom door and checked it twice. She eyed herself in the bathroom mirror. Her eyes were swollen from her crying, and she'd developed a splitting headache. She raised her eyes heavenward and whispered, "Lord, why did this happen to me? What did I do?" Tearing at her clothes, Dianna tried to rip them off her body.

Naked, she turned on the water and watched it for a moment before stepping into the tub.

The water was as hot as Dianna could stand. She wanted the hot water to burn away every inch of the betrayal she felt while it cleansed her of the evidence of Spencer's abuse.

She cried as she scrubbed her torso, barely noticing that it left angry, red blotches all over. Dianna wished she could just as easily erase her memory. She wanted to forget what happened. She wanted to feel like herself again. But as much as Dianna wanted to forget and move on, she knew that she never would—all hope for the future had died when her brother raped her.

## *Chapter 3*

Taylor was furious.

How could Spencer do something so vile? When they were growing up, his older brother had always been on the sneaky side—even had his share of troubles—but Taylor had trouble digesting the fact that Spencer had raped Dianna. He knew that his sister would not invent such a lie, however.

The Harris family had their share of damaging secrets, but their father had managed to survive the scandals of the past with his political career intact. That would all change if something like this came out. Taylor felt guilty at the thought of keeping silent in spite of how Dianna must be suffering.

She was a beautiful young woman and had a lot going for herself. Dianna was strong in her faith and diligent in her daily Christian life. Taylor was proud of her commitment to remaining abstinent until marriage. Their father had been hoping to marry Dianna off to Marc Baines, the son of a prominent Savannah and civil rights activist.

Taylor wasn't sure what Dianna would do now. Could God heal her spirit as well as her body? He worried that Dianna might not recover. His ire continued to rise as he drove the last two miles to his father's house.

He pulled into the circular driveway and parked. Taylor got out quickly and headed up the steps of the massive estate home. Using his key, he burst into the house and searched through almost every room looking for his no good brother. "Spencer, where are you?"

Taylor glanced up at a middle-aged woman coming down the stairs and asked, "Have you seen my brother?"

She shook her head no. "I had a doctor's appointment earlier and just got back not too long ago. He's not in his room, because I just changed the linen on his bed."

Taylor found Spencer swimming in the pool.

"Get out," he demanded. Taylor's body shook in his anger. The heat of his rage caused tiny beads of perspiration to pop out on his forehead.

Giving Taylor a wide-eyed, innocent look, Spencer questioned, "What's wrong with you, little brother?"

Standing on the edge of the swimming pool, Taylor repeated his command.

Spencer got out and dried off with a towel in a nonchalant manner. "Look, I'm not in the mood for a fight, Taylor, so whatever it is—I'm sorry."

Arms folded across his chest, Taylor eyed his brother. "It's not that simple."

Giving his him a cocky grin, Spencer asked, "What's your problem?"

"You."

Folding his towel across his arm, he questioned, "Okay, what did I do now?"

"Cut the innocent act. It's not gonna wash this time. I know what you did to our sister."

Spencer turned his back on Taylor. "You don't know what you're talking about."

Unable to contain his anger any longer, Taylor shoved Spencer. "You liar! You raped her, and *you know it.*"

Whirling around, Spencer pushed back. "Dianna is the liar. She came on to me and I rejected her. That girl needs therapy. I think she's doing drugs or something."

"Don't you dare talk about our sister like that."

"She is *your* sister."

Taylor shoved him again. "I oughta kill you…."

"What in the world is going on here?" A voice boomed from behind them.

Tossing a glance across his shoulder, Taylor eyed their father.

Daniel Winston Harris walked briskly toward them. His voice barely above a whisper, he demanded to know, "Why are the two of you acting like a couple of teenage boys?"

"Ask Spencer," Taylor responded tersely, his hands curling and uncurling into fists.

Their father looked to his eldest son for answers.

Spencer quickly replied, "It's nothing, Dad. Just a little misunderstanding."

Taylor sputtered with indignation. "Little mis… He raped Dianna."

Astonished, Daniel looked from one son to the other. "What?"

Pointing an accusing finger, Taylor said, "Spencer attacked his own sister."

Daniel looked as if he were about to collapse. He tossed an uneasy glance across his shoulder at the gardener. Although the man didn't appear to be paying them any attention, Daniel could not be sure. He called out to the gardener. "Jose, could you leave us please. You can go on home."

While the gardener gathered his equipment, the trio stood glaring at one another. Taylor kept his hands curled into fists. He wanted to choke the life out of Spencer. The smug expression on his brother's face was enough to drive him over the edge. Daniel's rigid composure was tinged with anger. He hated public scenes of any kind. No doubt he worried that he would see a photo of his sons fighting in the newspaper.

When the gardener left, Daniel inquired, "Where is Dianna now?"

"She's staying with me. I came over to pick up a few of her things."

He nodded. "I think that's best for the time being."

Taylor could hardly believe what he was hearing. "That's all you have to say?"

Carefully, surveying the area, Daniel responded, "I don't want to discuss this out here. Who knows how much the gardener's already heard? The last thing this family needs is more negative media attention."

"You're more worried about your political career," Taylor accused. "Dianna is your daughter. She's been violated. Don't you even care what's happened to her?" He failed to mention that he'd considered the very same thing earlier. Taylor couldn't help but wonder whether or not his father felt any sense of shame. He did. He was ashamed of his part in adding to Dianna's pain. Because of her blood ties to Congressman Harris, he had asked her to suffer in silence.

Daniel gestured to his eldest son. "Spencer, go on

upstairs and get dressed. I'll talk to you later."

"Dad ...".

"You heard me."

"I am not some child you can just dismiss like a servant. Dianna came on to me," Spencer lied. "This is all her doing."

Daniel glared at his son. "I said I will talk to you later."

Spencer gave Taylor a smug look before taking his leave.

Taylor eyed his father. "This is crazy, Dad."

"Spencer is my son. I will deal with him."

"Really? How?"

"You just take care of your sister. Leave your brother to me, Taylor."

Taylor gave a reluctant nod.

"Tell Dianna that she can never tell anyone what happened between her and Spencer."

"What hap ...," Taylor's voice died. His voice was filled with disbelief. "Dad, she was raped. *Your daughter was raped.* You make it sound as if she willingly had sex with Spencer."

"You misunderstood me." Daniel met Taylor's heated gaze. "What happened is tragic, to say the least. But this can't get out," he reiterated. "Am I clear on this? We can't afford to have this unfortunate situation become public. None of us want that."

"We do agree on that particular fact."

"We will never discuss this again. Do you understand?"

Taylor nodded a second time. *But if you don't take care of Spencer, I will,* he vowed silently. Dianna would have to live with this nightmare for the rest of her life and he was powerless to do anything about it, but Taylor swore he would see that his brother never escaped the truth.

## Chapter 4

Dianna rose to her feet when her father strode into the bedroom. Congressman Harris was a very brilliant and powerful man, but when it came to his children, he was always a very indulgent father. She respected her father and knew that he would have a solution to her situation. He would find a way to make things right.

"Daddy, I—."

He interrupted her by saying, "I know what happened, Dianna. All I can say is that I'm sorry."

She gave a slight nod.

"This may sound unsympathetic, but you are going to have to forget what happened, Dianna."

"I wish it were that easy," she countered.

"I will see that Spencer never comes near you again," Daniel interjected quickly. "But you must never discuss what happened."

"I didn't do anything wrong," Dianna argued. "Daddy, I was still a virgin. I did not seduce Spencer. I thought he was sick, and I did what you told me to do—I went to his room to check on him. He's my brother and I …." Her eyes filled with tears. "I l-loved him. I trusted h-him. I never thought he would…." She couldn't finish her sentence because of sobbing.

Daniel stood watching his daughter for a moment before reaching into his pocket and retrieving a handkerchief. He offered it to her.

Dianna wiped away her tears. She dropped down on the edge of the queen-sized bed and waited for him to speak.

"I think it's best that you stay here with Taylor. You shouldn't be in the house with Spencer." Daniel glanced around. "You seem pretty comfortable here."

Stricken, Dianna glanced up at her father. "You blame me, don't you?"

He did not respond.

"Daddy?" she prompted. Her heart rate slowed and she took a deep breath. "I can't believe this. I'm the victim and you don't want me to come home."

"I'm not putting you out, honey," Daniel quickly reassured her. He swallowed hard before asking, "Do you want to come home?"

Dianna shook her head no. "Not while Spencer still lives there. I don't want to be anywhere near him." Playing with her hands, she added, "Are you going to allow him to stay there?"

Her father looked uncomfortable.

"I see," Dianna murmured softly. She shook her head in disbelief and prayed she was wrong. Her father couldn't possibly blame her for what happened. Surely he wouldn't betray her in this way.

"Your brother ...," Daniel paused for a heartbeat, "Spencer has had a lot of problems. Losing his mother so young…it messed him up, Dianna. I didn't help much by marrying your mother so quickly afterwards. Perhaps if I'd spent more time with him.…" Shaking his head sadly, he added, "I should have spent more time with all of you."

"We all know how much your political career means to you, Daddy. As for Spencer—there's no excuse for what he did to me." Dianna chewed on her bottom lip. Folding her arms across her chest, she glared at her father. "There's something I need to know. How can you be so understanding towards Spencer?"

"I didn't say I understood anything about this," Daniel snapped. "I am furious about this … this situation."

His tone startled an already nervous Dianna, and she jumped involuntarily.

"I'm sorry. I shouldn't have talked to you like that."

Dianna didn't say a word as she watched her father pace around the room. She was so disappointed in him and longed to tell him so, but didn't dare.

Sighing in resignation, Dianna picked up a small round pillow and pressed it to her chest.

Daniel came and took a seat beside her. "Dianna, I'm so sorry. I want you to know that." He cleared his throat noisily. "It may not seem like it right now, but I promise you that in time you *will* get past this."

"I don't know, Daddy."

"You will," he insisted. "You're a Harris. We come from strong stock."

He looked as if he wanted to say more. Dianna waited; she wanted him to tell her that he was going to kick Spencer out of the house. She wanted her father to promise his protection going forward. She wanted her father to wrap his muscled arms around her and make her feel safe. Dianna wanted assurance that all would be fine again.

Instead, all she felt was betrayed.

Long after her father left, Dianna sat replaying his words in her mind. The pit of her stomach burned with the heat of her father's betrayal. Only Taylor really seemed to care what had happened to her.

A couple of hours later, Dianna ventured out onto the patio. It was late afternoon, but the sun was still shining bright. She stood outside admiring the landscape.

Taylor needed more color in the backyard, she decided. *Roses. Roses would be nice.* She loved flowers and made a mental note to ask her brother if she could plant some bulbs; maybe doing something she loved would help her feel better. Deep down, Dianna doubted that she would ever feel normal again.

## Chapter 5

Memories assailed Daniel during the ride home. He was furious with what Spencer had done, but could he truly condemn him, especially after his own sin? There was a time in his life when he was no better than his son. God had forgiven him, and Daniel was now a better man.

Despite the circumstances, his own lust mirrored his son's. He had stolen what once belonged to another man, but it hadn't stopped there. Daniel was an adulterer and had had many affairs. He didn't like to be reminded of those times in the past and struggled to shake those memories now. He'd paid lots of money to make sure his past never came back to haunt him or taint his political career with scandal. Sure, there had been rumors, but Daniel had been successful in keeping them squashed.

In his mind, he admitted that leaving Dianna with Taylor was born out of his own guilt. His daughter was very beautiful, and he had hopes that she would marry Marc. The Baines family had strong political ties—the type that could help him achieve his goal of becoming the next Governor of Georgia.

*Spencer*. What could be done about Spencer? Daniel felt like his hands were tied behind his back. He didn't know what to say to his own son. He hadn't even known what to say to Dianna. His daughter had been raped and now he was sitting in the back of a stretch limo contemplating how to handle the situation. For the first time in his life, Daniel felt helpless as a father. He had better success handling various problems in Congress than those of his own daughter.

Tears filled his eyes and coursed through his body. His little girl was hurting, and he'd banished her from his home.

Daniel wept silently as he prayed to God. He didn't ask for forgiveness, instead he said, *"Father God, help my Dianna through this painful time in her life. Give her the assurance of Your blessing and show her the way to move forward and live out her life without bitterness and fear. I pray that she will be able to not only forgive Spencer in time, but also to forgive me as well. Lord, please show her that hope is not lost. Amen."*

\*    \*    \*

"I don't want to go," Dianna argued. "I don't want to be in the same room with him." She had managed to avoid Spencer since that terrible day, and she wasn't ready to see him. It was too soon.

"Honey, I'm going to be right by your side. I promise." Taylor placed a comforting arm around her. "It'll be okay."

"I can't believe Daddy is forcing me to do this. I guess his political career means more to him than my feelings."

Taylor didn't know how to respond.

Sighing in resignation, Dianna uttered, "Don't mind me. I'm just feeling sorry for myself. And I'm angry because I don't want to face Spencer. At a party, no less."

"I'll keep him away from you."

Dianna nodded. "I guess I should get ready. Daddy's always prompt."

Two hours later, she and Taylor were ensconced in the limo with their father. Dianna released an audible sigh of relief when she found that Spencer would be arriving separately.

The first familiar face Dianna saw was Marc Baines. She pasted on a smile. "I didn't know you were going to be here."

"I wanted to see you," he responded. "I was beginning to think you were avoiding me."

"No ...," Dianna searched for something to say, "I've had a lot going on."

"Anything wrong?"

The conversation she'd had with her therapist concerning Marc came to mind. "I just need time to get myself together."

Taylor joined them, sparing her further explanation. He and Marc shook hands.

"Where's Spencer?"

Dianna and Taylor glanced at one another. Playing with the tennis bracelet on her arm, she answered, "He didn't come with us."

Marc didn't seem to notice how nervous she'd become. Feeling a chill, Dianna pulled her wrap closer around her. She didn't have to look around the ballroom to know that Spencer had arrived. His eyes were burning a hole in the back of her head. She moved closer to Taylor.

Her brother and Marc were engaged in heavy conversation and didn't seem aware of her anxiety. Dianna caught a glimpse of Spencer out the corner of her eye and then boldly met his gaze. His eyes still beamed hatred in her direction. The smirk on his face was too much to bear, so Dianna turned away.

Taylor's attention was on her. "You okay?"

Dianna cast a look Marc's way before responding, "I'm fine. Why don't we join Daddy at the table?"

Marc took her by the hand, surprising her. "I've missed you. I hope we'll get a chance to talk before the evening ends."

She gave him a brief smile and sent a pensive look Taylor's way. Dianna didn't know what to tell Marc. She knew she couldn't be totally honest with him—that's why she'd avoided most of his calls in recent weeks.

Spencer was already seated at the table by the time they made it over. Dianna sat down in the chair held by Marc. Taylor mumbled a greeting to Spencer, but Dianna refused to even acknowledge her older brother.

*I wish this night was over*, Dianna thought silently. Her therapist had prescribed anti-depressants for her, but the meds didn't seem to be working. Her anxiety was at an all-time high.

Taylor could tell Dianna was having a miserable time. This was the last place she wanted to be. His eyes traveled to Spencer. He sat staring at Dianna until Taylor cleared his throat noisily.

When he had Spencer's full attention, Taylor sent a warning glare to him.

His brother broke into a short laugh.

He felt Dianna's gaze on him, and Taylor decided to ignore Spencer for the rest of the evening. There would be plenty of time to make him pay for what he'd done. Taylor would never forget, and he would bide his time. Then, when Spencer thought all was forgiven, he would strike.

## Chapter 6

### Two years later

A drunken Spencer strolled into the oceanfront condo in Marina Del Rey owned by his family. Taylor followed his brother as they weaved their way slowly through the darkness to his bedroom.

Even in his drunken state, Spencer could sense that he and Taylor were not alone. He paused in the middle of the room, his eyes searching the dark corners. When he spied the outline of someone standing near the window, partially hidden by the drapes, Spencer turned to face his brother. "So you finally have the guts to come after me?" He gestured toward the stranger hiding in the shadows. "Or at least, have someone else do your dirty work."

"You have to pay for what you did."

Spencer dismissed the words with a wave of his hand.

Taylor no longer tried to hide the anger he felt toward his brother. "How could you destroy your own sister that way? She used to be outgoing and vibrant. She was going to be a doctor. Now Dianna is as skittish as a cat, and she hardly leaves the house. You ruined her life."

"She is your sister, Taylor. And she ruined me," Spencer complained. "I loved that girl until ... until...."

"Until you raped her," Taylor finished for him, his eyes burning with rage.

Spencer stared his brother straight in the eye. "Just do what you came to do. End this torture for all of us. That is, if you have the guts." He gestured to the lone man standing in the darkness. "This is why he's here, isn't it?"

Spencer could barely detect the sound of a gun going off. The only telltale sign was the gut-wrenching, burning agony he felt in his chest.

He tried to focus on Taylor as he fell to the floor writhing in pain. Spencer blinked rapidly and struggled to speak, but the pain was too great. The memory of Dianna's face was the last image in his mind.

Taylor eyed, without emotion, the still body of his brother lying on the floor. Without looking at the man, he said, "Now me. Hit me hard enough for it to be convincing."

The swift movement of the stranger and the brief flash of metal in the moonlight caught Taylor off guard. For a moment he feared that his plan would backfire and he might meet the same fate as Spencer.

Taylor felt a blinding pain in the back of his head and began to lose consciousness. His body spiraled to the floor beside his brother. "Forgive me," he murmured before darkness took over.

## Chapter 7

Dianna opened the door to find her father standing there. She was surprised to see him so early. Normally he didn't stop by to visit until dinner time.

"Have you spoken to Taylor?" Daniel questioned as he stormed inside the townhouse.

"Not today. I expect that he'll call me at some point." Dianna chewed on her bottom lip before asking, "Is something wrong, Daddy?" He appeared to be bothered by something. She thought she spotted a flash of pain in his eyes.

"Haven't you had a chance to catch the news?"

"No." In the pit of her stomach, Dianna could feel the spark of fear ignite in her quivering belly. "Why? Has something happened to Taylor?" She knew he'd gone to California a few days ago.

"Taylor is fine," Daniel grumbled. "He has a concussion, but he's going to be okay."

Dianna's fear flamed, spreading through her body. "Daddy, what happened?"

"Spencer is dead. Someone broke into the beach house."

Dianna stood before her father emotionless. She felt nothing over her father's words. Her older brother had died a long time ago in her mind.

"Oh. I hadn't realized he'd gone to California with Taylor."

"Taylor invited him to go along."

Her father made it sound like an accusation.

"He was murdered," Daniel announced. "According to the news reports, Spencer and Taylor had gone to have dinner with friends. When they returned to the beach house, someone was there. Taylor was knocked unconscious, and when Spencer tried to subdue the burglar—he was shot in the process. The official story is that he died trying to save Taylor."

"If you are looking for me to feel something—I'm afraid you're going to have a long wait," Dianna confessed.

Daniel's eyes filled with sadness. "I'm leaving tonight to bring my son's body home."

She nodded in understanding.

As soon as he left the house, her mind began to invent scenarios and tears filled her eyes. Taylor and Spencer had barely spoken to each other since the rape, so why did he invite him to the beach house? They had never been close, and the only time they traveled together was during family or political events, and that was only after their father issued an order.

Over the past couple of months, Taylor had become increasingly secretive and attended private meetings at odd hours. "Taylor, what have you done?" she whispered softly.

## Chapter 8

Dianna jumped every time the phone rang as she waited anxiously to hear from Taylor. She'd called the beach house earlier and spoke to a detective. She had even tried calling the hospital, but her brother had already been released. Reports of Spencer's death were on every channel but not much was mentioned about Taylor. There were a couple of glimpses of him dodging reporters as he was driven away from the hospital.

The media had camped out at the airport when her father arrived in Los Angeles. A somber Congressman Daniel Winston Harris declined to comment—however, he pleaded with the media to leave the family alone during this time of bereavement.

His request was being ignored. They followed his every move, including the somber task of having his son's body carried to the airport in preparation of bringing it home to Georgia. According to the media—Spencer was a hero.

Dianna knew better. Although there was once a time when she felt differently, Spencer wasn't anybody's hero— he was a rapist.

The telephone rang.

Dianna answered on the second ring. "Hello."

"It's me."

Her body swayed with relief. "Taylor, I've been so worried about you. Where are you?"

"I'm fine, Dianna. I'm staying at a hotel."

"Daddy's bringing Spencer's body home. I thought you would be on the plane with him."

Her announcement was met with silence.

"When *are* you coming home, Taylor?"

"I'll be there for the funeral but I'm leaving right after. I need some time to myself."

"I'm sorry. If I—"

"None of this is your fault," he interjected. "Spencer was a wild card."

"Come home, Taylor," Dianna pleaded. "Let me help you through this."

"I will … eventually. Just right now I need some time alone. Are you gonna be okay?"

"I'm fine."

"Are you planning to attend the funeral? We should all attend the service. As a family."

"For appearances," Dianna muttered. "I know." She didn't want to go to the service, but her father would be furious with her if she refused.

"I'll get in late tonight," Taylor announced. "I'll see you then, okay?"

"Have a safe flight."

They said goodbye and ended the call.

Dianna navigated toward the patio and peeked outside. Taylor had allowed her to plant a rose garden in the back. The yard was alive in vibrant colors and the air fragrant with the delicious scent of roses. She loved flowers, and working in the yard was therapeutic for her.

Spencer migrated into her thoughts. She refused to wallow in grief over his death. Dianna had found it in her heart to forgive him, but their relationship had long ended. Whenever she'd been forced to endure his presence, she did so in silence. Her brother had not tried to pursue anything more. Spencer moved around her as if she didn't exist to him. The rare occasions Dianna had caught him watching her—his eyes were so filled with hatred, it brought tears to her eyes.

Her tears were not for him though. They were for her. Spencer had turned her world upside down and he walked around as if she'd done something wrong. She'd left college and had practically become a recluse. Marc had just announced his engagement to be married to someone else. There would be no mate for her because she was ruined. Spencer had robbed her of the one special gift reserved for her husband.

Bitterness tried to take root, but Dianna struggled to keep it at bay. She didn't want to live out the rest of her life in anger. Her heart was troubled and sadness had become a constant companion. Dianna was grateful to Taylor for his support for her. She had no idea what she would do without him.

*     *     *

Dianna sat between her father and Taylor. She was thankful for the dark sunglasses that shielded her eyes and hid her contempt for having to put up with this farce.

Every now and then she would glance over at the huge photograph of Spencer. The fingers on her left hand trembled slightly, so she hid them in the folds of her skirt. She felt Taylor shift his position in the pew. He was just as uncomfortable as she was.

Dianna struggled to concentrate on the words of the pastor. She didn't want to be there. She crossed one leg, then shifted and crossed the other. Her father tossed a glance her way. She lowered her head and folded her arms across her chest.

Taylor's soft sigh caught her attention. Once again the thought that he could have murdered Spencer entered her mind. They had never discussed it, but in her heart she knew.

After the service, Marc came over with his family to offer his condolences. She'd heard he was involved with someone in his church, and Dianna wished him well. Her heart swelled with regret over what could have been.

Taylor wanted to vomit.

If the memorial service had lasted a moment longer, he would have embarrassed himself. Ever since Spencer's death, Taylor had become a ball of anxiety. His conscience haunted him day and night.

*Spencer deserved to die*, he kept telling himself. *There was no other way. But if that were true, why do I feel so guilty?*

His father knew the truth. Taylor could see it in his eyes. Daniel would never openly accuse him, but his actions indicated otherwise.

They stood side-by-side as friends, politicians and

other prominent figures offered words of sympathy but said nothing to each other. In one instance, Taylor accidentally brushed against his father, Daniel jumped as if a snake had bitten him.

Taylor took this rejection to heart.

## Chapter 9

Dianna studied her Bible. She knew that anyone who belonged to God should not feel as if they were facing a hopeless future, but she did. There were days Dianna didn't even want to venture out of bed. Two years ago, she had been a vibrant woman with hopes of marriage, babies and a career. Now all that was left of her was this weeping woman struggling with depression. The only thing left in her life that brought her joy was her rose garden.

Her thoughts centered on Taylor, and her heart went out to him. He was on his way to Canada. He was planning to spend sometime with their mother's family. In his last conversation with her, he'd mentioned how lonely he felt. Dianna understood, because it was the same way she'd been feeling for the past couple of years.

Her heart filled with guilt because it was her fault. *No,* she amended silently. It was all Spencer's fault. The media was still planted outside her father's house, hoping to interview him. The police were scrambling to find suspects in Spencer's murder.

Two days ago they'd attended a private memorial service for Spencer, and now her father was on his boat. He was taking the cremated remains of his son and burying him at sea. Spencer had always loved the ocean.

"Spencer...." Dianna shook her head. She didn't want to think about him. Not now—not ever. She had forgiven him, but she didn't want to think about him or about the way that he died or the reason he died.

It hurt too much.

## Chapter 10

Dianna found Taylor standing in the middle of the living room when she came downstairs one morning.

It had been three years since Taylor left Savannah. She squealed with joy and rushed toward him. "I can't believe you're home. When did you get here?"

He laughed as he embraced her petite frame. "I just walked in." He surveyed her face. "How are you doing?"

"I'm fine."

"Are you sure?" Taylor questioned. "You've lost so much weight."

She gave her brother a reassuring smile. "I'm going to be much better now that you're home."

"Tired of your own cooking, I see."

Dianna gave him a playful pinch. "I certainly didn't miss your horrible cooking. Granddad told me how you burned the pancakes."

Taylor grinned and embraced his sister once more. "I really missed you."

"I missed you, too." Dianna stepped away from her brother. "Have you spoken to Daddy? Does he know that you're back?"

He shook his head no. "I'm not sure when I'll be ready to take that step. So much has happened."

She nodded in agreement. "He really missed you, though."

"You wouldn't know it. He and I haven't had much to say to each other the whole time I was away."

"Maybe he just didn't know what to say to you."

"Maybe...." Taylor bent to pick up his suitcase. "I'm going to take my things upstairs. I'll be back in a few minutes. We can catch up over breakfast."

"I'll make all your favorites," Dianna promised.

While her brother was upstairs unpacking, she strolled into the kitchen and set about making pancakes, bacon and scrambled eggs. Taylor loved pancakes with fresh strawberries and whipped cream.

When he entered the kitchen almost forty-five minutes later, Dianna had finished cooking and was setting plates on the breakfast table. Taylor helped her.

When they were seated, Dianna prayed a short prayer of thanks.

"Amen," they said in unison.

"How long are you going to be home?" Dianna asked. She added more butter to her pancakes.

Taylor took a sip of orange juice. "I don't know. I'm taking it one day at a time."

"You can't avoid Daddy. You're going to have to talk to him sooner or later."

"I know." Taylor popped a strawberry in his mouth.

There was so much Dianna wanted to say, but she remained quiet. Taylor didn't look like he wanted to relive any of the past—truth was that she didn't either. She focused on her plate instead.

They finished their breakfast talking about Taylor's life in Canada.

"I thought that maybe you were mad with me," Dianna confessed.

Taylor glanced over at his sister. "Why would you think that?"

"A postcard every now and then. A phone call six times in three years...."

"I called you more than that," he countered. "I'm sorry, Dianna. I wasn't mad at you. I just needed some time away from family. We're a sick bunch, you know." Catching her expression, he amended, "You are probably the only one who truly has a good heart."

"Your heart is good, Taylor. Don't ever think otherwise." Her brother suddenly looked tense, so Dianna changed the subject. "Did you meet anyone special in Toronto?"

Taylor broke into a grin. "As a matter of fact, I did."

Smiling, Dianna uttered, "Good for you."

"How about you?"

She shook her head no. "I'm just not ready," Dianna stated briskly. "I'm fine with my life the way it is, Taylor."

"What do you do all day? Just work on those roses in the backyard?"

"I love flowers."

"But they can't become your entire life."

"I go to church. I have my Bible study. Taylor, I'm okay."

He eyed her in disbelief.

"I am," she insisted. "I am doing fine." Dianna lowered her eyes to her plate. She pretended to be interested in the remaining sausages and scrambled eggs.

Taylor finished off his breakfast and downed the last of his orange juice. She rose to her feet. "Would you like some more?"

"I'm full. Thank you for such a splendid homecoming breakfast."

"I'm going to clean up the kitchen. Why don't you go upstairs and take a nap or something. I'm sure you must be tired."

"Yeah, I am," Taylor confessed. "I can't do much sleeping on a plane." He pushed away from the table and stood up. "I'm going to make a few calls before I lay down."

Dianna washed up the dishes and cleaned off the countertop. Afterwards, she went into the study to get her Bible. She always read the Bible after breakfast. On the way to the family room, Dianna caught her reflection in the mirror that hung above the lowboy in the foyer. She was not surprised with what she saw. A woman with short dark hair, skin the color of sienna and there was nothing wrong with that … except for the hopelessness that regularly swamped her these days.

Dianna couldn't deny the gnawing void in her heart. A lump grew in her throat. She hadn't been totally honest with Taylor. Her heart ached for all of them. A chain of sin had woven itself through her family, and there was nothing she could do about it. She felt hopeless about the future.

The tiny voice inside her shouted, *God will not be consigned to a hopeless end. Do not believe this lie of Satan.*

Dianna prayed for strength and for the grace to believe the truth that God had the power to restore hope to the hopeless. Throughout the Bible, she had read stories that inspired Christians to hold onto hope rooted not in the events of life, but in eternity.

While she knew this truth—applying it to her own life had become a challenge.

## *Chapter 11*

Taylor hung up the telephone. His father had refused to speak with him. It had been three years since Spencer's death, and Daniel was still not talking to him. The only time they'd spent any time together was during special events or political fundraisers. The anger he once felt toward his father had since diminished and he yearned for a closer relationship, but the feelings of rejection lingered. Taylor painfully recalled the incident at the memorial service.

Although Spencer had been groomed to follow in Daniel's footsteps, it was Taylor who wanted to get involved with politics. He wanted his father to believe in him the same way he'd believed in Spencer. He didn't want to replace his brother in Daniel's heart—he simply wanted a place in his father's heart.

Taylor made a few more phone calls before settling down to take a morning nap. He'd spent most of the night on a plane and was exhausted.  Taylor fell asleep as soon as his head hit the pillow.

*       *       *

Taylor strode into his father's office without preamble. Daniel was on the telephone but hung up shortly after his son's arrival.

"Since you won't take my calls, I figured I'd just come see you. You can have me thrown out, but I'll just keep coming."

Daniel gazed at his son for a moment before rising to his feet. He came from around the huge desk and held out his arms. The two men embraced.

"It's good to see you, son," Daniel stated flatly.

Taylor knew deep down that his father's welcome was given reluctantly. The fact that Daniel refused to give him wholehearted forgiveness bothered him. His father claimed to be a Christian. God had not half-heartedly forgiven Daniel for his sins, and therefore his father should strive to be just as forgiving.

Rebellion was cast in his heart as he struggled to maintain his emotions despite the sting of his father's rejection.

"If you ask me, I'll tell you the truth," Taylor commented out of the blue. He dropped down onto one of the visitor's chairs facing the huge desk.

Daniel returned to the leather chair and sat down. "I don't need to ask. I've known from the moment I heard."

"Will you ever find a way to forgive me? I am your

son, too. Just like Spencer, I committed a terrible sin."

Daniel sputtered in indignation. "How dare you...." He waved his hand in frustration. "I don't want to discuss this now."

"What do you feel when you look at Dianna? Tell me that, Dad."

Glaring at Taylor, Daniel responded, "I said I don't want to get into this."

"We're going to have to talk at some point. I would think that you know better than anyone that at some point you're going to have to account for your actions."

"Guilty," Daniel uttered. "I feel guilty. She's my little girl, and I didn't protect her."

"And you didn't punish her rapist," Taylor threw in.

Daniel slammed his fist on the desk. "Keep your voice down."

"To the end, your only concern is what your constituents will think of you." Shaking his head in disbelief, Taylor said, "You are no better than me, Dad. While I was away, I learned a lot about you." Rising to his feet, he added, "You have no right to sit in judgment of me."

## Epilogue

Life had been good to Taylor. In the years that passed, he and Daniel were slowly rebuilding their relationship, and he'd been blessed with a wonderful wife.

Dianna was overjoyed for her brother who was now the father of three beautiful children.

"Here is your namesake," Taylor said. "She's a little cranky because she's getting over a cold."

Dianna held out her arms for the baby. "Just give her to me. She'll be fine." She took the infant and pressed her close to her heart. "Hello, little Dianna," she cooed. "I'm so sorry you haven't been feeling well."

Inhaling the powdery baby scent of her niece, Dianna raised her eyes to Taylor and smiled. "She's so beautiful. She's going to be a knockout when she's older. You'd better keep her under lock and key."

"Don't you worry," he murmured.

The childish laughter drew Dianna's attention toward her nephews playing nearby. The two little boys looked just like Taylor at their age. She smiled as they wrestled with each other on the floor.

Children were so free, she mused silently. They had no worries and were filled with a complete sense of security—especially surrounded by family. *This is the way it should be*, Dianna decided.

While the baby napped, Dianna took a stroll outside to her rose garden. The weather was perfect, and the flowers were just beginning to bloom. This was her favorite time of the year. The harshness of the winter season was leaving, and now the promise of spring had arrived in a profusion of colors. A couple of verses from the first chapter of 1st Peter came to mind. *All flesh is as grass and all the glory of man as the flower of the grass. The grass withers, and its flower falls away, but the word of the LORD endures forever.*

The birth of a baby and even the tiniest sprig of a flower bursting through the dirt always signaled new life and hope. Dianna had squandered a lot of time on regrets, and it was time to put an end to it. Each day she opened her eyes was a breath of hope—she realized it now. It was time to put her energy into reclaiming her life and not just in her gardening.

For the last several weeks, she'd been seriously considering going back to school and continuing her education. Taylor had been kind enough to provide for her all these years, but it was time for her to become more independent. Dianna had a job interview scheduled for the next day, and she was actually looking forward to getting back in the workforce. Even her therapist agreed that Dianna was ready.

Closing her eyes, she prayed. "Dear Lord, I believe in my heart that You were raised from the dead and that this guarantees that Your death was sufficient to pay for all my sins, and therefore You are for me and not against me. You have shown me time and time again how much You care for me. It is through Your grace that I open my eyes each morning and am given another day to glorify You. I pray that You will plant a sprig of hope in me. Help me to hope fully in Your promises so that in times of stress and anxiety I will be continue to be joyful. Amen."

# *Lust*
# *and*
# *Lies*

# *By*
# *S. James Guitard*

S liding my tongue into her mouth not only opened her up, but me, to a level of drama and trials I had never experienced before in my life. Night after night, the shapeliness of her legs and the voluptuous curves of her body kept calling me, so I kept calling her, the problem is, I've already been called—By GOD.

Tremendous, mind-boggling sex. Lustful rendezvous and misguided love have me lying in the bed, while lying to a woman who I know deep down doesn't really love me. Unfortunately, that hasn't stopped me from loving her, even if I can't trust her and my being with her conflicts with the Word of God that God has entrusted within me.

Sitting in the bed half-clothed, I watch her slowly parade across the bedroom floor wearing nothing more than a seductive smile. With a body like hers, it's hard to focus on her lips even when she's talking. Everything about the way she moves is constantly talking. When she says, "Look at me," I respond back with licking my lips and saying, "What do you think I'm doing?"

The rolling of her eyes and the placing of her hands on her hips are a sure 'nuff indication that she is not amused by my comment. "Look up here, Samson. I'm talking to you."

I honor her request even though my presence in her bed dishonors God.

"Samson, I have a question."

"Okay, what is it?"

"Baby, you are so powerful. Do you know that? You are a powerful, powerful MAN. If I have ever met a man in my life, then you are definitely IT. Baby, I wanna know, how you get to be the way you are? It is hard to be able to imagine anyone being able to hurt you. But if someone wanted to hurt you, not that they can, but if someone wanted to hurt you, what could they do?"

Though my body is ripped with muscles and the outward strength of my appearance exudes confidence and instills fear, it doesn't reflect the extent of how emotionally fragile my heart is. Silently, I continue to nod my head to her question, pondering and contemplating not the answer, but instead the purpose of her inquiry and the future we may never have because of it. Determined to not let her know that I suspect she may have ulterior motives, I slightly alter my sitting position on her bed so as to face the bedroom mirror. Right now, I need to face not only the implications of her question, but also myself, along with the fact that despite my proclaimed love for her we may never make it to the altar.

Long stares into the mirror haven't changed what I already know. I don't want to lose her, and I don't want her to leave me. That is unquestionable.

Earlier when she entered the bedroom, she made a point of slowly and glamorously spinning around so I could see her awesome figure while announcing that Delilah had entered into my midst. She could have easily said, "Sin. Temptation. Promiscuity. Lust and Danger," for she was all of them.

Her patience in awaiting my response to her question allows me some additional time to appreciate how beautiful her body silhouette looks resting its enticing wares on the king-size comforter. The more I look at her reflection, the more I can't help but reflect on my past failed marriage, the strip club dancer I had recently been with and how each woman, including Delilah, mirror a similar characteristic. They are all women with which I have been unequally yoked and who can't appreciate the level of calling that God has on my life. The reason we have been together, despite how intelligent I am, is because I'm so caught up in what I see that I don't see the implications of what being with a woman who is not meant for me can do to the ministry that God has given me.

Remaining calm in light of the storm of emotions that are raging within me, I give Delilah a look that indicates, I'm going to answer you but don't sweat me on the time. I'm thinking, just give me time. There are so many different thoughts running through my head, but the one that I can't run away from is the truth—I don't trust her.

Not telling her the truth is wrong, but so is being with her. With all the enemies I have and the number of people who hate me because of who I am, I can't afford to be weak, even if her beauty makes me weak in the knees. I am definitely in love with her and want for her to stay in my life, but I can't afford for my self-respect to walk out because of her.

The folding of her arms across her chest, the tapping of her right foot heel against the carpet combined with the motherly expression of impatience on her face are her way of signifying that she wants an answer from me—now. Delilah's nagging is a reminder of how far it is from Red Grape Valley where Delilah lives to Hornet Drive where my God-fearing and loving parents raised me.

Several years ago, when I first approached my parents about my desire to marry my former wife who is now deceased, their opposition was appropriate and filled with wisdom. But they had not been at Club Timnah during Sexy Bikini/Beach Night when we first met. Had my parents been there, they would have seen women with some of the best beach bodies imaginable. Women scantly clad wearing almost nothing but the impression of the sun's rays on their skin filled every level of the dance floor. My wife and I met on the upscale VIP buffet line featuring a variety of seafood delicacies.

All during the evening hours on any given night, the advertising for Club Timnah appears on almost every radio station. Though my parents had taught me well about the dangers of certain women and places, these are days in which everyone does what is right in their own eyes. In light of who my family is, the community I have grown up in and the history of conflict that exists between us and those who live near Club Timnah, I had no business traveling to a neighborhood where my mere presence could kick something off.

Known for putting on some of the best "worldly" parties, the club was packed with women everywhere you turned. The woman that I would marry definitely caught my eye that night, and I found her visually pleasing. The mermaid tattoo in the small of her back, according to her, was symbolic of the fact that she spent a lot of time swimming as well as it being a part of her family heritage. Since I work out regularly. Stay fit. Do a lot of push ups and sit ups, I have a set of abs that makes a woman turn her neck in mid stride just to get another look, and if she stares too long—she can even get turned on.

We decided to dance to a couple of songs then chill in the VIP lounge. I'm not sure what it was she was saying that connected with me the most. It might have even been the tone in which she spoke; I can only tell you that the soft, even tone of her body complexion was talking to me. The G-string bathing suit she was wearing had me totally strung out. She was so fine I knew right away that I wanted to marry her.

The club's strobe lights continually flashed a dazzling array of different colors across the walls as people of all different colors flashed money and other signs of materialistic success. The Club DJ came over the mike and announced, "This is the re-mix," as people swayed from side to side, lifting up a variety of mix/specialty drinks into the air. The dance floor was on fire; Club Timnah was heating up, and I needed some water with ice to cool my temperature down. I told the woman whom I would later marry to make her way to the bar. We made our way through a security detail comprised of men with thick necks and biceps that had the responsibility of overseeing a popular club thick with athletes, entertainers and celebrities. I caught the bartender's attention as he poured a drink for a man who by his demeanor you could tell was filled with ego, self-importance and everything but the Word of God.

Too much ice in my drink is always annoying. So it is with men dripping in ice, drooling over a woman that I am with. His I-live-just-to-sleep-with-a-woman-like-you look was met with an ice-cold stare from me that said you will die tonight if you step out of line.

The spirits/alcohol that was being served throughout Club Timnah did not compare to the level of spirit of lust that I was under based upon my decision to be at the club. How sad of a condition for a man such as myself who was blessed by God since birth and had the movement of the Spirit of the Lord in his life.

After ordering my water and her drink, we zigzagged through the crowd in order to get to a cozy loveseat in a dark corner of the VIP lounge. As is often the case when you are outside of God's will, I was in the dark about the troubled and turbulent future my wife-to-be and I would have together.

When I arrived at my parents' house to share with them the news about my desire to marry the woman who I met at Club Timnah, my mother immediately started slamming kitchen cabinet doors in frustration. She then began to lecture me in the presence of my father with statements like: "Samson, I can't believe this…You know better than to do something like this…We raised you better than that…Your father and I expect more from you."

My dad, every once in a while, would try to interject, but my mother was so hyped that she waved my father's attempts to calm her down away and said to me, "Samson, I didn't carry you for nine months in my womb for you to want to do some nonsense like this. You got no business wanting to marry some woman that you met at Club Timnah."

In an attempt to gain some support, I looked over at my father. He gave me a look back that said, I gotta really agree with your mother on this one. He then actually said, "Son, with all the women that you've grown up around who share the same values as our family, is there not one of them that you see qualities in that would suggest to you that they would be a good woman to marry?"

Recognizing that this was not a timeframe so much for me to respond to him, I listened further as my moms said, "I'm not telling you who necessarily you should marry. I'm just saying, with all the people that we know and all the networks of people that we have access to, I can't believe you are sitting here in front of me trying to tell me the only woman you can find to be with is a woman who, not only is not of the same faith as us, but is a woman who comes from a political, social and economic perspective of life that is detrimental to our family and community."

My father then said it more plainly to me, "Son, you know those people hate us and they're trying to destroy us. I'm not saying that you don't find her attractive or anything else like that. 'Cause I don't know anything about her except the fact that you say that you want to marry her. But look, you know our history; you know the situation that we're faced with right now in the country. I just don't know if that's the best decision to be making, son. I'm not looking down on where she comes from; I'm looking at what does she stand for and what does she believe?"

Any conversation that consists of what my parents' expectations have been for my life always, in a non-negative way, begins with reminding me about the circumstances surrounding my birth. My entire childhood leading into my current adulthood, I have always been reminded about what my birth not only means to my family but to the community that I come from.

My parents, in a joyful, testimony type of way, have instilled within me from birth a sense of pride and purpose in not only myself but in my history and culture. As I have gotten older, the magnitude of what my parents have gone through and endured has had greater meaning.

I am blessed to have the type of father who passes on the level of wisdom that he has shared, even if at times he is a little long-winded. Many a man or woman would long to have the fatherly wisdom my dad provides. His family history lessons are not only insightful about the past, but are important lessons for me to think about now and for the future.

\*     \*     \*

"Samson, you need to know that your mother and I know what it is like to have a lot of skills, talents and desires to achieve a particular goal in life, and despite all of our best efforts, we have found ourselves at different times—Barren. Our experience with barrenness, as well as your own experiences, can range from being professionally unfruitful, financially destitute, unsuccessful in relationships, to just being in a place in life where you can't give birth to anything that is good no matter how much you want it.

"Our barrenness was not the result of a lack of commitment or a lack of expertise. In some cases, your mother and I have had to come to grips with the fact our barrenness was the result of our disobedience to God, and subsequently we were not able to prosper in one area of our life because of what we had done in another. Praise be to God, however, that the God we serve, who is the one true God, is a forgiving God. A merciful God. What God wants from you and me, and everyone else who has ever sinned, is a repentant heart that is sincere and focused on Him; a commitment to do what's right, not in the eyes of the world, but through the eyes of God's Holy Word, the Bible. Samson, are you paying attention?"

I respectfully nodded my head and asked my Pops to please continue.

"Son, I won't pull any punches with you. Your mother and I are not sinless, but everyday we try to sin less."

"Pop, what is the key to coping with your barren times?" I knew the answer, but it always made my dad feel good when he had the opportunity to talk about God and what God had done in his life.

"Son, when you accept Jesus Christ as Lord and Savior, God will speak to you often through His Holy Word, the Bible, as well as through the conviction of the Holy Spirit. Always be careful; there is a lot of false biblical doctrine masquerading as the Word of God, but it is inconsistent with God's Holy Word. These lies seek to play on people's emotions and their need to be included or accepted by the world. God is real, consistent and powerful, but you have to seek God with sincerity, truth and humility, because God is Holy and worthy to be praised."

"Pop, I know all that. Tell me what happened with Moms."

"What happened with us is what you in your own life will experience with God. Not necessarily in every issue, but definitely at some time or another you will find yourself in a barren place in life and will hear God say to you through His Holy Word, His Holy Spirit, a song or some other means, the following: 'I hear your pain and know of your burdens, brokenness, bruises and the bumps of life that you have experienced.'

"Samson, if you stay focused, there's a certain amount of joy that comes from knowing that the God who knows all has seen your tears and knows your fears. If you know who God is, His righteousness, His grace and mercy, and come to grips with the realization that the God who is omniscient, omnipotent and omnipresent is knowledgeable and concerned about your barrenness, then you have accomplished one of the first steps of having peace in the midst of a valley. Samson, God not only knows where you've been and are currently, God knows where He is taking you. When God spoke to us concerning you, He not only confirmed His desire for your mother and I to be blessed, but also gave us an understanding of the purpose of the blessing. Is this making sense to you, Samson?"

"Of course it is. You know I've heard this a thousand times, but I still like hearing it."

"Samson, when God allowed your mother to give birth to a blessing in you, God revealed to us prior to your birth that He had a purpose for your life. People often become so absorbed in what they want from God, but spend very little time thinking about how will and does God get the glory for the blessing He has provided?"

My mother often during conversations like this would be listening in another room. You could occasionally tell that she was paying attention, because every once in a while she would pop her head in the doorway and say to me, "Listen to your father. He's a good man."

I would chuckle at what my mother said. She's always saying something as if she had exclusive groundbreaking news. I knew I had a good father. I liked the fact that she knew that she had a good husband.

My dad, in a caring but stern way, turned to my mother and said, "Let men be men, sweetheart. We're doing fine."

My mother gave my father a look that said, why are you not including me?

My father, sensing my mother's need to feel a part of this, told her, "Sweetheart, give us some time to talk, okay?"

My moms smiled at hearing the word "sweetheart" and

looking at the one whom she calls her "sweetheart."

My dad then turned back to me and said, "Samson, are you paying attention?"

"Pop, you know I am. Will you continue the story?"

"I'm just checking, Samson. Let me tell you about something that your mother did that will bless you if you adhere to its wisdom. Prior to your birth, God spoke to your mother and then to me and gave instructions as it relates to your birth. In light of who you were to be and the privilege of having you as our child, your mother took an oath to abstain from certain activities. She understood the nature of the blessing that you are and the need for you to be separate from the world, both in substance and symbolically, while you are still in the world. Do you understand what I'm saying to you, Samson?"

"Of course I do. If you don't hear me say I don't, then you know I do."

"Samson, in light of the level of what God was doing in your mother's womb, she had to abstain from certain activities that were reflective of what you would need to abstain from after birth. What I'm trying to emphasize with you, son, is that in the midst of awaiting what God is doing in your life or within you that is going to result in a major blessing, you may be led at times to consecrate your blessing prior to its arrival."

"Okay, Pops, elaborate on that some more."

"Son, some people who are pregnant don't know that they're pregnant and subsequently live in such a way that consists of a variety of poor diets and usage of different elicit drugs and narcotics. The impact of their behavior is that the child that is within them comes out often deformed, a stillborn or needs unbelievable levels of major attention. By the time certain pregnant women change their behavior, it's often already too late for the child that is within them."

"What is the point you're trying to make, Dad?"

"Son, God has placed something in you that is someday going to be birthed—the same concept of a woman giving birth—I don't know when, but I do know this—you are going to give birth if God said it because God keeps His promises.

"Samson, what you need to ask yourself sometimes is what type of womb am I developing within me to nurture the promises that God has given me? It took nine months from the time of knowing about your upcoming birth to the date you were actually born. How are you preparing for the blessing that God is going to give birth to in you?

"Remember, Samson, the key to it all is understanding that the blessing of what God is doing in you and around you is not for your fame and glory but that God may get the glory based upon what people see God doing in your life.

"With all that now said, Samson, what do you want to do with that woman from Club Timnah?"

"I still wanna marry her."

"Son, you will reap what you sow. Every man and woman has to make their own choices. My responsibility is that you receive sound, godly doctrine and have been shared the Word of God with power and truth. I will keep you in prayer for truly your body is strong, your intellect is sharp, but your flesh is weak."

*       *       *

My parents, while not supportive of my choice and decisions, nonetheless said that they would accompany me back to the neighborhood where my wife-to-be lives in order that they could be present at the wedding. Due to the ceremony preparations, we left a week and a half before the actual wedding.

We started off driving together on the highway, but due to the level of traffic and the fact that I didn't have a lot of gas, I decided to tell them to keep driving on so that they could get to the hotel and get some rest. What I was going to do was stop off at the ATM and there get some more gas. After arriving at the gas station, cranking one of the hottest songs of the year, I cavalierly made my way to the ATM in order to get out some cash to pay for the gas as well as to get some snacks.

To my surprise and out of nowhere, a member of the Young Lions, a gang on that side of town that is known for preying on people and seeking to kill and destroy wherever they can make their mark, appeared out of nowhere. Young Lions are known for their roughness, their ruthlessness, and the ravage way in which they go about stealing and killing.

Due to the size of the Young Lion member, my first reaction was to look for something that I could use to knock him over the head, but to my initial dismay, I recognized that there was nothing in sight that I could grab a hold of and was left to face the Young Lion all by myself.

While I had nothing to grab a hold of outside of me, a mighty level of power and strength from God felt like it took hold within me. I turned and struck the Lion with a devastating right hook that brought him comatose down to his knees. Uncertain of whether the Young Lion might have a gun or some other form of weapon, I didn't want to rely upon just hitting him with one blow, so I leaned over and grabbed him by the collar and pounded my fist again and again into his face and body until one of the blows that I hit him with knocked off the Young Lion emblem that was on his jacket. This is exactly the type of drama that I should know better than to get in to and is the direct result of the fact that I'm in a neighborhood that technically I don't have any business being in.

I jumped back into my car, sped away and told my parents nothing about what had transpired.

When I saw a sign that said "Club Timnah," I knew that I was within the vicinity of where my future wife lived. Her house was only a couple exits away from the club. When I saw her, she was looking as fine as can be. We talked for a bit, and all I could say when I looked at her beauty was that she pleased me well.

\*       \*       \*

A couple of days later, on my way to see my future wife, I found myself once again traveling down the main thoroughfare that leads to Club Timnah. I came across an SUV that had been turned upside down in a ditch. Not knowing the circumstances for why it was there, I grabbed my cell phone and made my way over to see what had happened. Due to the lateness of the hour, I looked around and noticed I was the only one on the road. As I

approached the vehicle, I saw a duffel bag hanging halfway
out the back passenger seat. The license plate said,
"YL4LIFE," an indication that this was most likely an SUV
that belonged to one of the Young Lion members. After
close inspection of the roadway, I didn't see any headlights
for quite a distance. So, I went up to the vehicle, stuck my
hands into it and opened up the duffel bag. Inside the duffel
bag were lots of small bills wrapped up in rubber bands.
What appeared to be possibly crack vials and powered
packages were scattered across the backseat. I grabbed as
many of the large denomination bills as I could fit into my
pocket, then double-checked to make sure that no one saw
me and hurried back to my car without calling the police. It
appeared, by the bloodstains and bullet holes in the front
seat and on the driver's-side door panel, that somebody or
several somebodies had been shot and most likely had died.
The amount of blood was massive. It made me wonder
what had happened to the bodies. The SUV with the doors
open reminded me of a carcass.

When I eventually caught up with my parents later on
during the next morning. I decided I would treat them to a
wonderful dinner out, take them on a shopping spree and
give each an envelope with a substantial amount of money
in it. What I did not do is inform them of where the money
had come from.

*     *     *

By the seventh day of my marriage, the only thing that
remained fine was her. Whether it was our joyous wedding

day or the day that I came to understand that she had betrayed me, the one thing that remained constant was that she was a gorgeous woman to behold. It was just her ugly ways that I couldn't stand.

The wedding day and reception were beautiful. All during that week we had activities. People kept on coming up to me and saying, "Samson, y'all sure 'nuff know how to throw down. I ain't never been to a party like this one. Y'all sure spent a lot of money on this." There was a ton of people and a ton of food.

The friends of her family were ghetto-fabulous. By their behavior, you could tell that while they were dressed in designer clothes, they were not clothed in their right mind. There were about thirty of them in particular who must have thought that this was a baller convention. They clearly mistook the fact that we were having the reception at a five-star diamond hotel to mean that they were to come to it wearing lots of diamonds. They had diamonds in their watches, on the crosses on their neck, in their ears and on several fingers.

I just couldn't figure out what was the purpose of all the blatant excess of materialistic gluttony. Since I doubted they could either, I decided that I would pose a high-stakes wager with them that would result in my freeing them up from the amount of tackiness that they thought was symbolic of having class. I came up with a complex way to engage them in an enormous financial wager that would result in them having to put up a lot of their diamond-studded attire just to enter into the high-stakes level of gambling that I was presenting to them. They were game and thought that they would school me.

Unbeknownst to me, they had told my wife that if she didn't help them win the bet, they would kill her and burn her father's house down. In addition, I later on found out they thought that they had been invited to the wedding so that they could be made fools of and so the money they brought with them could be taken away. All I know is that I came home one night and was startled to see my wife balling in tears.

I said, "Sweetheart, what's going on here? Baby, what happened, what happened, what happened?"

She didn't answer me at all. The only thing she did was continue to curl up on the sofa in a fetal position, shivering and sobbing in tears.

I'm like, "Baby, what's going down? What happened, what happened? Talk to me. What's going on?"

She then responded back with, "Samson, you don't love me. You only hate me."

In my mind, I'm like what the hell is she talking about? I'm clueless about what would make her say such a thing. Here I was, just recovering from a feast where I drank alcohol that I should not have been drinking, marrying a woman who my parents didn't even approve of, taking all types of risks with the ministry that God had given me with the hopes that it wouldn't backfire on me, and she comes out the blue and was like "you hate me." I'm like, I can't believe her accusation, but because I don't know the basis for it, I just ask her more questions to find out what would make her say such a thing to me.

She then said, "How you going to enter into a major,

high-stakes, financial wager with people who are connected to my family and not explain to me how you gonna win it?"

I gritted my teeth, tried to maintain my composure, and not let the awesome strength of my size and my body posture negatively affect what I was trying to share with her in light of the fact that I didn't understand why she's saying what she's saying.

"Is this about the money?" I asked.

She said, "No, it's not about the money. It's about the fact that you didn't tell me that you were going to do that, and now that you have, you haven't shared with me how you're going to win."

I tried to contain my anger, and in the nicest way that I could put it, I said to her, "Look. I've not even told my parents—mother or father—how I go about winning major contests that have high-stakes money involved. They gave birth to me, and I keep them in the dark as it relates to things like that. Why would you expect that I would tell you?"

She showed no signs indicating that she understood my position. I showed her that I'm not only physically strong but can be headstrong at the same time, and therefore took the approach of, go on and cry then, with the hopes that eventually she would let this issue go. I was dead wrong, and it would only be a little while before she would also end up dead.

For our entire honeymoon, all she did was whine and complain about this issue over and over and over again. We would be at dinner at a fancy restaurant—specially prepared cuisine, a live, private orchestra, a spectacular view of the oceanfront. Having worked out and lotioned up, my muscles were all protruding and bulging through my clothes, making women all around go, "D#!%, he fine". But I was always just keeping my eyes on her. And she's always keeping her eyes filled with tears.

"Samson, are you going to tell me the answer to the wager?"

"Baby, I can't believe you still on that. It's been several days since then. Why are you still harping on that? That's personal business. That don't have nothin' to do with you. I don't understand why you are making this such a big issue."

All she said was, "If you loved me, you would tell me."

I'm like, "If you loved me, you'd stop asking me."

We spent another lovely-looking evening without any love being shared.

The next day I thought would be different. We had a ton of activities to do. I had paid for an all-inclusive tour plan of the island. Everything was being done at the highest possible level. There was no expense that I wasn't willing to expend within the boundaries of the amount of money that I had. I was going to let everyone see that the beautiful woman with me had all the wonders and beauty that life had to offer.

We spent a good part of the day walking hand-in-hand, laughing, giggling. We got in some long, romantic kisses. Tourist couples would take photos of us and talk about how beautiful of a couple we were, how dazzling her appearance was, how well built I was.

Later on in the evening we went to a poolside party. I took off my shirt and almost started a stampede amongst the crowd. Women were running to see what was all the oohing and awwing about. It was as though people thought there was a fire and were making a mad dash for the exit. I wanted for her to see how appealing people saw me in light of how appealing I saw her. I watched women be almost moved to tears when I took off my sweats.

*     *     *

Despite the earlier fun that my wife and I had, she was back to pressing me again about the wager and how disappointed she was that I had not shared the information with her. Her constant nagging was really getting on me.

During the evening, I looked forward to partaking in the intimate joy of relations with my wife. I knew that should definitely make her smile. Yet, even in an area in which the only tears that I would ever expect to see from her were tears of joy, all that I got were question marks before we went to bed and tears of disappointment afterwards because I had not told her the answer to her question. And here I thought the only reason she would be crying was because of how good I made her feel.

I had enough of it and said finally, "Sweetheart, you want to know the answer to the wager? In order that we can cut off all this whining and pressing me every day, here is the answer...." I just wanted peace.

It turns out that she then (when I was out of the room) made a long distance call to her family friends and told them how to win. What she did not know is that the only person that could have known the answer was her. So, when they later on that day got in contact with me in order to meet and share with me the result of our wager, I knew right away that she was the reason. Her backstabbing, nonsupportive, unwife-like behavior had now cost me a lot of money. I was steaming mad.

I decided I would make my way to the casinos that were on the island and went on a massive gambling spree in order to recoup the money that I had just lost to her family. In the midst of my gambling binge at the hotel, a group of people gathered in the main lounge. You could tell by the way they carried themselves that they came from the same neighborhood as her family friends. They kept on looking at me. I was in a hyper mood anyhow and was like, "Whatcha lookin' at?"

"Who you talkin' to?"

"I'm talkin' to you. Who you think I'm talkin' to?"

"You don't want none of this."

I was like, "Bring it," because in the end I knew I was going to end up taking from them enough of their money and jewelry that it would compensate for any level of drama that I was entering in to. They thought because I was by myself they could handle me. I ended up beating all of them down in a massive slugfest.

Luckily for me, nobody had any guns because we all had gone through several metal detectors to get to that part of the hotel due to the high level of security. This was just a downright, old school throw-down. I beat each one of them to the point of death and left them there, took their diamond watches, pendants and rings, and left them sprawled across the floor in blood.

After it was clear that my wife had betrayed me by revealing the answer to the high-stakes wager, I thought it was best that we take some time to separate from each other in order to calm down the amount of tension. My intent was that later on we would mend our disagreements and get back together. I had a lot of vacation time that I had not used as well as frequent flyer miles. I decided to catch a flight and use one of my hotel vouchers in order to spend some time away.

After reflecting on it for awhile, I had reached a point where I had calmed down. I decided to get my wife a small gift and go visit her to express the fact that though she did me wrong, I still cared for her and wanted for us to work things out.

When I arrived at my in-laws' house, her father would not permit me to go in. Technically, I could have beaten him down to the ground, but I was at a point where I wanted to work things out and didn't think that pounding him to the earth was the best solution.

Then he said to me what I couldn't even believe, let alone fathom would come out of anybody's mouth. He told me that he thought that I hated his daughter, didn't care anymore about her, didn't want to have anything to do with her, and that the marriage was off. I never said any of that. I just needed some space in order to calm down.

The next thing he said to me ended my ability to be calm. He had the audacity and the unmitigated gall to tell me that in the short period of my absence, a friend of mine who was the best man at my wedding, was now sleeping with my wife. They were now having a relationship behind my back.

He then muttered something about the fact that this wasn't his only daughter and what did I think about how beautiful her sister was. He obviously knew that I was greatly moved by a woman's beauty, but nobody in their right mind would think that this was the appropriate time or place to say something so stupid. Everything he told me made me steaming mad. I decided to go into the heart of their community and beat down every single person that I came across who I thought was in any way possibly connected to that family.

The level of rampage I went on caught the attention of the people whose property I was destroying. Nobody challenged me. When they saw my size and the level of rage I was under, all they could do was ask who I was. The result was that while they were afraid of me, they were not afraid of my wife nor her family. So in response to the level of damage that I did to their neighborhood, they decided in retaliation to kill my wife and my father-in-law.

When word got back to me that they had killed my wife and her father, I was grieved and decided to take revenge in return. So I started an all out war against them. If it was conflict they wanted, it was conflict they got.

The word got out about where I came from. So they then sent people to my neighborhood in order to try to track me down and to kill me. I went to different neighbors in order to hide out, but it turns out they had already been co-opted and had made plans to turn me over in order to avoid themselves getting caught up in a major altercation.

I was surprised by their pathetic response, and even in one case went along with it initially just to take the pressure off of the fact that people thought they might be helping me. So I allowed for them to give information about my whereabouts. I was then supposedly ambushed. When I found myself under attack, I prayed that God would allow for me to be able to make it out of the battle. God, as He has throughout my life, answered my prayers, and I was victorious once again.

\*     \*     \*

So stressed out from all the issues that had been going on in my life and all the levels of violence that I had been partaking in, I wanted to spend intimate time with a woman as a way to relieve some of my tension.

I went to a popular strip bar and met a woman there who I found to be very attractive. This was a poor decision to make and was not reflective of the level of blessings that God had given me and the type of decision-making that God would be happy with. But I was under so much stress and still mourning the recent death of my wife despite the issues that went down between us that I just wanted to be with someone. I wasn't interested in her past, I just wanted her in the present to be able to share some affection with me. So we spent the night together.

It would be several months later that I would meet Delilah.

\*     \*     \*

All this reminiscing about what happened in my past has distracted me from the question that Delilah posed to me soon after entering the bedroom. I was still uncertain about how I would respond to her inquiry about the source of my power. I know I love her; I know I don't trust her; I know her patience is running out, and she's waiting for me to respond to her. She keeps checking back on me, giving me a look like, are you going to answer me?

I keep telling her, "Give me some time to think about it."

I can't believe that as much as I love love, love hasn't loved me. On the issue of love in my life, so many people have shown up claiming that they have love and are love that love almost has gotten a bad name because of them.

I decide that instead of telling her the source of my power and how I got to be where I am in life, I will give her seven things that a person, if they were to do simultaneously, could impact me in a negative way. When you have as many things going on as I do, an attack can range from the physical to the professional. The things that I told her that could hurt me, could cause damage but ultimately they would not bring about my destruction. I thought it was better to give something that would hurt me but would not destroy me.

\*     \*     \*

Delilah and I are laying in bed with me being half-asleep, and all of a sudden Delilah shakes me and says, "Samson! Wake up! Wake up!"

I jump up, startled and say, "What's going on? What's going on?"

She says, "Look at the T.V.."

I turn to the television screen, and there's a major announcement about seven viruses that are impacting certain computer networks across the globe and that are expected to have a major impact on global commerce. "The company that will most likely experience the greatest loss due to these viruses appears to be Samson Enterprises. We will return with the latest breaking news as soon as it becomes available."

I look at Delilah with disbelief. How could she have done this? How could a woman I love so much take information that I gave her and then turn around and use it against me? I want this relationship to work so badly. Doesn't she understand how much I love her, is what I keep pondering in my head over and over again.

"Samson, what are you going to do?"

"I got it under control."

"What do you mean you have it under control? According to what you told me, if those networks were to ever be affected, it would have a major impact on your power base."

"That's true, but I still got it under control."

"Samson, you know I got your back. If there's anything I can help out with, let me know."

"I appreciate that."

"I mean it, Samson. I'm in your corner."

# S. James Guittard

"I love you, Delilah. You mean the world to me."

I'm hoping that she recognizes that though I know that she is the reason behind these viruses, I'm not seeking the destruction of her nor our relationship. Allowing her to do something that I know was intended to harm me and then ignore it as if it didn't happen with the hope that my response would help cement our relationship is my way of trying to tell her how much I care for her.

I slide out of the bed, make my way over to the laptop computer, connect to the Internet, access my personal website, enter in a series of passwords and begin fighting back against the viruses that are attempting to break through my computer firewalls. While the viruses are potent and would impact the majority of companies, and are even expected to impact my own, the level of talents and skills that I possess intellectually as well as physically are of such that I have things well within my grasp. I have people so caught up on my physical appearance that they often overlook my level of intelligence.

Samson Enterprises' success is the result of combining my intelligence and physical alluring appearance together in order to create a company that has global appeal and creditability both in corporate America as well as in the urban streets.

After countless hours of counterbalancing the onslaught of the viruses, I proudly close the computer and get back into the bed. Relaxed and business-stress free.

While a part of me is free, Delilah will not let go of the fact that she thought that I had given her the ultimate tools to bring about my destruction. For some people, it would be

188

giving them alcohol, for others it would be giving them some form of narcotics, for some it's flattery—the things that can exploit a person's weaknesses can vary.

Delilah says, "Samson, what you told me could not have been the truth. Why did you lie to me about what those viruses would do to Samson Enterprises? I can't believe you don't trust me and would make a mockery of me."

I say, "It's not about that."

"Then what is it about?"

"I don't want to talk about it."

"Why can't we talk?"

"I just don't want to talk about it."

"If you love me the way that you say you love me, then you would keep me informed about the intimate details of your business as well as not lie to me about issues concerning you."

Not wanting to turn the relationship sour, I decide to tell her that the issue wasn't that the viruses didn't have impact, it's just the type of viruses they used were not strong enough. I then go on to tell her, "As in many things, it's not what you take but the amount of what you take. Whoever sent the viruses had the right idea; they just didn't understand the strength of the viruses they would need. That's all."

"Then, Samson, why didn't you just say so?"

Later that evening, I go into the shower to wash away the level of betrayal that I'm finding myself under once again. I can't wash away the pain nor the hurt no matter how much I lather up. Neither can I wash away the level of disappointment that I have in her. All I can hope for is that the level of love I have for her is of such that she appreciates it.

Through the half-open bathroom door, I hear on the television set once again, "We have a new breaking report on the computer viruses that are sweeping across different networks. It appears that these viruses are particularly targeting the networks that carry information by Samson Enterprises. Our reporters have been able to determine that the extent of the earlier viruses has now been compounded. The viruses appear in a newer form that is much more potent and expected to now have a major slowdown on the ability of Samson Enterprises function. This could have dramatic, negative implications on the power base that Samson Enterprises has in the industry. Stay tuned for further news. We return you back to the regularly scheduled programming."

While I know that this won't hurt me because it's not the real source of the strength of Samson Enterprises, I'm still nonetheless hurt. I focus on utilizing the towel on the bathroom rack to wipe off the remaining drops of water on my body while recognizing that the tears that are starting to appear in my eyes will not be so easily wiped away. Apparently my love has not wiped out Delilah's betrayal.

I then hear Delilah say, "Samson, can you hear the latest report?"

I tell her, "Yes, I can. I'll be out in a few."

It had just been a few hours earlier when I gave her the rationale for why the previous viruses didn't work. Now I'm faced once again with having to overlook something that clearly I see is a problem in the hopes that what she'll see is how much I love her and how much I'm willing to overlook in the name of love.

I come out of the shower with a towel wrapped halfway around my waist and go to work on the same computer as before. I diligently plug away at the computer keys and once again, defeat the viruses.

I then get dressed and prepare for what clearly looks like is going to be an extraordinarily busy day. Since being with Delilah, my prayer life has deteriorated. I don't study God's Word like the way I used to. I'm more likely to hear shouts of her screaming out in ecstasy in bed than I am to hear someone shouting out how good God has been to them. Instead of being stretched out before the throne, I find myself more and more everyday stretched out in her bed, seeking comfort in the sweetness of her body versus in the sweetness of God's grace and mercy, which He has provided me so often in the course of my life. It is God who has allowed for me to overcome the various obstacles in my life. I have been raised and have come to understand the importance of holding on to God's Word, but now I spend my time primarily focused on how to hold on to her. If the level of attacks, both on Samson Enterprises and me, keeps up, it will be difficult just to hold on to my peace of mind.

Delilah comes over to where I'm at sitting on the couch and says to me, "Samson, are you okay?"

"I'm all right."

"You seem a little moody."

"I just got a lot on my mind, Delilah."

"I can understand that."

"I think I'm going to go work out for a while in order to remove this tension that I have. People always comment about what great shape I'm in; if they had to run an enterprise like Samson Enterprises, they would find a recreational outlet, too."

"Do you want me to come with you?"

"Nah. I just need some time with myself just to cool out."

"I have a question for you before you leave out. Do you love me?"

"What do you mean, do I love you?"

"Do you love me, Samson?"

I think of all the levels of things that have went down in this relationship that are wrong, but nonetheless I still try to do the right thing even though I know that I'm in the wrong place. It's amazing how someone who's doing you wrong will try to turn the tables on you to make you feel like you've done something wrong. Despite how selfish that is, I try to do what I think is an unselfish act in the name of love and try to ignore even that. It hurts, but I'm trying to. The only thing it appears that I've been consistently ignoring is the level of call that God has on my life by my refusal to call love, love and lust, lust.

"Samson, are you paying attention to me? I want to know why are you constantly lying to me over and over again?"

Deep down I want to know, why is it she is lying to me? One thing I can't lie about is how beautiful she looks and how impacted I am by her presence. When she starts to give me a certain look that says, "Samson, I love you, I love you, I love you," all I want to do is believe in it and share in it.

"Samson, I really want to know, as a part of confirming that you really do trust me and love me, for you to tell me what is going on, how can I help you and why aren't you being totally honest with me?"

I had given her almost everything that I had to give in the name of love. I was now going to give her the key to what is connected to my success.

I tell her to let the issue go for now and I'll deal with it later. She does for the moment. But then begins pestering me daily. I still don't tell her the source of where my strength resides. But that doesn't stop her from asking me constantly.

Spending so much time with Delilah has resulted in me being away from church when I know I am supposed to be there. I miss Bible studies, Sunday School lessons and general worship services. More important than any of those, I miss private time that I used to spend praising and worshipping God. I have allowed the love I have for Delilah in many ways to become a pagan god in itself. I wanted that love from her so bad as a part of validating who I am, who I'm not and who I want to be. And I've been willing to do almost any and everything to get it.

*       *       *

Cuddled up in my arms, exactly where I want her to be, Delilah asks me again about what is the key to my power and my being a powerful person, both personally and professionally.

I tell her that it is the miniature cross I wear around my neck. My parents had this for me before I was born and gave it to me at birth. The cross symbolizes my relationship with God, my commitment to His Word and the awesome blessing that God has in store for me. It is a constant reminder to the world and to myself about who and what I live for. I don't tell people all of what it means to me, but it is the most important thing that I have and is the source from which, when I'm in trouble, I rely upon. It has been with me through so many battles.

Several nights later, while lying in the bed next to Delilah, she whispers in my ear, asking me to remove the cross from around my neck because it is cutting her when she lays up against my chest.

She says to me that she can't be as close to me as she would like because of that cross. "If you want me to be as close to you as you want for me to be and love me the way that you say you love me, then you won't allow for that to come in between you and me and the love that we share. I wouldn't let anything come between you and me. I can't picture you wanting something to come between us."

Troubled as I am by what she says, I allow for her to remove the cross from around my neck. She then presses her body tightly against mine as I listen to her heart and her saying, "Trust in me."

I can't help but think about what my parents told me early on: Trust in the Lord with all your heart. I just hope I don't end up heartbroken.

The next thing I know, I hear a pounding at the door.

"Open up. It's the Federal Marshals."

I make my way to the door before they break it down, look through the window and see news camera crews and Federal Marshals all around the house.

They repeat, "Open up, or we'll break the door down."

I reluctantly open the door and am told to back away slowly and to keep my hands in sight. I agree to their request and slowly slide back as Federal Marshals rush throughout the entire house.

"We are serving you with a warrant for corporate fraud. Everything that you have is being placed in an escrow account. You have to come downtown with us. All the items in the house are being confiscated. You have to come with us right now."

I look over at Delilah and ask her to call my family attorney to meet me downtown. She just smiles at me, shakes her head and begins to laugh with one of the Federal Marshals. I overhear the Marshall say "we wouldn't have been able to make this case without you. Thank you for your assistance." Delilah responds, "when do I get the reward you promised? I've lived up to my part of the agreement."

I can't believe this is happening to me. After all that I have done for her. She is lying about me. I reach for my cross, but it is not there.

*　　*　　*

During the upcoming weeks, my company's stock plummeted. Negative news stories about me appeared inside the press. Stand-up comedians on late night shows and comedy clubs made jokes about me. I was featured on every magazine cover in a negative way. My heart was broken; my self-esteem was crushed. To make matters worse, I was given my cross back while sitting in the detention center as a gesture of how empty it was of the power to protect me. The jail cell that I languish in has given me an opportunity to see how the choices and decisions I have made have imprisoned my future. It makes me think about the choices I've made and the choices that I've allowed people to make in my life.

I start to think about the cross that I allowed to leave my neck. People are now, as a part of their stylish look, wearing crosses with everything as a way of highlighting their wardrobe. The cross is an additional fashion accessory. The contradictions between what the cross symbolizes for believers in God and the way in which it is often featured as a part of a materialistic ornament draped in diamonds in conjunction with the subject matters in which the cross is shown is blasphemous. The cross should never appear to support highly sexually explicit messages or materialistic themes that now can be found everywhere. Giving me back my cross was a way of indicating that the cross had no power.

What they did not understand that I understood when they gave me the cross back is that it didn't have any power because the cross itself is a symbol of the relationship that a person has with God. The cross is not the source of the power, the relationship that one has with God is the source of the power. The cross symbolizes the crucifixion of Jesus

Christ and His resurrection. To the extent that you have a relationship with Jesus Christ as Lord and Savior, then you have access to God's grace, mercy, strength, power, and love that can only come from Him.

When I was willing to remove the cross, I was symbolically suggesting a removal from the type of relationship that I wanted to have with God. So, while I now have the cross back, I still don't have the level of relationship back until I'm willing to repent for my sins before God in order to restore the relationship that I had with God. I need not the cross, I need the relationship that the cross is symbolic of. That is why I'm seeking God's forgiveness, not tomorrow, but right now.

I have to get back on track. God has given me a ministry to lead that I have been avoiding. There are so many people have a relationship with Church, but don't have a relationship with Christ. They have churchianity, not Christianity. They are filled often with religion, but not by the Holy Spirit. They have the outward appearance of being righteous while living unholy lives. They have taken the symbols and perceived images of what being godly looks like and studied ways in which to be seen as having a relationship with God versus allowing people to be able to see God within them by the way in which they treat others.

I, however, am grateful and thankful to know that all have fallen short of the glory of God but can repent, and restore their relationship with God by acknowledging one's sin, seeking forgiveness from God and trying to daily live a life that is pleasing in God's sight. As my father said, never sinless, but every day trying to sin less.

My power is already on its way back. I will use this experience as my Friday prior to the resurrection that God is going to do inside of me through His power, and when God restores me I will look back at today as *Good* Friday only because of the power of God to make me whole.

Until then, I will meditate on some of the lessons learned.

*Blessed is the man who walks not in the counsel of the ungodly, nor stands in the path of sinners, nor sits in the seat of the scornful; but his delight is in the law of the LORD, and in His law he meditates day and night. He shall be like a tree planted by the rivers of water, that brings forth its fruit in its season, whose leaf also shall not wither; and whatever he does shall prosper. The ungodly are not so, but are like the chaff which the wind drives away. Therefore the ungodly shall not stand in the judgment, nor sinners in the congregation of the righteous. For the LORD knows the way of the righteous, but the way of the ungodly shall perish.*
*Psalm 1:1-6*

*Blessed is the man who endures temptation; for when he has been approved, he will receive the crown of life which the Lord has promised to those who love Him. Let no one say when he is tempted, "I am tempted by God"; for God cannot be tempted by evil, nor does He Himself tempt anyone. But each one is tempted when he is drawn away by his own desires and enticed. Then, when desire has*

*conceived, it gives birth to sin; and sin, when it is full-grown, brings forth death.*
*James 1:12-14*

*Who can find a virtuous wife? For her worth is far above rubies. The heart of her husband safely trusts her; so he will have no lack of gain. She does him good and not evil all the days of her life.*
*Proverbs 31:10-12*

*For the lips of an immoral woman drip honey, and her mouth is smoother than oil; but in end she is bitter as wormwood, sharp as a two-edged sword. Her feet go down to death, her steps lay hold of hell.*
*Proverbs 5:3-5*

*The way of the fool is right in his own eyes, but he who heeds counsel is wise.*
*Proverbs 12:15*

# Sword of the Lord

## By

## Terrance Johnson

# Sword of the Lord

I've done well for myself and have never had to look back on Bishop Joseph's family—my family. I thought the chances of me ever speaking to them again were as slim as an anorexic snake. But what are the odds of the vindictive past that I buried eighteen years ago rising from the grave to propose an alliance? If I had bet against it, I would've lost big today when my half-sister came as the family emissary to the arena three hours before my mixed-fighting tournament.

She pried open a part of me that had been slammed shut, the days when I was nobody to somebody. A time that I remember forgetting, back when Momma had no religious training and sampled any and all hedonistic heathen activities. Her vice grip was money and sex, which translated into selling her body as a stripper and then straight-up prostituting.

Bishop Louis Joseph—my Dad. Well, his holy record was extensive: first pastoral position at twenty-one; founded Word of God Nondenominational Assembly in the southern Illinois town of Louisville at thirty (an assembly with traditional teachings and a charismatic worship service); and eventually the leader of five other churches in South Holland County. He was untouchable on the educational level, too: Bachelor of Arts in Psychology, Master's in Business Administration and a Doctorate in Divinity. From what I've been told, he was faithful in his marriage to Martha until he met Momma thirty-seven years ago.

Even with Momma and Dad on opposite ends of the moral spectrum in the same town, their paths crossed on a soul-winning campaign in the streets of Louisville. She accepted the Lord as her God and joined his church. Her impoverished spirit coupled with her vivacious body provided just enough temptation at just the opportune time in Bishop Joseph's life for him to slip and get a little bit of tarnish on that spit-shined record of his.

He confessed his sin, and because it was the Bishop, the church forgave him. Surprisingly, his good name wasn't scandalized. Everyone figured that Momma tempted him and that the fruit of her womb was an accursed thing. When Dad moved to Chicago to assume a new pastoral position, me and Momma followed behind him from Louisville. He tried to graft me into his family, but the wife and kids were having no parts of the illegitimate Joseph Jephthah Lewis. Whenever the Bishop's head was turned, I was mauled and verbally assaulted by his children. Finally, Momma had enough ostracism, deciding to step out of his life and the area when I was only five years old.

Fourteen years later, we went back to see the Bishop.

I didn't have a strong relationship with him, but I still needed to be there to somehow offer my final farewell. Bishop Joseph's eulogy listed all of his accomplishments in the ministry. The number of souls born again through his ministry was innumerable, including Momma, but she wasn't honored as a sister in the faith. Listing his children should have been an easier count—fourteen. But I wasn't included.

The tension was thicker than the anointing oil when me and Momma were discovered on the last pew during the home-going service. Although funerals are supposed to be an opportunity for friends and relatives to console each other, we were content to anonymously pay our respects to a man who was a part of us.

We kept our distance at the repast, but as fate would have it, Princess Drusilla, Momma's youngest daughter, and Jackie Joseph, Dad's youngest daughter, connected like little girls do. After skipping in unison all over the church, Drusilla dragged her new friend over to meet us, providing just the opportunity for the Joseph children to stink bomb us. I still remember the scene and the words like it was yesterday—years hadn't smoothed the edges. Aunt Hazel snatched Jackie up and insisted, "You can find something better to play with." She didn't even categorize us as people, let alone family.

Justin, the eldest brother of the legitimate Joseph children, warned, "I know you ain't expecting any part of our inheritance."

"Lewis ain't Joseph," bellowed my other brother Narcissus who is the same age as me. And to think, there was a time in my youth when all it took was a comment like that for me to have some gangstas sweep the streets of South Chicago with his head.

Jason, Dad's younger brother, insulted, "We don't have any dealings with hookers in this sanctified church."

Cousin Ruby suggested, "Why don't you take your ghetto rats home."

I had withstood bullets by that time in my life, so I was most definitely not fazed by their personal insults. But once they dissed my Momma and sister, in my mind I got dressed up with my make-up, oversized shoes and colorful suit, because it was clowning time. Rising a good imposing foot above them, I promised, "If one more insult is slung this way, I will open up the floor and bury the person who utters it where they stand."

Jason soughed just loud enough to get my attention.

"What, fat boy, what?" I reacted as I flashed him the glare of death.

He wisely looked away.

"You ready to jump, Justin?" I asked, throwing my hands to the side as I stepped a good inch away.

His eyes blinked rapidly as he backed up.

I turned to Narcissus and said, without holding anything back, "I oughta drop you in that spot." Apparently he lost heart also, because he blushed into what looked like fearful silence. "Where are the antagonizers?" I asked, doing a revolution of the still fellowship hall.

Drusilla and Jackie were left staring in bewilderment as their friendship was sunk before it could set sail.

Without another utterance, I led my family out of the

sight of the Josephs for what I thought was the last time, vowing never to return.

I knew they didn't want any parts of me. So, I spent my young adult years acting like I didn't have family on my Dad's side. I didn't want to ever see them again. Not only was I determined to never go back to my family, but I also promised to do something that would shame them, not caring much about how I would look. Banging is what I knew and that's what I would do, just harder, straight up cold-blooded. They hadn't seen anything yet. By the time I turned twenty-one, I hadn't been able to keep my promise. Turned out that my gangbanging wasn't glorified or documented in the mainstream. With all of my street fighting, I didn't even have an arrest record. None of my scandalous activities had scratched the good Joseph name.

As easy as it was for me to be in charge on the streets, I knew it was time to make a change. Fighting for the win was my talent, my gift, and I needed to use it in a way that was going to do more good than what I was throwing down, so long as I didn't forget my street family. When I bonded with my boys in our crew, I had promised them that I would somehow open up doors of opportunity and prosperity, and they trusted me. My notoriety came after finishing undergrad in three years a` la Momma, and graduating law school magna cum laude on my way to a well-publicized career as a defense attorney and civil rights lawyer, bringing me to this time and place, sitting in this room waiting on my bout to kick off.

As I was meditating on the victorious exploits of the warrior Jephthah in the Bible, my trainer came to tell me that there was a Ms. Jacqueline Holland waiting to see me. I couldn't think of anybody by that name, so I told him to tell her she had the wrong person. A minute later my trainer tells me that it's my sister, Jacqueline, and ushers her into my dressing room. And there she is, standing in my presence, my family, my blood, my sister who I don't know but feel something for her. I don't know what to say. She is all grown up. The last time I'd seen her she was running around after Dad's funeral playing games with the other kids.

I gaze bewildered at her familiar features. She's as yellow as the summer sun at high noon, and her hair is a mushroom-cloud afro-puff, but her elliptical green eyes have it. My eyes are a matching orb-like forest green. My father had the same freaky configuration to his soul windows.

"Holland, not Joseph, huh?" I ask.

She smiles. "I married a Holland and didn't want to hyphenate it."

"Your features will always give away your Joseph heritage," I tell her.

"Are you married?" she asks me.

I tell her about my wonderful wife that God hand-picked for me and about my beautiful daughter that has her eyes.

The exchange and conversation are initially warm and sincere, but then she states that not only are the backbones of the community, the churches in South Holland, being uprooted, but the citizens are being displaced by the state because they want to build a new prison and other related commercial entities. She tells me that some of the older people will have no place to go since they don't have enough money to buy a new house or enough to move into a retirement community. People are frightened and need help but can't seem to get any. She knew the law was against the poor residents and no other lawyer would even consider representing them.

"Why should I help you? The family wants no dealings with me."

Jacqueline looks down at the floor and doesn't utter a word.

"This Joseph," I start to say before remembering who I am, "I should say Lewis is doing just fine without my so-called father's family."

Jacqueline assured me that the future would be different. I had no reason to believe her, but I did, I wanted to, maybe needed to. "You know that I will have to speak with the elders at the church before I agree to do this," I advise, air boxing in place so that I can stay loose.

"I know," Jacqueline affirms with a nod.

I promise to help and she leaves my locker room after dropping the plea for help. I plan to discuss it with her further in my office on Monday, but I am prepared to assist them in some way, even though I don't know exactly what that means. All I know is that I'm a fighting attorney who keeps my promises.

A few minutes later, my corner-man gives the signal that it's time to throw down in the ring, so I rise from my stool and throw the hood of my robe over my head as I reach the engulfing doorway. With the trumpet of my soundtrack signaling the start of my theme music, I quote Hebrews 11:32, "I do not have time to tell about Gideon, Barak, Samson, Jephthah...," transitioning to rhyme mode as I Crip Walk in cadence with the gangsta beat to the ring.

"But Joe can put on a show
Going blow for blow
Take a chance at romance
Let's dance
But the cost is a right cross to the jaw and tooth loss
Can you manage the damage
And risk entering eternity on a gurney by an attorney
You can't taint Saint Lewis
Reviewing and chewing you like bubble gum
Check out my shotgun arms
Leaving you charmed, alarmed and harmed
As I blast you into the past
Traveling back fast into time to kick you past your prime
Leaving you punch drunk with the wine of wrath
With knuckle prints and head dents as the aftermath
No man can wing it in my ring
Ping ponging and stomping you like King Kong
You're wrong to bet against Jephthah
The gladiator of the midwest
You failed the taste test of death
So sweet dreams as I lay you to rest in pieces."

I climb through the ropes and leave my robe on as I bounce around to keep the circulation going.
"In the purple corner, standing 6'2", weighing two-

210

hundred-forty-five pounds, with an amateur boxing record of twenty and zero, and a mixed martial arts record of six and zero, hailing from South Holland and fighting out of Chastity, Illinois, the second advent of the Brown Bomber, The Minister of Pain, Joseph 'Saint' Lewis," the announcer bellows, triggering an explosive applause from the packed arena.

My opponent is the former NCAA wrestling champion and Olympic runner-up known as The Bear. At 6'4", two-hundred-ninety pounds of mean muscles and merciless aggression, he has put most of his opponents in the hospital with broken bones or concussions. He's the favorite to win since mixed martial arts no-rules competitions favor the grapplers, but God favors me.

It's questionable whether I have a death wish or a sadistic desire to kill the opposition, but sometimes the line is blurred between faith and foolishness. I do know that fighting is fun to me, especially when the odds are against me. Whether opposing the justice system as a lawyer or battling a bigger foe in a tough-man contest, there is no greater thrill than mixing it up in the ring. When the task is easy, the burden of success can easily rest on talent; when the task is impossible, the outcome is in the Divine hands that are wrapped around my soul.

*       *       *

Odds and favorites mean nothing when you go into battle with the killer instinct. I sit at my desk Monday morning, reveling in the beating I put on The Bear Friday night. I swing my thoughts to a new battle, the one I agreed to do in the legal arena for my sister. I peer up at the customized clock with the sword hour hand, dagger minute hand and gavel second hand that ticks away against a scale backdrop, which reads a quarter to five and ponder out loud, "Eighteen years is a long time," as my mind travels back to when we fled South Holland the first time.

When Momma and my five year-old self escaped from Bishop Joseph's world, Jim Crow-segregation-at-all-costs like laws were enacted in the suburbs of Chicago for her. She couldn't be in the same proximity as Dad without her rep getting lynched and the possibility of her body being burned. We drifted from hood to hood all over Cook County, and when she finally landed in Chastity, I had seven issue-laden siblings, and Momma had eight absentee baby's daddies.

In bouncing from area to area I gained a notoriety and credibility in the mean streets. As opposed to the certain gangs recruiting me as a neophyte, they flocked to me like sheep without a shepherd. I had the closest ties and the most loyal foot-soldiers in my crew, while at the same time, the favor of the Lord. Amazingly, there were no gang war casualties on my set, and there was a peace in the area between the rivals.

Our exploits included robbing the liquor stores owned by immigrants, burglarizing the stores of the Eastern merchants, and thrashing the European warlocks who were used to casting their spells in our hood. But it was all different when it came to our neighbors. We protected the women and children of the community from the negative elements and influences. It was like family looking out for family; the way it should be.

The core of warriors who are a persevering link to my inner circle consist of Buck "Yuck Mouth" Tucker, who used to suck down both edibles and inedibles, while uttering the most vile things in his gangster rappin' days; Jimmy "The Vet" Mason, the former Corvette jacker and hubcap snatcher; Leo "Chicken" George, a coward who had no business bangin' back in the day, but is courageous as a king after hooking up with the Lion from the tribe of Judah; Mark "Hammer" Head, whose hands used to hammer heads; Herman "PeeWee" Johnson, a 6'8", three-hundred-fifty pound unfriendly giant; Trent "Glock" Myers, who used to smoke suckers, is now on fire for the Messiah; Marvin "Hard Knocks" Locke, who served ten hard years on lockdown in the penitentiary, is now a prisoner for the Lord. All of these are my brothers that I will live and die for; all of them saved by the mercy of God.

I'm a fighter, a warrior. Wherever there's a brawl, I try to be in the center. My street record is 53-2-1, with the draw coming against five thugs and my two losses coming from my ex-fiancée and my brothers when I was a kid.

I've defeated corporate giants such as United Motors in regards to hiring, promotion and discrimination practices; the Happy Hungry Hamburger restaurant chain on the preferential treatment of non-colored customers and even the city of Jerryville for the concessions that excluded black contractors. Those are my money-making lawsuits. My career-making battles are the pro bono cases that look bleak and even the most diligent lawyers won't touch with golden gloves and an unlimited flow of cash because it would break their careers.

Most of the litigation that I do for free has to do with young black men accused of a heinous crime that's blasted in the media to the point where he's guilty as charged by public opinion even before his trial begins. I've taken some cases after a public defender jacked things up and the defendant was either sent away for a few life-times or lined up on death row. DNA evidence has been a powerful weapon to prove my arguments, but usually it has been the investigation that laid the foundation of innocence.

The state wants to evict the citizens of South Holland and erect a prison. Of course the developers have already mapped out how the town will be booming with businesses funded by the souls of inmates, which I suspect to be mostly black men. The state will accomplish their plan only after taking me out, which they may try to do.

With all of the fight within me, all of the passion and all of the winning experience, I need the Lord at the center to assure victory with this legal battle. That's why before I go forth in this cause, I'm seeking Him. I'm in the battle even if it's not His perfect will, because the town is worth fighting for. He'll either permit me to battle or He'll stop me, but I'm determined to lay the smack-down or go down swinging, taking some folks with me. And I won't be alone. There are many ways in which I plan to attack, but the first plan is to go lay the spiritual groundwork.

After catching up on some paperwork, I leave the office and swing northwest to Mount Sinai Hospital on the

West side of Chicago to have dinner with Momma. I'm used to my mother getting leers from men as we step down the hallway. Thankfully the looks are brief enough to grant mercy and no catcalls are made, because I wouldn't know what to do if a high schooler hollas at my mother.

"Scarlet," one of Momma's fellow nurses calls as she fixes her wary gaze on me. "You checking out?"

"Lunch, Mendy," she states with an exasperated grin. "See you in an hour," she amends and steps a confidential breath away from Mendy and affirms, "and tell the Nosy Knows that this is my oldest son."

Embarrassing. "Some things never change," I express as we break the threshold of the door and make our way to the car.

"Don't hate me for being beautiful," Momma jokes as I let her in.

Her statement is true as I recognize in a sincere, not lustful sense. Framed around a smooth, creamy skin tone and fire red flowing hair, her features are soft, innocent and welcoming. Dirty old men step to her because they think she's a teenager with a hot body. Boys stumble over their tongues because they think she's a wet dream and a good conversation piece for the prom.

"Did you fight Friday night?"

I nod, chuckling at the recollection of an easy night of fights as I pull out of the parking lot.

"It's hard to tell when you don't have any visible bruises or scars," Momma tells me.

"I can't get bruised if I get the first hit."

"So did you at least break a sweat?"

"I gave the Bear the right hand of fellowship for a twenty second TKO," I assure, slapping my right fist into my left hand and quickly getting my hands back on the steering wheel before Momma throws a fit. "Shannon 'Dragon' Lee kissed my hand and got put to sleep after he tried a round-house kick at the one minute mark. The last fighter forfeited when I raised my right hand, so I only put in a minute and a half night's work."

"Did it at least relax your mind?"

"Not at all. I was distracted and disturbed. That's why the matches didn't last any longer," I confess as I dwell on the spiritual apostasy of South Holland. Although I didn't witness it in person, the unorthodox teachings and practices of the churches were well documented, broadcast and publicized. "The churches had a minister of music who smoked the ritual blunts, contacted the dead and practiced fortune telling; a school superintendent who suggested circumcision and animal sacrifice to atone for sins; a preacher who cursed everyone who ate pork; and one elder who was a proud, practicing homosexual and another who was a known adulterer. The congregation was taught that having sex before marriage is okay so long as you wear a condom. According to the special on PBS, they have an usually high percentage of teenage pregnancies in that area. And I won't mention the ecumenical alliance with the False Witnesses and the Last Day Believers. It's a wonder fire from heaven didn't come down on South Holland."

"In spite of how we left the area, it is hard watching it go down," she says, shaking her head as she pops in the Deitrick Haddon CD.

216

"I didn't realize how many liquor stores and gun shops moved in and how the factory and business district faded out, causing unemployment, foreclosures and desolation, the perfect ingredients for the developers to make a killing within only eighteen years. It wasn't even subtle. It's like the earth opened up and Hell swallowed up South Holland. I don't even know who to wage war with, where to start or who to sue. All I know is it's not fair that the land is being snatched up."

She reaches over and rubs my shoulders. "You'll do fine."

"It doesn't look good," I confess, shaking my head.

"How does it look through the eyes of faith?"

"I think I need glasses, but regardless, you know how much I like to fight, so I'm going in to win anyway."

"But it seems to me that you're not the fighter, the Lord is," she says as she leans over and pecks me on the cheek. "You're the sword in the Lord's hand."

The tension in my spirit is immediately loosed, and I ride on in reflective silence as we listen to 'Hold On 2 Your Faith.' Momma is a corner-man to me, firing me up in between the rounds of life and assuring me that I can knock 'em out when I get back out there. She knows from experience.

Once she graduated from carnality to spirituality in the Christian faith and moved to a higher level in her relationship with the Lord, she found herself completing her GED and pursuing her lifelong dream of being a nurse. With six kids, public assistance and financial aid, she finished her studies in three years with a 3.8 G.P.A.. Two years after landing a job at Mount Sinai, she landed Reverend Dr. Paul Peterson MD, an affluent man of honor who saw Momma as a born-again woman of virtue, not the eternally soiled sinner that the South Hollanders saw.

"You and Doc still on for Hawaii next month?" I small talk as I open the door to Home Run Inn.

"Aloha."

"I need to get away, too," I note wistfully, letting out an exhausted sigh.

"What's stopping you?"

"Work and War."

"Joey, you'll learn to relax and enjoy life one day before you get old and gray," she promises as the hostess leads us to a non-smoking section.

I mull over her statement as I peruse the menu. All work and no play makes Joe a tired boy for sure. Indeed, getting away wouldn't hurt. After all, I am starting to feel the wear and tear, and the gray strands are a testimony of my labor woes. After the waitress takes our order, I meet the stare of a middle-aged couple who are smiling approvingly at me and Momma. I return the smile and a nod. Momma verbally greets the couple. The man nods and the woman tells Momma, "You look just like your father."

My jaw drops slightly as I stare at Momma, and her countenance cracks into a jubilant grin.

# Sword of the Lord

## Part Two – By Faith

I accepted this monster of a case and the more I try to get my arms around it, the more it wiggles loose. I don't know whether it's all good or not, but I am back in contact with my Dad's family. It's been bittersweet. The more I get to know about them, the less I wish that I did know. My somberness from the recent news that my brother, Pastor Narcissus Joseph, was found guilty of money laundering and will serve at least four years in a federal prison, sags from my whole body like a wet jump suit. The blow of his ordeal just punched me flush in the gut as I return from dropping my teenage daughter Chastity off at her maternal grandmother's house in the city. Even though there's an open issue between me and him, I take no pleasure in his situation. It discredits the Church and my Dad's name, the part of me that I've tried to drown but keeps floating back up.

The corrupt capitalism in the Community of Churches is just a microcosm of the ugly history of the city. Black genocide is just one of its offspring. Unbeknownst to the Josephs and other black visionaries who thought they were reaching a promised land in the southern suburbs, they were steered to South Holland as opposed to the neighboring Lilydale.

As a result of the diabolical, Blockbusting scheme in which word spread through the community that with the addition of folks of color moving in, the pure white area would be defiled, the Italians, Polish and Irish who had lived there for decades made a small profit from selling their homes, while the agents and developers turned around and sold it to the blacks for triple the market value. While a handful of the European-Americans stayed in the area, most scattered in all directions. Many who did leave were unwitting of the plan. With the white flight, the value seemed to decrease because the mortgage and insurance companies refused to issue loans or insurance in the area. The immoral scheme was obvious, but not proven or challenged in a court of law.

Once the town was established as a black mecca with thriving businesses and good schools, the negative elements slithered into the area. Like dandelions, the liquor stores owned by foreigners started popping up. When the social services were cut and school funding decreased, gang recruitment increased and two prisons were built in neighboring counties to handle the wave of new residents.

There is religious freedom in South Holland. While I disagree with some of their practices, I will defend their right to worship their god, even in the Community of Churches. However, I draw the line on the ecumenical philosophy and joining in their worship. We can agree to disagree, but I will not give them credit for having some of the truth when they deny the validity of the Gospel. Unfortunately, that's what has paved the road to their impending downfall. Sanctifying the Church was the initial step that was already started before I came in, now the legal drama is what remains.

After researching the current state of affairs, I circulate petitions, schedule demonstrations, give several media interviews, organize protests and assign several investigators on the case to determine the magnitude of the dirt. When the results come back, the liability is spread out and shared by the state, county and city, the police, prosecutors, developers and real estate agents. I telephoned them all, querying them on their involvement. As it turns out, none of their lawyers take me seriously, so I pray, "Lord, bring to light all the darkness, for Your glory and honor. I promise that the first piece of good news that is received in my house I will give back to You—totally abandon and walk away without looking back. I will give not only a tenth to You, but the whole blessing, no matter what it is."

Now I'm ready to file my civil suit against the State of Illinois for trying to take the land. I will also do a class action lawsuit against Luci's Developmenters Incorporated, who are contracted by the State to bring their vision to fruition and were directly responsible for the gentrification through unethical and illegal practices.

To make bad matters worse, the developers and the state aren't the only problems that have to be dealt with. The churches are falling apart just when I need them to have their act together. In a state of emergency, all formalities are thrown out the window. In addition to Pastor Narcissus religiously out of commission, Bishop Justin's serial adultery and drinking has him too tangled in a web of controversy to continue in his station, so he is resigning to get help, leaving the churches without a leader. I've stepped up and put in my bid out of necessity, not interested in the title and recognition that comes with it. My forte isn't preaching in between the four walls of a building, but helping people Monday through Friday with a tangible need and street witnessing on Saturday with a good discernable word. Most people outside of my circle of friends don't know that I am a licensed minister, and I don't verbally advertise myself as such. Normally when a new leader is installed at a church, there is a lot of pomp and circumstance. If I'm selected, there will be no hypocritical celebrations in my honor.

I utter a silent prayer as I exit my Chevy Suburban and make my way through the doors of Watchtower Church. I went the whole day without eating—choosing to meditate on the Word of God, pray and peruse my two favorite books: "Without Sanctuary" and "Foxe's Book of Martyrs." My second oldest brother, James, who owns a bookstore, insists that I'm morbid after finding out that I seek books that give accounts of people getting killed just for being black and for being Christians. I don't have a sick lust for blood, I'm just awestruck and inspired to read of every day people who were tortured to death for something as simple as a belief or a racial classification. And when I'm inspired, I'm determined and focused.

While many folks who died on the battlefield of various wars—whether natural or spiritual—are celebrated and remembered after death, more often than not they are obscure and anonymous during their life. I recognize that the combat beforehand could be bloody, and although I am resolved to fight, I must set the record straight and make peace with my own family before officially declaring war.

In my amateur boxing days, I would enter a zone fueled by anxiety, adrenaline, excitement and expectation, rendering my nerves mute and my strength magnified. I am currently in that zone.

When I break the threshold, I am escorted to the back where the leader's office is. The stout usher takes my coat as he opens the door to the bright, spacious elder's chamber. The paneled walls are lined with several plaques and notable photos, including that of my father. I almost sink into the gold, high-piled wall-to-wall carpeting. The ministerial staff is gathered to the sides of the exiting Pastor Narcissus and Bishop Justin, resembling knights waiting on the king's word. Peering at the thirty clergy men and women, I settle my glare on their Bishop.

"Before I address the assembly and give my decision, I need a word with you and Pastor Narcissus."

He closes his eyes and nods, ordering the ministers to "Meet us in the sanctuary."

They file past me in a straight, dignified line, leaving the two officials seated. When the door closes, I take a deep, passionate breath and launch my verbal, improvised anger at them.

"Atlanta, Georgia, April 23, 1899, according to the account in 'Without Sanctuary,' Sam Hose—a black man who was falsely accused of killing planter Alfred Cranford and raping his wife—was stripped of his clothes, chained to a tree, soaked with kerosene and oil. Before they applied the torch, the lynch mob cut off his ears, fingers, and genitals; skinned his face, and plunged knives into his flesh and then baptized him with fire. Ironically enough, he cried 'Oh, my God! Oh, Jesus.'

"Louisville, Illinois, September 15, 1998, history

repeated itself when you suggested to the community that I was gay. That, my friend, was more than an assassination attempt on my character; that was like spiritual and moral castration of my identity," I declare with restrained, confident fury as tears pour from my eyes.

The octaves in my voice burst through my restraint as I step to Bishop Justin's face and yell, "That's what you did to me; you castrated my character and lynched my persona. You cut my soul and it hurt like hell, but by the grace of God—just like Sam Hose before me—I can say 'Lord have mercy.' In my heart I forgive you, but know you shot a hole in my soul that has tortured me," I emphasize, letting the power of my words sink in.

He trembles briefly and gulps with the subtlety of a collapsing skyscraper as the sting of the slanderous remarks is fresher now than when it first happened five years ago.

Men of Valor is my non-profit organization designed to salvage the souls of men. It has a prison ministry that not only goes into the penal systems with worship services, but it provides necessities to the inmates' families and a highly developed transitional system to assist prisoners in adjusting to freedom through shelter, job placement and skill building. The work is personal to me, and my blood and faith brothers twisted my noble cause into a perverted lie. But lies die, the truth rises and Men of Valor is still marching strong.

Sticking my hand out as an olive branch gesture, I ask, "Are we cool now?"

Bishop Justin peers at my hand for a moment, nods and extends his into mine and assures, "We are brothers," he tells me.

I pull him from his seat and into an embrace, which Pastor Narcissus joins.

The Joseph bridge was burned down years ago, but the blood bond is too strong to resist crossing the turbulent waters together. "Now let's go," I order.

Bishop leads me and Pastor Narcissus out to the full, restive sanctuary where the members of all five churches patiently wait for the word. After a brief prayer and a short biography from Bishop, I step to the podium.

Clearing my throat, I peer out at the expectant congregation, registering each of the faces while at the same time taking in the group as a whole. "It's no secret to this denomination and to the town that I am the illegitimate son of the founder, and that eighteen years ago I was rejected. In spite of the ugly history, I loved and still love my family, and I love the Lord, the same God you love. I wasn't welcome here, but it was home to me even though I wasn't present. There may still be some who don't want me here."

"We want you here," a voice from among the multitude trumpets.

I nod and continue. "I will defend the land regardless of my title or station in this Church and town, but the battle will be much easier if I am not only fighting as your lawyer, but as your Pastor. Understanding that I won't accept this position if I'm not truly wanted."

"We can vote now," a woman in the front row motions, seconded by, "All in favor of Joseph Jephthah Lewis leading us, raise your hands," from an older gentleman on the deacon's row.

Amazingly and flatteringly, all of the hands are raised, almost moving me to tears.

"So it's official," exiting Bishop Justin announces as he walks beside me.

"It's official. I'm on the frontline."

\*         \*         \*

I waste no time in putting the word out on the march around South Holland. Invitations are mailed to hundreds of churches across the city and it is announced on all of the Gospel radio stations. The initial response is quick and overwhelming. However, I know that the majority will back out when it comes time to go soul winning.

The rally is right on time. Of course my ministry is down with the program, and my bosom buddies gather the men from their congregations and jobs. Another one hundred fifty men from my new church are present. Even saints from different denominations put their differences aside and unite, although there are a minority who want to make an issue of the ritual cleansing formulas, babbling in different languages, and works of the law.

It's time for me to lay down the real deal so I let the words flow. "Expect any and everything out there. You don't have to strain your imaginations either. No one is an alien to the inner city woes; sin ain't so uncommon that it shocks us, so don't trip out when you come across brothers smoking their blunts or sisters selling their hotcakes. You will hear cussin', fussin' and all types of ruckus; you will cross thugs, see drugs; folks will be drunk, high and low, hot-headed and cold-hearted. We know what's going on. If you have a weak heart and can't handle going on the offensive, I suggest you go fry some chicken or bake some cakes, because this is war. And while you're at it, sit in on a couple of Sunday school classes and go to prayer meeting and ask God for some more faith. No one joins a team to ride the bench, and no Saint should enlist in the army of the Lord to warm the pew," I state with emphasis as I scan the crowd of five hundred men, all saints.

"If you know the Truth, if you are righteous, if you are eager to spread the Good News, if you have faith, if you are saved, and if you know the Word of God, then strap on your armor and let's pray," I beseech, and then lead the soldiers in prayer before starting our prayer march around the town.

After closing out in the name of God Almighty, I charge, "Soldiers march in the name of the Lord," and we proceed to circle South Holland as a symbolic gesture that we're about to lay claim to it.

After the rally is over, I am pumped and ready to win this thing, although the odds aren't in our favor. Nobody in their right mind goes up against the state, but then again that's what I do. I ease down the highway letting the Church, the rally, and the task at hand penetrate. I call my wife to fill her in on the latest events and promise to see her soon. The forty-five minute drive home feels like a day. I have come to learn that God is where faith is.

When I drag myself to the doorway, the hands of hope immediately snatch the ill mood from my bosom. My wife,

Faith, has obviously entered the house since I left.

For some people, prayer is a formal religious exercise; with others it's a duty that they check off on a daily basis. Faith doesn't fit in either category. For her prayer is an experience, a fellowship, a lifestyle. There isn't a lot of repetitive babbling or big words uttered, but she reaches Heaven. Sometimes the volume is high enough to hear behind the door; most often the dialogue is at a confidential tone. The only evidence of God's answer is when she affirms what she hears, followed by a confirmation in the scriptures that she immediately flips to.

Her coos are inaudible, so I tiptoe to her den that doubles as her prayer closet and gently push open the door. The half-smoked Frankincense incense floats up with her petitions toward Heaven and through the ceiling as she paces backwards and forward on the floor. The sweet fragrance eases through my nostrils and allays my nerves even more as I absorb the view of her virtuous beauty. Intensity permeates her being, but distress is absent from her countenance. The words are not to me, but they are for me, so I listen.

"My Lord, I'm laying my concerns for the Word of God churches before you. It's a burden to me because they are in the family of faith. They're important and have a purpose in the community," she pours out.

*"Yes, You know their deeds, and they have forsaken their first love.* The report says that the doors of Word of God Church will be shut...*Yes, yes, but You say, 'What I open no one can shut, and what I shut no one can open,' "* she utters as she flips the pages. "But will this destroy

Pastor Joseph?"

She flips the Bible as she utters, "*Lord, you 'chasten those you love and judgment begins in the house of the Lord.'*

"Lord have mercy on them, I'm concerned about their salvation. Okay Lord, *'For no one can lay any foundation other than the one already laid...If any man builds on this foundation using gold, silver, costly stones, wood, hay or straw, his work will be shown for what it is, because the Day will bring it to light. It will be revealed with fire, and the fire will test the quality of each man's work. If what he has built survives, he will receive his reward. If it is burned up, he will suffer loss; he himself will be saved, but only as one escaping through the flames.'*"

My heart smiles, relieved that my new church is in God's hands. Even though the former leadership was in error and He has a chastening hand on them, I take no solace in knowing an enemy person is suffering. I have a friend in Faith, and I was blessed with the wisdom to recognize my need for her in order to live a victorious life. I gape in reverential awe as I ponder how God protected me in the streets and brought me to this place of direction and purpose. So far from where I was when me and Momma put the Josephs out of our lives after the Bishop's funeral.

At the time, it was the right gesture, but it didn't solve all of our woes. Only a month after being alienated from the Josephs, I was expelled from school senior year for fighting and I buried the mother of my daughter after she was killed in a car crash. I realize now that the beating I took was meant to prepare me for the war I'm fighting today, but I didn't know it back then. Through it all, my steps were ordered to the church, which I joined before the sermon was preached and the invitation was extended.

After I accepted the Lord, Minister Mark Singleton and Faith were assigned as my prayer partners and guardian angels who took me through a religious boot camp. Chastity, my daughter, took an immediate liking to the maternal Faith, and I couldn't help but follow suit and be drawn to her gentle spirit and full bosom. Whereas Mark taught me how to spiritually fight and apologetically defend my beliefs—going over the pillars of the faith, salvation, the unity of the Lord, the Angel of the Lord, the Spirit of God, and the scriptures, Faith taught me how to open up my heart, soul, mind, and might to the Lord and how to live a godly life. After constant exposure to doctrine and virtue, I was transformed into a man of valor even though I was ignorant of the change. Through all of the scriptural studies, I recognized that God's Word is bond.

Whenever the church doors were open, Faith was there like a permanent fixture, with her alluring figure. Initially, my faithfulness rested on my desire to see Faith. Every succulent inch of her body worshipped the Lord, and her gold-tone face was illuminated with the glory of God. The warm hugs after service kept me carnally honest and our frequent lunches in between services drew us closer.

Eventually, I was there for communion with God. His Word spoke to my deceived heart about the eternal security of my salvation, demolishing the commercialized false doctrine that had me feeling safe. I once believed that my salvation rested on my good works, which I fall way short of enough to merit eternal life. That next year was dedicated to courtship and religious reprogramming. After that, my blessing was a bride more precious than jewels and the Bridegroom known as the Messiah who will usher me into eternal glory.

Faith winds down her prayer by praising, "Lord, just as you took Enoch to heaven without him dying, I know that you will snatch some of us up when you come. Praise and glory and wisdom and thanks and honor and power and strength be to You."

With my mood seasoned with inspiration, I grin as I stealthily ease my way beyond the door.

"Come dance with me, my Brown Bomber and Mighty Warrior," she beseeches before I can step all the way out the door.

"How did you know I was in here?" I question as I step into her line of vision.

"I can feel your strong presence," she affirms as she jubilantly glides over, embraces me and plants a kiss on the old stitches just below my left eye.

"You know I can't dance, and besides I have a lot on my mind."

"Don't sweat the issues," she encourages, taking my hands in hers as she pulls me over to the CD player, adding, "Celebrate the victory that the Lord has ordained even before you start fighting."

My reluctance to celebrate melts as "In Your Will," by Light of Love softly plays. She gently ushers me into the center of the floor, into her bosom and into a slow dance, consumed by faith.

231

*Part Three - Power of the Vow*

The class action suit only shined a light on all types of corruption and exposed folks of repute and people of anonymity. When the audits were finished, there were enough crooks singing the sweet sound of truth to fill three mass choirs. Of course I received death threats, but oddly enough, the folks who were somehow connected were winding up dead.

Victory was sure, and Luci's offered to settle for an amount that would have been appeasing for me and the people, but the suit had to run its course of exposure and annihilation in order to not only repair and restore what was broken and ravaged, but to set up a monument in honor of the Lord so that the inhabitants of the Community of Churches would never forget. The process was an abbreviated three years and seven months, with the judge finally ruling in the Lord's favor for South Holland and twenty other surrounding cities, and punitive damages in excess of two billion dollars in the civil suit against the state. Word spread like a plague when the verdict was read, and before I made it home that evening I was an international celebrity.

A letter from Lang County sticking out of the mailbox, followed by "A Balm in Gilead" by Karen Clarke Sheard greets me at the door. My daughter isn't too far behind and rhythmically bounces into me.

"Hey, Daddy," she says, "What kind of a rhyme do you have today? I know you have something after winning."

"You know I do," I say as I gladly open the envelope and my heart to lay down a rap with my only child, the apple of my eye.

"J to the E to the P to the H to the T to the H to the A
to the H
Coming your way
Earthquaking and dominating like the Lakers on a
championship trounce
Bouncing in the south
Can you pronounce the sound of slaughter
Better yet measure the magnitude of the attitude
Of the Righteous Jedi Knight of Light
Nice and enticing like chocolate icing
Rhapsadizing Chastity rappin' 'bout the Shiloh's Bad Bro
Catch Joe's M O to go for broke
Smokin' and smotin' the jokers
And clowns getting downed like a frown
Da Brown Bomber's coming to town
Beating a path of destruction of the constructions of the
enemy's schemes
You know what I mean
The Seed of righteousness laying claim to the promised
land is the aftermath
In lieu of Joe Lewis' right cross
But by the power of the sword of the Lord
You heard the Word
You're down by the law
And he can still break your jaw

You're dissed and dismissed
By the victory of the vow
And the power of the promise,"

The lyrical content causes my joy to overflow, only to have the cup of my persona tip over, spilling out all of my positive passion.

Listening to my daughter recite back as much of the poem as she can, I read the letter. It confirms what I was hoping. I would finally own Chastity outright. I already own several structures in the Chastity community: thirty houses, ten condominium buildings, eight commercial properties including two malls, and fifty acres of undeveloped land. There are undefiled lakes, streams and ponds in Chastity, with scenic access to the two major expressways. Then it hit me like a ton of bricks, I had to walk away from it because that's the promise I made to God for letting me win the case. Why did the letter have to come today? When I settled here two decades ago, the area was underdeveloped, with only a few shacks and a couple of stores. Much has gone into the building up of Chastity, and the bid I put in to buy the town at auction won easily, as I knew it would. I planned in my heart to give Chastity to my daughter, for her name's sake. It was my great desire. Owning a town was guaranteed to keep her from having to go through the agony of banishment from your home because somebody didn't want her around. All of the work and hopes that I'd put into making this place a reality are gone. It's mine and I can't have it. I hinted to her that this town would one day be hers. At this moment, I sit grieved because I won't be able to give the town to Chastity—her rightful inheritance, something I had no taste of from my Dad.

"The letter is bad news isn't it?" she questions, snapping me out of my depression.

I hug her and assure, "The letter is da bomb."

"Daddy," she asks, "then why is your face hanging all of a sudden, as if you have food poisoning?"

With my heart aching and my head hemorrhaging, I exhale. "Sit down, Chastity." We park on the sofa and I show her the letter, explaining, "Chastity is now my city."

"Daddy, that is great. We finally get to own it. It finally happened, just like you said that it would. I can't wait to tell my friends. I can't believe that this will be my town someday. Daddy, thank you so much. I love you," she tells me full of giddy teenage enthusiasm.

"Wait, Chastity," I hate saying, "but there's something else I need to tell you."

"More good news? Wow!"

"The city is mine, ours, but I wish that it wasn't mine until next week; next month; next year.

"From the time we moved out here, I had a vision of a beautiful community that I could not only raise you in, but pass on to you as an inheritance. Today, my dream came true, only I'm awakening before I can give it to you, which makes me want to die," I say with tears streaming down my cheeks. "Before I took on the case and filed suit, you knew the odds were stacked against me."

She nods, her eyes welling up as she peers at me.

"The only way to win was by the Lord winning. No

other way. It wasn't my skill, my influence, nor a matter of us being right. It was the Lord's doing. I knew it going in. So before I went to battle I prayed to the Lord, promising to walk away from, totally abandon the first piece of good news that was received into this house and winning the bid to buy the city for us is the first good news." I can't look at her sad little face without breaking down. "We'll have to move."

"Daddy, I don't want to move."

"I'm sorry, but we'll have to move and let the Lord use the town as he chooses."

Turning her wet face away and looking down, she methodically cries, "Daddy, I'm going to miss my friends and my school. No more music, no more martial arts, and no more dance lessons. We won't be able to live here any more?"

She is precious to me. I sacrificed for her, but in giving to her abundantly, I never forsook the Lord God. I didn't live a loose life in her sight. I pay my tithes, minister and advance the Kingdom. Now I have to honor God in her presence so she knows how to do it when her time comes.

"It will be hard to go," I tell her.

"Okay, Daddy, I know we have to go, but can I stay here for the rest of the summer so that I can be with my friends?"

"We can stay for the rest of the summer. After the next two months are up, we'll leave."

"Thanks, Daddy. I love you."

The only thing better than winning battle after battle is having my only child know me as her Daddy, never having to apologize for who she is and how she came into this world. The demons of my past are finally dead, and I no longer have to prove myself to anybody. I am God's man chosen for whatever task He puts before me. I am a fighting warrior with victory in my blood.

# The Best
# Of
# Everything

# By
# Victoria Christopher Murray

he's torturing me." Hannah slammed the car keys onto the granite kitchen counter.

"Honey, what did she do?" Brandon rushed behind her, folding his arms around her waist. "Sweetheart, what did Renee do?"

Hannah closed her eyes, reliving the scene from church this morning. Remembering how Renee had walked up to her. Taking slow steps with a wide grin. All four children in tow.

"Hannah, I don't know why you're upset. You were this way through the entire service."

Hannah sighed and turned to face her husband. "She's always bringing the children...."

Brandon stepped back a bit, although he still held her. "The children are supposed to be in church. They're there every Sunday."

Hannah nodded, but lowered her glance. That's one of the problems, she thought.

"I thought you loved my children."

She lifted her gaze. "You know I do," she said as she hugged him. "I love Robert and Stella and Greg and Susan. I love all of them." Before she uttered the last word, her arms fell away from him. She sauntered across the wide space to the family room and settled into the softness of the cream leather couch. The smooth surface felt cool against her bare legs even though the August sun shined, full of promise, through the windowed wall. She closed her eyes when she heard Brandon's footsteps clapping against the limestone floor, edging toward her.

Brandon leaned against the back of the couch and let his fingers rest on his wife's neck for a few seconds before he began kneading the tightness. Hannah allowed her head to slump free, seamless like a rag doll. The tension eased, first from her face, then her neck, and next she felt the tightness loosen in her arms. She rested her head against Brandon as he continued to free her from the pressure that enveloped her muscles.

For long minutes, she escaped. But then the blackness behind her eyes filled with images. Her mind dragged her back to the church steps where she had waited as Brandon parked the car this morning. She smiled and kissed other parishioners as they filed into the church; some she knew by name, most she knew by sight only from Sunday services and Tuesday night Bible study. As she leaned over to kiss Miss Pearl, she saw Renee rushing up the steps toward her.

"Good morning, Hannah," Renee said as she tugged at five-year-old Susan, pulling her along. She paused as if she had to catch her breath, then added, "Everyone, say hello to your…stepmother." She spoke the last word as if it were the punch line from a Queens of Comedy joke.

Hannah wasn't even sure if the children had obeyed their mother's command. All she could think about was why did Brandon's ex-wife have to attend the same church?

Suddenly, Brandon's fingers felt heavy against her neck. She opened her eyes and slipped from his grasp, moving to the French doors that led to the patio. The sun's brilliant rays shimmered against the pool's water, an inviting sight, a peaceful oasis—so different from what raged inside of her.

"You know I love you, Hannah," Brandon whispered.

"This I know. I've never doubted it."

"All that matters is that we're together. And, that I can make you happy."

Hannah turned to face him, fighting the water that threatened to spring from her eyes. She didn't want to cry again. She wasn't sure if she could. There had been so many tears shed. "Brandon, I want to make you happy, too."

"Sweetheart, you do. I'm happier than I've ever been in my life. How many times do I have to tell you this?" When his wife remained silent, Brandon shook his head. "When are you going to believe me?"

"I believe you…." She paused, knowing that her tone wasn't convincing.

Brandon turned away. "Hannah, I don't know what else to do." He pressed his hands against his forehead.

"We can't go through this every time we see Renee and my children."

"I know, Brandon." She rushed to his side and took his hands. "I don't want to do this either. It's just that you've given me so much. All of this...." Her eyes scanned the massive family room filled with designer pieces. She wanted to run through all five-thousand square feet of their home that Brandon had designed and built and just remind her husband of all that he'd done. "I want to give something back to you. I want to give you a baby."

"I want that, too, Hannah. But you know what? If it doesn't happen, I will be just as happy, because I didn't marry you for that. I married you because I love you more than I've ever loved anyone."

Hannah wrapped her arms around Brandon's neck. "I love you, too," she whispered before she kissed his cheek.

As Brandon pulled her tighter and nestled his nose in the curve of her neck, Hannah closed her eyes. She was in the arms of her soul mate. She knew this within minutes of their first meeting. He'd walked into the law office where she was an associate attorney. She'd been standing at the receptionist desk when he introduced himself. When she took his outstretched hand to shake it, she was sure an electrical surge had seared through her. She'd checked his left ring finger for the symbol of marriage and became more excited when she saw none. But her excitement was diffused with his next words...when he asked the receptionist to let Calloway Powell know that Brandon Carrington had arrived. Calloway was one of L.A.'s most prominent divorce attorneys.

She saw Brandon often in the weeks that followed, always managing to be around whenever he came into the office. But when he suggested that they go to lunch together, she declined. She didn't know his business, but she knew enough to figure out that he was getting a divorce. No matter how her heart fluttered when he spoke her name with that rich tone that could rival Barry White, or how her knees shook when he smiled and the dimple in his cheek winked at her, she refused to be on the bad end of a rebound. But seven months after his divorce was final, Hannah's resolve faded, and they had their first date. Seven months after that, they were married in a beachside ceremony in Maui.

Hannah never doubted Brandon's love. He was a faithful man of God who had loved his first wife – until he found out that she'd been sleeping with his best friend. After hours of counseling with his pastor, and even more hours of prayer, Brandon was able to set aside his bitterness for the sake of the children. The divorce was amicable, albeit still painful for Brandon who wanted to save his marriage. But it was Renee who insisted on the divorce, telling Brandon that it wasn't him – it was just that she felt stifled after having four children. In a heart-wrenching declaration, Renee had proclaimed that all she wanted was her freedom...and six thousand dollars a month in child support and alimony. Hannah always thought that was odd – just how much freedom could a woman have with four children living at home? But she would give anything to have just a quarter of the off-spring that Renee had.

Hannah hugged Brandon tighter. He had proven his love for her – from the diamond marquis she wore on her finger to the home he'd built for her on the ocean's edge in Manhattan Beach. His actions went beyond his words to let her know how much she was cherished. But long shadows of doubt rested over her. How could they be happy if their family was incomplete?

"I love you," Brandon whispered once again into her ear.

Hannah nodded, but said nothing. She closed her eyes and prayed that his love would be enough.

*     *     *

The minutes moved forward at a snail's pace as Hannah weaved her way between the office window and the doctor's desk.

"Sweetheart, are you training for the marathon?"

She turned, facing her husband, but her grimace didn't match Brandon's smile. He reached for her and she took his hand, settling into the chair next to his. The large cushions were designed to bring comfort. But as she sank deeper into the chair, her hopes dropped with her as she imagined all that the doctor would say.

"I'm sorry, Mr. and Mrs. Carrington, but there is no way that you will ever have children." Then, Hannah envisioned the doctor turning to her with a sneer of pity. "God has closed your womb."

"Honey, don't...," Brandon began in a voice so gentle that Hannah was sure he'd heard her thoughts. But he stopped as the office door opened.

Doctor London swept inside as if she suddenly remembered that she had two people waiting anxiously for her news. "I'm sorry I kept you waiting," the doctor said before she sat behind the pine desk that seemed to be standard furniture for medical offices. "I just wanted to make sure we had all the test results."

From the moment the doctor entered the office, Hannah's gaze followed the manila folder tucked under Doctor London's arm. She took a deep breath and Brandon squeezed her hand, trying to share his calm with her.

"Just give me a moment," Doctor London said, pulling her eyeglasses from a leather case before resting them on the bridge of her nose.

It felt as if the air had lost its oxygen as Hannah forced deep breaths through her nose. She watched the doctor's glance glide across the papers. Doctor London turned the pages, her expression staid, absent of emotion. Absent of any signs that would give them the news before she was ready to divulge it. Hannah pressed her body deeper into the chair, praying it would be enough to keep her from jumping up and snatching the folder from the doctor so that she could read the results for herself.

"Well," Doctor London began.

She's not looking at me, Hannah thought. Oh, God. It must be really bad.

"I have good news."

Hannah frowned, but remained silent.

"We performed almost every test known to man to determine the reason why you haven't been able to conceive. And," the doctor held a pink paper in front of her face before lowering it and continuing, "from the hysterosalpingogram to the ultrasound, it all looks fine, Hannah. Your hormone levels are normal; you don't have any scar tissues or adhesions. This is really good news."

Oxygen returned to the room, and Hannah breathed, relieved.

"Brandon...." It was the way the doctor said his name that made Hannah hold her breath again.

"We did find a bit of a problem for you," she paused, then added quickly, "It's a small one. Your sperm count is slightly low, but I'm not too concerned about that."

"Well, if it's not a problem, Doctor, why did you mention it?" The question exploded from Hannah before she could stop it. She regretted her words and tone as soon as Doctor London and Brandon stared at her. "I only meant...," Hannah paused, giving herself seconds to settle before she added, "It must be a concern or else you wouldn't have mentioned it."

"I understand your thinking, Hannah. But that's not true." The doctor leaned forward on the desk, crossing her arms in front of her. "I believe in full disclosure. I want my patients to know everything that we find on tests." She looked from Hannah to Brandon. "But as I said, this really isn't a problem."

Hannah leaned back into the chair, but she felt little relief. She had imagined the doctor entering her office with droopy eyelids and slack cheeks expressing her sympathy at the pitiful state of Hannah's dysfunctional uterus, ovaries and fallopian tubes.

"God has closed your womb."

Those were the words she'd heard over and over in her mind. But, that wasn't it. If anything, this was Brandon's fault. She wanted to look at him, to see what he thought about the doctor's disclosure. But she'd been unable to move her gaze from the doctor since she'd entered the office.

"Actually, I don't believe that Brandon's sperm count has anything to do with this. After all, he has fathered four children."

Hannah blinked. She had almost forgotten about that. This couldn't be Brandon's fault. God had allowed him to have children. God hadn't allowed her.

"My professional opinion is that there is no conceivable reason why you're not pregnant now." She chuckled as if her pun would lighten the mood. But Hannah and Brandon sat still, without smiles.

"But, Doctor, there must be some problem." Brandon spoke his first words. That was fine with Hannah because it had become difficult for her to breathe again.

"No, Brandon. I really don't think there is a problem. There are no medical abnormalities as I told you before."

"Then, what?" Brandon continued to ask the questions that were inside Hannah.

"Well, there is something. Actually, there is a small group of women who are just unable to get pregnant without explanation. But, it's such a small group, and I really don't believe that's what's happening in this case. Actually, it wasn't worth mentioning."

Hannah wanted to stand up and scream. Why did the doctor keep saying things that supposedly didn't matter? Hannah was sure of it now – she would never be a mother. She belonged to that small group that wasn't worth mentioning.

"So, Doctor, what should we do?" Brandon asked.

"I would give it a bit more time." She looked down at her chart. "Has it been a year yet?"

Hannah couldn't believe the doctor's question. Didn't she remember? Not only was she Hannah's doctor, but Sheila London attended the same church. She was sure the doctor had seen her and Brandon at that altar many times over the year, whenever Pastor Ford called for couples who wanted to conceive. Yes, it's been a year, Hannah yelled inside. It's been more than a year. "It's been almost two years, Doctor." The words squeaked from her.

"I see," the doctor said without a hint of apology. "But, that's still not a long time, considering that you've just been married two years, and getting settled into a new marriage can bring with it its own stress that can lead to challenges…."

"We don't have any problems," Hannah interrupted, then added a bit softer, "except for not being able to get pregnant."

"No, honey," Brandon said turning to her, and then looking to the doctor. "You might have a point, Doctor London. It's been a whirlwind two years. Not only did we get married, but we designed and built a house. We've just been in our home a few months."

The doctor nodded.

"And, Hannah stopped working. That has to be part of this, too," Brandon added.

Hannah sighed inside. How could not working be a problem? If anything, there was less stress in her life since Brandon had declared that he preferred for her to stay home. She had gladly traded her tailored suits for sweat suits, exchanged her corporate bob for shoulder-length mahogany-tinted twists and filled her days with church committees and volunteer work at the Children's Hospital.

"So Doctor, there have been quite a few changes in our lives," Brandon finished.

"See," Doctor London exclaimed with such joy that Hannah was sure she was about to clap her hands. "I think the two of you are fine. Now that we have the test results, my suggestion is that we wait a few months before we explore other options." The doctor jotted a note onto the top sheet in the folder. "Hannah, let's touch base again in three months. We'll talk and proceed from there."

"Doctor, the other options…I've been reading about other ways of conceiving," Brandon said. Hannah raised her eyebrows in surprise. She didn't know that he'd been researching this. She'd often wondered if he wanted a child as much as she. Maybe he did. "That can be expensive, right?" he asked.

Hannah wanted a Q-tip to clean her ears. Surely her architect husband, who paid more than two hundred thousand dollars in taxes last year, wasn't asking how much he'd have to pay for the privilege of becoming a parent. She was right – he didn't want a child.

Doctor London nodded. "It can be. But we're not there yet. The two of you have been worrying and wondering if there was anything medically wrong. I think now that you know everything is fine, the stress may go away. And who knows. I may see you in less than three months. In a week or two you could be back here getting a pregnancy test." The doctor stood and leaned her fingers against her desktop. "There's one thing you can't deny. Trying to get pregnant can be a whole lot of fun." She laughed, but her words sounded stale as if she'd spoken them often.

Brandon stood and chuckled. Hannah stood and held back tears.

He took one look at his wife and turned to the doctor. "Thank you, Doctor London, for all of your help. We'll be in touch."

The doctor noticed the water that filled Hannah's eyes. "Mrs. Carrington, please don't give up. I will do everything I can to help you on my end, but remember the greatest doctor is the Creator of life. Remember to take this to God."

Hannah nodded, knowing that tears would flow if she uttered a single word.

"Thank you, Doctor," Brandon said as he put his arm around Hannah and escorted her from the office just before the first tear left its trail down her cheek.

*          *          *

In the darkness of their bedroom, Brandon held Hannah close, as he'd been doing all evening since their return. But his tenderness brought little comfort to Hannah. She couldn't stop crying.

He'd tried to help her find peace from the moment they'd left the doctor's office. "I don't understand, Hannah," Brandon had said softly as they sat in the car. "Doctor London says there's nothing wrong. We'll have our baby."

She had shaken her head. "Something is wrong. There is no medical reason...and yet...." She had turned to face Brandon in the front seat of the Jaguar and taken his hands into hers. "You know what scares me the most," Hannah said through her sobs. "Maybe God is punishing me for something."

Brandon shook his head. "God doesn't work like that."

"But if we don't have a medical problem, then...." She turned away from him and looked out the window. The sun that had shone when they went into the doctor's office was now hidden by low-hanging clouds shrouding the light. After a few moments, she said, "I feel as if God has closed my womb." It was the first time she'd said the words aloud, and her tears gushed forth like an erupting hydrant.

"Don't say that, Hannah. God is in the business of blessing."

"Then explain it to me."

Brandon hadn't answered her as he started the ignition. "Let's go to Houston's or the Cheesecake Factory," he said.

She was silent.

"I could really use a piece of banana-cream cheesecake."

Hannah had shaken her head, not even able to find pleasure in the thought of her favorite eateries. "I just want to go home."

They'd driven the rest of the way in silence. When they began their nightly devotional, it was only Brandon who read. He tried to bring comfort to both of them with scriptures showing God's goodness and mercy.

"Hannah, there is one thing I know. And that is, God wants us to have the best of everything." Brandon turned the pages of his Bible to Psalm 84:11 and read, *"For the LORD God is a sun and shield; the LORD bestows favor and honor; no good thing does He withhold from those whose walk is blameless."* He paused and put down the Bible. "We need to stand on this, Hannah. It bothered me earlier when you said that God had closed your womb, and I don't believe He works that way."

"Then how would you explain this?" Hannah had asked through her tears.

"I don't think God causes these kinds of things. He is allowing us to go through this for whatever reason, but I don't think He is the cause."

"It's the same thing to me," Hannah said. "If God wanted me to have a child, I'd have one by now. He knows the desire of my heart, and He's not letting me have it." She paused for just a minute to wipe the water from her face. "Maybe He doesn't think my walk is blameless."

Without responding to his wife, Brandon turned again to his Bible. *"Let us hold unswervingly to the hope we*

254

*profess, for He who promised is faithful,"* he read from the book. "Hannah, we have to hold on to what we believe. Just like one of the Psalms says, children are a reward from God, and if we just hold tightly to that hope, I know God will fulfill what He has promised. We just have to believe that it will happen. But in God's time, not ours."

The reading of the scriptures had dried her tears, but only until they'd lain together in their bedroom. The silent, black space filled Hannah's head with thoughts of curses instead of blessings, and her cries returned.

"I just don't understand why," Hannah exclaimed. "We can give so much to a child."

Brandon had held her tighter, his embrace his answer to her despair.

"I just want to give you what Renee already has."

"I told you that my love for you has nothing to do with us having a child."

She sat up and leaned over him, peering into his eyes. "Don't you want a child?"

He sighed, his first response to the question that he'd answered a million times. "I want what you want," he said hoping that a different answer would ward off further objections. It didn't.

"You're not answering my question."

"I don't know how many ways to say it. I would love for us to have a child, but it's not the end for me. I love you, and I'll be happy with whatever plans God has for us."

Hannah bounced back against her pillows, this time a few inches away from her husband's grasp. "Maybe that's our problem. Maybe we're having challenges getting pregnant because only one of us wants it."

Brandon jumped from the bed. "Hannah, I am trying to be patient. But this obsession of yours...it's making me insane."

"And not getting pregnant is doing the same to me." She turned on her side, her back to her husband, no longer holding her sobs. When Brandon reached for her, she jerked from him. "Leave me alone."

"I'm only trying to...."

"There's nothing you can do for me."

It was minutes before he said, "Hannah, you have me. Isn't that better than having even ten children?"

Her silence was her answer, and she stayed with her back to him.

"I don't recognize you anymore, Hannah. I don't recognize us."

A while later, she heard his muffled footsteps in the carpet; then the guest bedroom door across the hall from their master suite closed.

Her tears flowed. But her cries were not for her estranged husband. It didn't matter to her that Brandon was upset. It didn't matter to her that this would be the first time they'd slept apart since they'd been married. If she couldn't have a child, there wasn't much that mattered at all.

\*　　　\*　　　\*

"That was brilliant," Etta-Marie said. "Telling Brandon that there was nothing he could do for you. I guess you plan on making this baby by yourself."

Hannah yawned and leaned back against the couch in Etta-Marie's office. She'd had very little sleep after Brandon left their bedroom. Even when he'd awakened this morning and come into their room to dress, she'd been wide awake. But she lay still, pretending to be asleep. And he'd showered, dressed and left, pretending to believe her soft snores.

"You know, Hannah," Etta-Marie continued. "You're acting as if you're the only one affected by this. Brandon has told you that he wants a child, too."

Hannah stared blankly at her best friend. Actually, Etta-Marie was more of a mother figure – having been one of her mother's best friends. But when her mother passed away when Hannah was only sixteen, Etta-Marie had practically moved Hannah into her home, teaching her and guiding her and taking her through the rites of womanhood that her father was too male and too grief-stricken to worry about with his only child. Hannah couldn't remember a time when Etta-Marie wasn't there for her – from being at every graduation from high school to law school and even walking down the aisle at her wedding as her surrogate mother. But although Etta-Marie had always provided wise counsel, today Hannah didn't want to hear any of her friend's wisdom. After being with Etta-Marie for just minutes, Hannah knew she'd made a mistake. Etta-Marie wasn't saying anything that Hannah wanted to hear.

"Did you hear what I said, girl?" Etta-Marie pushed. "Brandon wants a child as much as you do."

"He has children."

Etta-Marie stared at Hannah and shook her head as if Hannah's last brain cell had just died. "I'm telling you, girl. Your attitude is going to push that good man away. And you ain't had him but for a minute." She paused to take another bite of the bagel smothered with cream cheese and lox that Hannah had bought as an offering when she called Etta-Marie and told her she needed to speak with her. "You better listen to someone who knows."

Hannah looked down at the bagel she held, still untouched, and dropped it onto the plate that lay on the long table in the reception room of Pastor Ford's outer office. She glanced at the clock on the wall behind Etta Marie's desk and sighed. She'd already been here for thirty minutes and knew that soon her friend would be kicking her out of the office, needing to return to her responsibilities as Pastor Ford's assistant. And still, she hadn't heard what she needed. She wanted Etta-Marie to tell her that all would be fine. She wanted Etta-Marie to tell her that she would continue to pray for her. She wanted Etta-Marie to be on her side.

"Maybe I'd better go," Hannah said.

"Why are you so eager to leave? Because I haven't said what you wanted to hear?"

"Well, you're not helping." Hannah stood. "I come here for a little advice, a bit of comfort, and all you can tell me is that I'm wrong."

"That's because you are wrong, girl. You're blaming Brandon for something that is not his fault. The man has done nothing but stand by you. He's given you everything you've ever wanted...."

"Except for a child."

Etta-Marie held her hands up as if she were surrendering. "Go on, then. Just go on home. There's nothing more that I can do with you." She turned back to her computer and began punching the keyboard. Even when Hannah wrapped her sweater over her shoulders, picked up her umbrella and turned to the door, Etta-Marie kept her eyes away from the child that she'd come to love as if she'd birthed her herself. Even when Hannah placed her hand on the doorknob, Etta-Marie's eyes remained fixed on the computer screen.

"I just want someone to understand," Hannah said turning back to Etta-Marie. "I want someone to understand the pain that God is causing me. I want someone to hear my cry."

At that moment, the door to Pastor Ford's office opened and the pastor entered, leaning against the door's frame.

Etta-Marie stood. "Pastor, I didn't know you were in your office."

The pastor smiled. "I came in through the outer door." She spoke to Etta-Marie, but her eyes were on Hannah. "How're you, Hannah?"

Hannah looked at her pastor, then lowered her glance. She tugged at the hem of the short tunic that she wore, pulling at it to cover her hips and wondered if the pastor had heard anything she'd said. No, she thought. She couldn't hear through the walls.

When Hannah looked up again, she knew she was wrong. Her pastor's eyes told her that she'd heard all of Hannah's words. She straightened her shoulders, stood taller and looked directly into her pastor's eyes. She didn't care what the pastor heard. She'd only spoken the truth.

"I'm fine, Pastor," she said finally answering the question. "I'm sorry. I didn't think you were in today, and I just wanted to bring Etta-Marie something to eat."

Pastor Ford glanced at the table where Hannah had left her uneaten bagel. "It seems to me that you brought her a little something more than food." She stepped back making room in the doorway and motioning toward Hannah. "Why don't you join me?"

Hannah hesitated, then shook her head. "I really need to be going...."

"This won't take long." Although Pastor Ford's lips were still spread, the smile was gone from her tone.

Etta-Marie glanced at Hannah, then turned her attention back to the computer. Hannah could almost hear her friend's thoughts: Pastor's gonna get you now. Well, no one was going to do anything to her. She couldn't help it if she felt like God had turned His back on her. She wondered how they would handle it if they were standing in her size-eight stiletto mules.

Hannah looked directly at Pastor Ford as she said, "I'm sorry, Pastor. But I don't have time right now." Hannah stepped through the door opposite Pastor Ford. She kept her head high and her shoulders squared as she moved through the sanctuary, but she didn't dare turn back to look at the shocked stares that she was sure covered Etta-Marie's and Pastor Ford's faces.

*     *     *

It had been almost three hours since Hannah had left the church. Even though Los Angeles had been ambushed by a rain storm, she'd woven through unfamiliar, nameless streets before she had turned to the freeway. After driving aimlessly, she decided to return home, too tired to continue.

Hannah tossed her purse onto the couch and sauntered toward the living room's windowed wall. She stared into the ocean's waves, crashing hard against the sand. This was the place where she often found her peace. But the normally soothing sounds from the Pacific brine were gone, replaced by the roar of the storm. It matched the roar inside of her – a bellow she couldn't stop. She'd been this way since she'd left Etta-Marie and Pastor Ford.

She turned away from the window and settled onto the couch, allowing her thoughts to drift through the twenty-four hours that had passed since she and Brandon had seen Doctor London. In that time, she and Brandon had their first real argument, and she was sure Etta-Marie would prefer not to hear from her for a few days. Even Pastor Ford was probably more than a bit annoyed. It was like she was driving away everyone who loved and cared for her.

But that's not what she wanted to do. She loved Brandon more than she ever thought she could love a man. And Etta-Marie...she was more than grateful for her friendship and guidance. She never intended for her desire to have a baby to be a wedge, separating her from those she loved. All she wanted was for everyone to understand.

She reached for the telephone, but before she could pick it up, it rang, startling her. She glanced quickly at the clock. It was after one. This was the time that Brandon called her everyday. She smiled; he'd called her before she could call him.

"Hello, Hannah."

Her hopes for reconciliation with Brandon disappeared. She took a deep breath before she said, "What can I do for you, Renee?"

"Oh, are we having a bad day?" Renee snickered.

Hannah pressed her lips together, fighting to hold back the curses she wanted to throw at Brandon's ex. Finally, she said, "Look, if you don't want anything, I'm going to hang up."

"I guess we are having a bad day. Anyway, I was calling to speak to Brandon."

"You know he's at work."

"Is he?" Renee asked as if she were surprised. "That's odd. I just remember when he was married to me Brandon always came home early on Fridays." She paused. "But I guess that's because there was so much to our lives. You know...with our family. With our children and all."

Renee's words barged over Hannah, flattening her to nothing more than road kill. She had to struggle to keep her voice steady. "Do you want to leave a message for Brandon?"

"No, that's okay. I'll call him at the office. Poor man, he's just working because he doesn't have anything else to hold his attention."

Hannah pressed her teeth against her tongue until she was sure she'd draw blood. Finally she said, "Goodbye, Renee."

"You know, I just wanted to tell Brandon something about our daughter," Renee continued as if she didn't hear Hannah's farewell. "Susan completed the most incredible project in Vacation Bible School." Renee paused, and Hannah was sure it was just to extend her torment. A moment later, Renee continued, "Oh, I apologize. I always find myself going on and on about the children. I guess I'm just a proud mother. I forget that women who don't have children are just not interested in hearing from those of us who do."

"Renee, do what you always do. Call Brandon at his office." She slammed the phone into the cradle before Renee could utter another word or before she could say something that would surely twist the little harmony their extended family had into permanent turmoil.

Hannah fought to keep her tears away, but she couldn't. Her heart was a target, the mark for the missiles that shot from Renee's tongue. Every time Renee spoke, Hannah's heart exploded into millions of pieces.

She stood, opened her mouth and released a piercing holler that surprised even her. But although the first seconds stunned her, she continued, giving voice to the anguish that seemed to have permanently settled inside. She wanted to rid herself of the pain that her thoughts forced upon her. That she didn't measure up – that she wasn't quite a woman – that she would never be if she couldn't birth a child. But when long minutes had passed, she felt only the soreness of her vocal cords. Her screams were over, and she was still motherless, childless, without any hope.

She reached for the telephone and dialed quickly. But when Evon, Brandon's assistant, answered, Hannah remembered what happened between them last night and how Brandon had left this morning. She pressed the off-button without saying a word.

How can I call him? she wondered. By this time of the day, he had usually called her several times just to say that he loved her. This was the first day since they were married that she heard only his silence.

Hannah grabbed her purse, reached for the car keys and ran out the door.

\*        \*        \*

"Etta-Marie will be right back," Angie, the church receptionist, sang in the sing-song voice she reserved for anyone entering Hope Chapel's doors between Monday and Friday. "You're welcome to wait in her office."

"Thanks," Hannah replied before she started toward the back. A second later, she turned around, just in time to see Angie disappear around the corner. Hannah hesitated then moved toward Etta-Marie's office. Pastor Ford was sure to be gone by now. Fridays were the one day she took some time to herself.

Hannah paused at Etta-Marie's door. When only the hum of the computer and the ticking of the clock hanging behind the desk met her ears, she flopped onto the couch.

"I'll wait five minutes," she mumbled as she picked up a *Christian Life Today* magazine from a stack resting on the table. She flipped through the pages, her eyes only scanning the article titles. But one caused her to pause: "When God Doesn't Make Sense."

She leaned forward a bit and began to read:

For those of us who have a personal relationship with God, we know that our Heavenly Father, like our earthly one, only wants the best for us. After all, Romans 8:32 tells us, *'He who did not spare His own Son, but gave Him up for us all – how will He not also, along with Him, graciously give us all things?'* So we march around knowing that God will give us all things. All of our needs will be met, and our desires are just pleasures-in-waiting. But what happens when that doesn't happen? How can we explain when we have wants, desires and wishes that we pray for...that we have all of our prayer partners focused on, and we don't get the results we expect? Is God not listening to our prayers? Or worse yet, has God heard us, but turned away? Is this a sign...a punishment?

Hannah was almost on the edge of the couch. This article had been written for her.

"I've been waiting for you."

The magazine slipped to the floor when Hannah jumped up, shocked by the voice. Pastor Ford stood in frame of her office door just like she had this morning.

"Pastor, I'm sorry...I thought you were gone...I was just waiting for Etta-Marie...."

Pastor Ford held her hand up, stopping Hannah. "No need to explain. I was waiting. I was sure you'd come back." She stepped aside making room in her doorway. "Are you ready to join me now?"

Hannah frowned a bit. Why had the pastor been waiting for her? She hadn't planned to come back. And she certainly didn't return to see Pastor Ford. She glanced toward the door across the room that led to the sanctuary, hoping Etta-Marie would suddenly appear, giving her a reprieve, providing an excuse for her not to have to face her pastor. But when there was no sign of Etta-Marie, Hannah knew there was no escape this time.

She avoided the pastor's eyes as she entered her inner office. But once inside, she stood frozen – as if she didn't know what to do. It didn't matter that she'd been in the office countless times. Today, the space felt foreign to her – as if she didn't belong.

Wordlessly, Pastor Ford motioned for Hannah to take a seat, and after a few seconds, she moved to the chair in front of the desk. She remembered the many times when she'd sat in this space, when Pastor Ford had comforted her (like when her mother had passed away) or provided her with words of guidance (like when she was leaving home for the first time for college.) Some of the most important hours here were when she and Brandon were engaged. Pastor Ford had counseled them for months before she united them in marriage. Hannah never questioned her pastor's love and commitment as her spiritual leader. Yet, she was sure that Pastor Ford would never understand what she was going through now, and she couldn't be held responsible for what she might do if she heard the words "Be patient" once again.

But Pastor Ford had guided her through so much. Maybe she had answers. Maybe she could help her understand what she had hoped to find in the article she'd started reading. Maybe Pastor could explain why God's indifference was directed at her.

The pastor's smile was back when she looked at Hannah. "This morning, I dropped by the office to pick up a few things. Then, I planned to go back home and enjoy the day." She paused, keeping her gaze on Hannah. Her stare caused Hannah to lower her glance. "When I heard you and Etta-Marie talking, I knew there was another reason why God drew me here today."

Hannah opened her mouth. She wasn't sure what Pastor heard, but she needed to defend herself. She was sure she sounded out of her mind; she'd felt that way for weeks, maybe months now. But still, Pastor had to know what she'd been going through.

Pastor Ford held up her hand, keeping Hannah silent. "I feel like you're going to try to explain, and you don't have to do that. I understand."

Hannah's eyes opened wide. "You understand," she whispered. It was the first time that Hannah had heard those words. Without explanation, the tears came again. Her deep sobs brought Pastor Ford from her desk to sit beside Hannah. When the pastor put her arms around

Hannah, she released all the sorrow she'd carried. It was minutes before she was able to speak.

"Pastor, I just feel so bad about what's been going on," she said through the pulsing in her head that had come with her tears.

"Tell me about it."

"I can't have a baby."

"The doctors have told you that?"

"No. They say there's nothing wrong, but they can't give me an explanation as to why I'm not pregnant. And that just leads me to believe...." She paused as the words choked inside her throat. She turned, not able to look at her pastor as she conjured up courage to utter the next words. "I feel like I'm being punished by God. I keep thinking that maybe, somehow, someway, He closed my womb."

The pastor used the tips of her fingers to lift Hannah's chin, bringing her glance to hers. "Hannah, I see your lips moving, but I can't believe this is you. You know that's not true. After all these years, after all God has carried you through, you know He doesn't work that way."

"Then explain it to me, Pastor. Why can't I have a baby?"

"I don't know the answer to that, Hannah. Only God knows the answers to all the mysteries of life. But the one thing I know is that God didn't close your womb. He may be permitting it to happen, but He didn't cause it."

The pastor's words were similar to the ones Brandon had said trying to comfort her. "I guess I don't understand the difference, Pastor."

"It's a difficult concept to grasp, and we're not going to understand it all because as humans we have limited understanding. But, it's like what happened to Job. He was attacked and allowed to go through great suffering. It was clear that his troubles were from the hands of Satan. God didn't cause Job's misery; He was aware of it, and He allowed it, and ultimately we know that God is in charge of everything. But that evil came from Satan."

"I understand that, Pastor. Because the Bible says that Satan caused Job's problems. But how do I know that God's not in the middle of my troubles? How do I know that God isn't the one making sure that I can't have a baby?"

"Hannah, the Bible is filled with scripture after scripture of God's goodness and His mercy and His promise to give us all good things."

Hannah thought back to the article she'd been reading and how the author had quoted Romans 8:32. In her heart, she believed that. She just couldn't understand what was happening to her now.

Pastor Ford continued, "But I think one of the most important things that the book of Job teaches us is how we must get to the point of the ultimate acceptance of God's plans. Job told his wife that they couldn't just accept the good things from God and not accept the bad things that come from this life because the world is full of sin. Job's position was a hard stand to take, but one that I believe most of us, in our Christian maturity, come to understand."

Hannah remained silent, letting her pastor's words enter her ears and hoping they would settle into her spirit.

"One thing that I do know is that the sin in this world didn't come from God. You believe that, don't you?"

Hannah nodded.

"And, I also know that when the devil uses his evil intentions for harm, it provides an opportunity for us to show our faithfulness to God and for God to show just how faithful He is to us. Whatever the devil meant for evil, God will turn it around for good. That's how I know God didn't close your womb. But He will use this situation to show His faithfulness – either one day you'll have a child, or you won't. But in the end, you'll know that God is sovereign and He is faithful. You'll see His hands all in this."

Hannah shook her head as if she heard the pastor's words but didn't believe.

Pastor Ford squeezed her hand. "Sometimes when we're in the midst of trouble we forget to stand with what we do know about our Lord. We forget about all He's done. It's easy to move away from our faith."

"I haven't moved away, Pastor. I keep talking to God. I've poured out my soul to Him. I keep begging Him to give me a child."

"Maybe the better prayer is for His will to be done."

The pastor's words made a lump fill Hannah's throat. "Suppose His will is that I not have a child?" She asked the question softly, as if she were carefully placing it into the atmosphere.

Pastor Ford hesitated for a second before she asked, "Would you want a child if it wasn't God's will; if that wasn't His purpose for your life?"

Her heart felt like heated wax, slowly dripping away. She shook her head. "No, no...I don't think so."

"Like I said before, I don't think God is holding a child back from you," Pastor Ford said. "But sometimes we have to ask and answer the tough questions. And then when we go to God in prayer about the desires of our heart, we have to pray perfectly, and that is for the fulfillment of His will. We have to pray and want for the Lord to be magnified."

Thy will be done, Hannah said inside.

Pastor Ford took both of Hannah's hands into hers. "Hannah, I want to pray with you. But before we do that, I have to ask you this...do you trust God?"

"Yes, I do," she answered almost before the pastor had fully asked the question.

"I mean, do you really trust Him? Do you believe that no matter how this turns out that God wants the best for you?"

One of her favorite scriptures flashed through her mind. *For I know the plans I have for you, declares the LORD, plans to prosper you and not to harm you, plans to give you hope and a future.*

Hannah had stood on that promise so much throughout much in her life. When she couldn't imagine a future without her mother. When she prayed that she'd make the right choice about college. Even when she had prayed for God's will for the right man to come into her life. She had turned that promise into a prayer, asking the Lord to always prosper her and not harm her and to give her hope and a future. He had always answered. He'd always been there. She did trust God.

"I trust Him, Pastor." She trembled.

"Then, let's turn this over to Him." She closed her eyes and Hannah followed. "Father, in the name of Jesus, we come to You with praise and thanksgiving. We come to You with knees bent and our tongues confessing that You are our Holy God. Father, we come to You with heavy hearts today, not understanding why the desire for Brandon and Hannah to have a child has not yet been met. But, we know that You are almighty and all-knowing. We know that You only want the best for us, and we pray for Your best and for Your will to be done. We pray for wisdom and understanding, and we pray, Father, that You open our eyes, especially Hannah's, so that we can come to understand and accept the plan You have for our lives. Comfort and correct us, Father, as You reveal Your perfect plan. You said in Your Word that You would not withhold anything from those of us who walk upright, and we believe You, Father. We trust You. We want You to be glorified. We want You to be exalted. And because of You, we know we have the victory, in Jesus's name."

Tears had left a track through the make-up on both of their faces when they looked up. "Hannah, I want you to go to the Lord. Find that quiet place and talk to Him. He has all the answers. All you have to do is ask Him the questions, in faith. And, I pray that you find the perfect peace that our Father in Heaven wants for you. And that He grants you all that you have asked."

Pastor Ford pulled Hannah to her, and they held each other for long moments. When Hannah stood, Pastor Ford said, "I know you're ready to leave now. Go in peace."

\*     \*     \*

She was still crying. And the pulsing beat in her head continued. Yet, she prayed all the way home.

"Dear God, please forgive me. All this time I've been whining about what is missing in my life. I've been complaining that I've been cheated because I haven't been able to conceive. Please forgive me for not realizing all that You have blessed me with. I thank You, Father, for all You have given me. For my wonderful family: my husband, my father, Etta-Marie and everyone You have put around me. I thank You, too, Father, for Pastor Ford and all that she brings to my life. Thank You for speaking to me through her heart. But most importantly, thank You for helping me to see that You are present; You are here; You have always been here. Thank You for being in my life and for accepting me as your child, even with all of my ungrateful ways." She had to pause for a moment to let the tears flow freely.

"But now, Father, I am asking You to hear my cry. Hear my plea, oh, Lord. I know that You've said that children are a blessing from You, and I'm asking You to see me, to know my heart and to bless us. I hold this up to You, Father. I pray that You will bless Brandon and me with a child that we can then turn over to serve You. Father, I promise that if You bestow this blessing onto us, this child will serve You all the days of his life." She paused as she remembered the pastor's words about the acceptance of Job. "But more than that, Father," Hannah continued, "I promise that I accept Your will."

She was still praying when she veered into their curved driveway. She rested in the soft leather seat of her Escalade minutes more, meditating on all that Pastor Ford had said. And all that she'd asked the Lord. She thought about the promises that she'd made to God and prayed that He would give her the strength and wisdom to fulfill all of them.

She sat and waited – until the last tear streaked down her cheek. She waited until the pulsing that had invaded her head stopped. She waited until she had turned every one of her heart's desires over to God. Then, she got out of her car.

By the time she put the key in the front door, there was no trace of tears. Instead, Hannah's face was dressed with a smile.

*       *       *

Darkness had long ago descended on the Pacific coast, and Hannah peeked again through the curtains that cascaded in front of the window. From the moment she had stepped into the house, she'd been planning their evening. She was going to ask for her husband's forgiveness – over and over again.

She contemplated what she was going to say. "Sweetheart, please forgive me. I have been out of my head with my desire to give you a child. But I know now that the way I was going about this was all wrong. I have turned this over to God. And, whatever plan He has for our life, I will accept. In the meantime, I want you to know that I love you, and if it comes down to it being just the two of us, I will make sure that our lives are full and happy."

After she told him, she would show him. She'd prepared shrimp quenelles, Brandon's favorite. She'd learned to make this dumpling dish during her last semester in college – as an exchange student in Paris. It was the first meal she'd ever prepared for him, and Brandon had told her many times that she could make the same thing for dinner every night.

"Not only do I love the way this tastes," he'd begun the last time she'd made the shrimp quenelles, "but it reminds me of the night I fell in love with you."

She prayed that tonight he'd be reminded again.

That was just the first part of the plan. The music that softly filled the downstairs was also part of the design. The CD was one that Brandon had burned and played for her on Valentine's Day – all day. Tonight, Luther Vandross would serenade them through dinner, Freddie Jackson would fill their ears as they sipped wine afterwards on the couch, and finally, they would waltz into their bedroom to the smooth crooning of Teddy Pendegrass.

She had been smiling all evening as she prepared, but now her cheer was gone. The dumplings had long ago cooled, and the cinnamon-rose candles that she had placed throughout the living and dining rooms had filled the house with their sweet scent, but no longer carried the hope of romance.

It was eight o'clock. Since they'd been married, Hannah had been able to set her watch by Brandon – he was always home by six. And the few times he wasn't, he'd called within five minutes of the hour to let her know he was on his way.

But tonight, there had been no call. She hadn't spoken to him all day – another first. Hannah moved through the room, blowing out the candles in the dining room before they became only stiff wicks. She covered the casserole dish with plastic wrap, letting it remain on the counter, praying that the evening that still danced in her mind would somehow come to be. But as she sat on the couch and watched the clock tick to eight-thirty, her hopes faded. She picked up the phone and dialed Brandon's cell. He answered on the third ring.

"Brandon, it's Hannah," she said although she knew he'd seen their telephone number on the Caller ID screen.

"Hello."

She stiffened at his tone. "I was beginning to worry." When he remained silent, she asked, "Are you all right?"

"Yes. Hold on a moment."

She frowned as she heard laughter in the background, then the muffled sound of Brandon's voice as if he had placed his hand over the receiver.

"I'm sorry, I'm back," he said.

"Where are you?"

There was a slight pause. "I'm at Renee's." He paused again as if he was trying to decide if she deserved an explanation. "Susan wanted me to see a panorama that she'd made, and then I decided to stay and help the children with their lines for the program at church tomorrow."

"Why didn't you call me? I would have gone with you."

Again, he hesitated before he responded, "Hannah, I'll talk to you about it later."

"Well, what time are you coming home?"

"I don't know. Listen, I've got to go. I'll see you...in a while."

She returned the phone to its place, dazed by his words. Since their engagement, she didn't know of a time when he'd gone to see his children without her. It was so important to him that she always be there.

"I want you to be a part of their lives," he had said from the beginning. "I want you to be with me every moment that I spend with my children."

That was what he said, but Hannah knew there was more inside those words. He wanted her around every time he saw Renee. That was his way of letting her and Renee know that there would never be any secrets – nothing would be kept from his wife. Those words and his actions had always made her feel secure.

Until tonight.

She moved like a robot as she placed the untouched dinner into the refrigerator, blew out the rest of the candles, turned off the music and then went into their bedroom. It was almost nine o'clock now, much too early for her to sleep. But she couldn't sit up and wait. Watching the clock would make it much worse.

As she undressed, she heard Brandon's voice again. Not his words, just his tone – so distant, so removed. She almost didn't recognize him. She paused at that thought. Isn't that what he had said to her?

"I don't recognize you anymore, Hannah. I don't recognize us."

She didn't try to hold back her tears as she slipped into her nightgown. She glanced at the Bible sitting on the nightstand – Holy Bible with Daily Devotionals for Couples. This would be the first night they wouldn't share that special time together.

A day full of firsts.

She sat on the bed. Had she driven Brandon away? She tried not to think of the way he'd left her in their bed last night. She didn't want to think about how he hadn't even kissed her goodbye this morning or that he hadn't attempted to contact her at all today. She wanted to block out the distance that she felt when he talked to her – when he talked to her from Renee's house. For an instant, she thought about Brandon and Renee together, uniting when they were man and wife, loving each other as they made babies together. Did Brandon remember those times? Was he thinking about that now as he sat with his ex-wife in her home? Did he have a desire to return to that life?

No, she screamed inside. Brandon wanted her. And furthermore, it was God who had brought them together. But now, she had to pray that He would keep them – even in the midst of this turmoil.

She scooted to the edge of the bed and fell to her knees. This afternoon, she thought she had turned over all that was important to God. But now she realized she had a lot more to hold up to Him. She had to hold up her marriage. She prayed, first in English and then in the spirit until no more sounds came from her. Still she stayed on her knees until she ached, knowing that she didn't have to speak out loud – the Lord would hear the cries from her heart.

When she slipped under the down comforter, she closed her eyes, willing sleep to rescue her, but she tossed, studying the clock until she finally heard Brandon drive into the garage. It was almost midnight.

She held her breath as she waited for Brandon to come into their bedroom. When he stepped inside, she breathed. She sat up and turned on the light.

"I didn't think you'd still be awake." He looked at her for a moment then turned away as he shook his jacket from his shoulders.

"I was waiting for you."

"You didn't have to do that." It was his shirt that came off next.

Hannah tried to keep her glance away from his naked torso. The way the muscles in his back flexed as he undid his belt made her want to run to him. "I wanted to wait up for you."

Brandon returned his glance to his wife. "I'm sorry I'm so late," he said as he slipped off his pants.

She blew a stream of air through her lips as she stared at him standing in front of her, almost as if he were posing for a Hanes ad. He was oblivious to the fact that he could rival any of the models or athletes companies paid millions to show off their briefs. "I'm glad you had time with the children," she said finally. Her gaze grazed over his body. "Is everything all right with them?" she asked, forcing her eyes from his chest.

He nodded, then slowly walked toward her. She turned back the covers, inviting him into their bed. He paused, but only for a moment before he slipped between the sheets. He turned to her, and she closed her eyes, waiting for his kiss. After his lips gently grazed her cheek, she felt him move away. It took seconds before she opened her eyes. Brandon was resting on his side, his back to her. She waited a moment, expecting him to turn back. To open his arms, inviting her to rest on his chest, just as he always did. It was the way they fell asleep every night. When he made no move to her, she called his name.

He released a deep sigh. "I can't do this tonight, Hannah. I don't want to talk, I'm tired."

She wanted to protest. To tell him that what he was thinking was wrong. Everything was different now. She wanted him to hear what she had prayed. She wanted to pray with him. But after a few minutes passed, she said nothing. She turned off the light on the nightstand and laid still until frustration, indignation and exhaustion fused to give her rest.

\*     \*     \*

Hannah's hand glided across the sheet before she opened her eyes, but she felt only the coolness of the satin. She opened her eyes. When she sat up in bed, she listened for sounds from her husband, but there was none of the stirring that she usually heard when he awakened before her on the weekend.

She slipped into her robe before she hurried down the stairs. Still silence. The family room and kitchen were as empty as she'd left them last night. She opened the door to the garage. Her Escalade sat alone. She sighed. How was she going to fix what was between them if he wouldn't spend any time with her?

She turned back to the kitchen and noticed a slip of paper on the counter: Hannah, I've gone to put gas in the car. I'll be back by noon so that we can go to church for the children's program.

She glanced at the clock. It was almost ten. Surely, it didn't take two hours to go to the gas station. But at least he planned to come home for her. That was something.

She took a deep breath. She wasn't going to let the emotions that had threatened to overtake her last night return. Pastor Ford had told her to find some quiet time, and that's what she was going to do. As she slipped from her nightgown, she prayed. She asked God to forgive her for the strain she'd put on her marriage. She asked Him to open her heart to His will. She prayed that Brandon would hear her and believe that she was truly putting this all into God's hands now.

In the shower, her prayers continued when she asked for the strength that she knew she would need and that would only come from God.

By the time Hannah heard the garage open, she was sitting on the couch reading her Bible. She had always cherished the time she'd spent reading the Word, but she couldn't remember the last time she'd done it. It was like her desire for a baby had taken her away from her life – from everything that she knew was right.

She was smiling when Brandon walked into the family room.

He paused at the door. "Hello." His greeting was tentative, as if he were afraid any more words would lead to a conversation he didn't want to have.

"Hi, sweetie." She stood and walked to him. She brushed her lips against his. When he stood stiff, she pulled back, but kept her smile. She hesitated before she said, "I'm really looking forward to seeing the children today." She reached for her purse, but Brandon was still standing in place. "Oh, aren't you ready to leave?" she asked glancing at her watch.

"Yeah." He spoke as if the word had three syllables. But still, he didn't move. "Are you all right?"

She cocked her head slightly. There was so much she wanted to say, so many reasons to apologize. But she couldn't count the number of times she'd told her husband things would be different. That she was going to focus on just the two of them. That it didn't matter if she couldn't have a baby. Her words had meant little then, and she knew he would feel the same way now. "I'm fine," was all she said. "I just wanted to be ready when you got here." She tossed the strap to her purse up her shoulder. "I was thinking we might stop at Starbucks first."

"Okay." Again, his word was slow as if he didn't believe what he was hearing...or seeing. But Hannah saw her first glimmer of hope when a glimmer of a smile flittered across his face. Starbucks was Brandon's favorite spot on Saturday mornings. Today, they wouldn't have a chance for a leisurely chat over their caffeine, but maybe the smell of the roasted beans would be just the aid that Hannah needed. "Let me change my shirt," he said.

She smiled as she watched him trot up the stairs. When he looked over his shoulder, she wiggled her fingers in a small wave. She stayed until he disappeared down the hallway to their bedroom.

As she waited, she looked out the window. Although the storm had ended, the bright blue canvas that hung over the Pacific Ocean in August had been replaced by corpulent clouds parading proudly down the coast. The hazy days of summer still had not returned, but Hannah had a feeling they'd make a come-back soon.

Even though she heard his steps behind her, Hannah stayed in her place. She knew he was watching her, and she wanted him to see her calm, feel her change.

It was moments before he spoke. "I'm ready now."

When she turned around, he wore a smile that matched hers. She felt as if she were a baseball player and had gotten her first major league hit. But that's just the first one, she thought. She was determined that by the time she returned home tonight, she would make it around all the bases.

In the car, she chatted as if they hadn't spent hours emotionally apart. "So, did you enjoy the kids last night?" she asked without a hint of judgment.

"Yeah, I had a great time." She could feel him peeking at her through the corner of his eye. "I stopped by to see something Susan had made, and then she wanted me to help her practice her poem for today. Soon, they all wanted to join in showing me what they were going to do."

She continued to ask questions and he responded until their talk transformed to the easy flow of conversation they were used to sharing. At Starbucks, they sat for a few minutes, and Brandon told Hannah about a new client his firm acquired to restore an old Beverly Hills mansion. It was something he would have normally shared during one of his calls from work. But Hannah was pleased that Brandon was willing to fill in the blanks from yesterday, still wanting to share the moments of his life.

At ten to one, they pulled into the church's parking lot, still talking, filling each other in on the hours they'd spent apart. Brandon got out of the car and opened Hannah's door, helping his wife from the car. He kept hold of Hannah's hand, pulling her close as they stepped across the gravel of the parking lot. By the time they reached the front door, their laughter filled the street.

When they looked up and saw Renee and the children waiting on the top step, Brandon squeezed Hannah's hand. But, she kept her eyes on Renee. "Hi," she exclaimed as if she were greeting her best friend.

Her cheer caused Renee to pause, but only for a moment. "Hello, Hannah." Then, a smirk filled her face, the prelude to her standard line. "Children, say hello to your...stepmother." But Hannah's response turned Renee's grin into a grimace.

Hannah laughed as the children greeted her. "Hey, everyone. I'm so glad to see you."

Her back was to both Renee and Brandon as she hugged all of the children. But she didn't need her eyes to imagine the expression on their faces. She was sure that shock wasn't an adequate description. It wasn't that she didn't love Brandon's offspring, it was just difficult to show it when Renee was hovering, using each child to remind her that she had none of her own. But she had prayed all of those feelings into a year's worth of yesterdays. And that was where they would stay. Nothing Renee could say or do would matter. She'd turned even Renee over to God.

When the children ran off to get ready for their performances, Hannah turned back to Brandon. He was smiling; Renee was not.

"I'm so looking forward to this program," Hannah said taking Brandon's hand and leaning into him. She kept her smile aimed at Renee. "Brandon told me about working with the children last night. So today, I'll get a chance to see how great they are myself."

Renee looked at Hannah, then turned her glance to Brandon. She smiled at him as if they shared a secret. "Oh, did he mention that he was with me last night?"

Hannah frowned. "No, Brandon never mentioned that." She paused as a smile began to spread across Renee's lips. "Brandon told me that he spent the evening with Robert, Stella, Greg and Susan. He didn't mention you at all. Were you there?"

Her smile disappeared, but it didn't stop Renee's words. "Maybe he didn't want you to know."

"Quit it, Renee," Brandon said and took Hannah's hand, leading her down the aisle.

Hannah wanted to dance up to the altar. She'd made it to second base.

As the program started and she stood with Brandon through praise and worship, Hannah couldn't help but glance across the aisle to where Renee stood on the end, glaring. *I wish I'd known it was going to be this easy,* Hannah thought as she met Renee's hostile stare. It seemed as if the torture tables were turning.

When the program began, Hannah pushed thoughts of Renee aside as she beamed through Susan's recital. Then she swayed with the crowd as Greg and Stella gave a soulful, youthful rendition of Amazing Grace with the young adult choir. And then she was on her feet, clapping when Robert stomped his way across the stage with his group, Anointed Steps.

At the end, when all were brought onto the stage, Hannah was one of the first to rise to her feet, joining with the other proud parents and well-wishers in the standing ovation.

"Weren't our children wonderful?" she asked, still applauding.

The grin that had filled Brandon's face faded.

"What's wrong?" she asked.

It took a moment for him to shake his head. "Nothing," he said. He drew her into his arms. "Yes, our children were wonderful."

She closed her eyes as he squeezed her tight. Her husband was back. She had made it to third base.

When she opened her eyes, Renee was staring at her. This time, Hannah didn't feel the triumph that she'd felt just a few hours before. Now, the only thing she felt was sorrow for Brandon's ex-wife.

*       *       *

"I had such a good time. You were all terrific," Hannah gushed as she lifted Susan into her arms. "I want to see it all again."

"I'll do my poem." Susan giggled before she began to recite the first line.

"No, we're not going to do that," Renee said, taking Susan from Hannah's arms. "I need to get you all home so that we can get ready for church tomorrow."

"Mom, it's only six o' clock," Stella whined. "I wanna go out and do something." She turned to her father. "Daddy, can we come over to your house?"

"That would be a great idea," Hannah said before Brandon could respond. "We can stop at Baskin and Robbins for ice cream and cake and have sort of a celebration...."

Renee interrupted, "No, that's not a good idea," she snapped. "I said I needed to get my children home."

"Daddy," both Robert and Stella whined at the same time.

"Guys, I agree with your mother. It's been a long day. Let's do this," he began putting his arm around Hannah's waist. "Tomorrow after church, we'll all go out. My treat," he added before Renee could protest.

287

"Yeah," the children cheered.

"Then it's a plan." Brandon slipped his hand into Hannah's. "Are you ready, honey?" He seemed rushed.

She frowned just a bit, but nodded. It took minutes for Brandon and Hannah to hug all the children and for Brandon to reassure them that they would celebrate tomorrow. Before Brandon pulled Hannah away, she said, "Goodnight, Renee." She stopped and then added, "Have a good evening." It had been a long time since Hannah had wished anything good for Renee. From the moment she'd entered Brandon's life, Renee had made it clear that they were not going to be anything close to friends. But tonight, when Hannah spoke those words, they were from the center of her heart.

In the car, she said, "I was surprised that you didn't want to spend some time with the children tonight. They all performed so well, I wanted to celebrate."

Brandon's face was stiff with seriousness. "Oh, don't worry, baby. We're going to celebrate."

It took a moment for Hannah to understand her husband's words. She smiled. She had rounded the bases. Pastor Ford had prayed that she would have the victory. Well, no matter what happened with a baby, she was already the victor. "Well, let the celebration begin."

*     *     *

The celebration had begun - from the moment they'd entered the house, giggling like teenagers. The garage door had barely closed before they embraced, impatient lovers.

Their laughter was gone, replaced with moans of expectancy. They swayed to a beat that their hearts scored as they sought to satisfy their desire. Their love dance shifted to the stairs, and with lips still connected and discarded clothes flying through the air, they left a telling trail from the family room to the bedroom.

They were almost naked when they wilted onto their bed. When Brandon slipped the last piece of lace from Hannah's body and lay with her, she was sure she'd explode. She moaned as his fingertips teased her, tracing her curves, exploring as if this were their first time. His breath was hot when his tongue followed the trail his fingers set, tantalizing every nerve ending until she freed herself through her screams.

"I want you now." She was barely able to breathe.

His tongue found hers, and he kissed her so deeply Hannah felt as if their skin had fused. They were one.

They joined, as husband and wife, fulfilling the cherished promises they'd made the day they married. They loved, as man and woman, each desiring to take the other beyond the boundaries of pleasure. They surrendered, as lovers, their passion springing forth in piercing cries of ecstasy that bounced off each wall in their bedroom.

They laid together, exhausted. The air conditioning blew cool throughout, but Hannah still breathed deeply, her skin moist from the heat of their love. She felt Brandon's short breaths streaming softly into her ear. She smiled. Minutes passed before she realized that this was the first time she hadn't wondered if they'd made a baby. She was just grateful that they had made love. It was the icing on a very delicious cake.

\*     \*     \*

Hannah laid in the dark, wrapped in Brandon's arms. She heard his soft snores, but she stayed still, not wanting to disturb him. It was like this most nights when they shared themselves. Brandon fell asleep, but she lay awake, her mind filled with thoughts. Tonight, it was the same – except her thoughts were different. She thought about how she had prayed for God to put the right man in her life and how He had gifted her with Brandon. She recalled her husband's words of commitment to her, and how she never doubted his love. She remembered how he said that all that mattered to him was her love.

She had no thoughts of a baby. She didn't have to – she already had the best of everything.

She smiled when she felt Brandon stir.

"What's wrong? You're still awake?" he asked through eyes that were still at half-staff.

"Yes, I was just thinking."

He turned slightly from her as if he were preparing for the baby questions that always followed their lovemaking.

"Brandon," she started then paused, waiting for his protest. When none came, she continued, "I just want to tell you that I'm sorry." She twisted in his arms to face him. "I know now that the way I've been handling this hasn't been right."

He brushed his fingertips across her lips. "Sweetheart, you don't have to explain. I understand."

She thought about when Pastor Ford had said almost those exact words. That was what she wanted to hear then. It was all she needed to hear now.

Brandon continued, "I wish I'd been more understanding before."

"Oh, no," she protested. "I went on and on about having a baby, and I never considered that there was so much more to life, so much more to us than a child." She took his hand into hers. "I know I've said this before, but I'm fine with whatever plans God has for us. From now on, you will have all of me."

He kissed her hand. "I love you, Hannah." He pulled her into his arms, wrapped the comforter around them, and together they slept knowing they'd finally found the peace of the Lord.

*     *     *

Hannah wasn't sure what she should do. Should she be sitting on the couch or waiting at the door or be nowhere in sight? She'd been trying to decide for hours. It didn't seem to be a big decision, but she wanted these moments to be perfect. Maybe she should be standing at the door with a glass of wine, a sign that they were about to celebrate. But no, that wouldn't work. She wouldn't be able to do that. At least not for a while.

She jumped; the squeak of the garage door surprised her. Well, there wasn't any more time to plan. She sat on the couch and leaned back, crossing her legs. She tossed her twists over her shoulders and smiled. But then, she stood up. She wasn't trying to seduce him. She laughed at that thought. That had already happened.

"Hey, sweetie," Brandon said, catching Hannah before she could stage another scene.

She almost tripped over the table as she rushed to him. "Hi, sweetheart."

He wrapped his arms around her waist. "How was your day?" he asked as he moved toward the kitchen counter and lifted the mail. He began shifting through the envelopes.

She smiled, thinking of all the ways she could respond. She'd had a great day; she could tell him that. But there was only one way she could answer that question now. "I'm pregnant." It wasn't filled with the romance that she'd imagined, but the look on her husband's face told her that only words were needed.

The envelopes slipped from his hands. He stared at her. "What did you say?"

It didn't seem possible, but her smile widened. She nodded, knowing he had heard her.

His steps to her were slow, as if any quick movements would change what she'd spoken. "Are you sure?"

She nodded again. "I bought one of those pregnancy kits and...."

"But, do those things really work?"

"Yes, because after the symbol turned blue, I called Doctor London and she tested me." She paused as she took his hands. "It's true. We're going to have a baby."

She'd dreamt of his expression at this moment from the day they married. But her imagination couldn't capture the fullness of his emotions. It was even more than she'd hoped to see.

He grabbed her. "Oh, baby, I can't tell you how happy I am." His embrace was so tight, she gasped.

"I'm sorry," he said pulling back. "Did I hurt you?"

She shook her head.

His hand moved in slow motion before he rested his palm on her stomach. "I didn't hurt the baby, did I?"

She laughed. "No, Brandon. We're both fine."

"Well, come over here." He nudged her along, full of concern as he led her to the couch. "How long have you known? Why didn't you tell me?"

She sat, still holding his hands. "I suspected last week, but I didn't want to get my hopes up. That's why I took one of those home pregnancy tests. But when I got the results, I called Doctor London and she took me right away. I found out this morning."

"Why didn't you call me?"

"Because I wanted to tell you in person." Her fingertips traced the lines between his eyes and his mouth. "I couldn't wait to see your face."

"Hannah." He pulled her to him once again. "I love you so much."

She closed her eyes, wanting to take this moment into eternity. For more than two years, there was nothing else that she wanted. And she would have done anything to make this happen. But for the last month, she'd made no effort – except for her conversations with God. She'd kept this desire lifted up to the Lord, thanking Him for already granting her prayer. But more importantly, she had lived to do His will.

Brandon brought his lips to her. His kiss and touch were soft, the caress of one handling precious gems. Hannah wasn't sure how long they'd held each other. It was only the ringing telephone that made them slip apart.

"I don't want to answer it," he whispered, then let his lips graze her ear.

"We have to. It might be one of the children."

He smiled. "They're going to be so excited. I can't wait to tell them."

She picked up the phone. "Hello."

"Hannah, this is Renee. Is the father of my children there?"

Hannah laughed. That was a new line from the woman who lived to torture her. But the edges of Renee's weapon had been dulled. She couldn't hurt her anymore. It had been that way for a month. "Yes, he is. Hold on a second." She lifted the phone toward Brandon, but then pulled it back. "Renee, I just wanted to tell you to have a nice day." She'd been saying those words to Renee for weeks. And each time, she meant them. Especially today. The only thing she wanted for Renee was a good life. She would keep that lifted to God.

Hannah handed the telephone to Brandon and watched as he chatted with his ex-wife. Slowly she walked over to the window. The sun hung proudly over the Pacific sky, heating the September day to almost ninety degrees on the coast. But she didn't need the earth's light to warm her. She was glowing in the midst of their news, flushed with the blessedness of their life.

She recalled the times she'd spent standing in the same space, wondering why God wouldn't answer her prayers, feeling as if she'd been deserted. But, she'd always known in her heart that God would never leave her. He was always there, just like He promised.

Thank You, Lord, she said inside. Her hands moved to her waist, and she rested her palms on her stomach. And like I promised, Lord, this child will be dedicated to You for his entire life.

A tear hung at the corner of her eye, but it wasn't like any of the cries she'd had before. These tears carried the fullness of joy.

Brandon came up behind her and hugged her. She hadn't even heard him hang up the telephone.

"Is everything okay?" she asked.

"Yeah," he said softly. "Renee just wanted to tell me that she was having the kitchen redone." He paused. "I wanted to tell her our news, but I didn't."

Hannah turned to him. "Why not? We don't have to keep it a secret."

"I wanted you to tell her." He grinned.

"We'll tell her together."

Brandon frowned just a bit. "I thought you'd be glad to let her know this news since she's been after you for years."

"That's Renee's thing, not mine. There was a time when I wanted her to disappear deep into the Pacific. But now I just want her to be happy."

His smile returned. "That's why we're so blessed."

He held her close again, and Hannah knew her husband spoke the truth. They were truly blessed, because God was faithful. He had heard...and answered her prayers.

## Discussion Guide
## "Baby Blues"

1. Why does Sarah ask Gayle to have her husband's baby? What do you think about Sarah's rationale and her choice of Gayle?

2. What are Gayle's motives for having Carl's baby? Are her intentions consistent with the will of God? How do you know? How do you know when your motives are in line with God? (*see Galatians 5:13, 19-23*)

3. Compare Carl's and Sarah's faith in God. Who's faith in God do you identify with more? Why? What lessons about faith can you learn from their experience?

4. What is the role of envy in the story? What does the Bible teach about the consequences of envy? (*see James 3:14-16 and Proverbs 14:30*) How is Sarah's and Gayle's friendship as well as their interactions after the birth of the child impacted by envy? When have you experienced envy? What have been the results?

5. How do Carl and Sarah finally resolve the issue of Gayle and Chris? Is it really over? How do you know? What issues in your life continue to surface even after you dealt with them? What is the appropriate biblical response to your situation?

## "Baby Blues"
### Bible Study/Discussion Guide
### Genesis 16:1-15; 17:15-22; 18:1-15; 21:1-14

1. How did Sarah take the matter of having a family into her own hands? What were the results of her actions? When have you pursued your own solution to a matter rather than looking to God for the answer? What were the results? What lessons can be learned from Sarah's experience and your own?

2. Abraham agreed with Sarah's plan. When have you agreed to a plan that did not come from God and what were the results? How should Abraham have responded to Sarah's idea? As a husband, did Abraham have any special responsibilities regarding the plan to have a child through Hagar? What does the Bible say about a husband's and a wife's respective roles in the family? (*see Ephesians 5:22-23*)

3. After Hagar became pregnant, how did she change toward Sarah? Why? When have you changed toward someone and why? How were your actions consistent or inconsistent with God's will? How do you know?

4. How much time passed between God's initial promise to make Abraham into a great nation (*see Genesis 12:2*) and the birth of Isaac? How have you responded when God's promise has not been immediately fulfilled? What lessons can we learn from the story about God's faithfulness? What lessons can we learn about what we should and should not do as we wait for God to fulfill His promises?

5. Who do you most identify with in the story? Why? How are you similar? How are you different? What lessons can you learn from this person that can be applied to your own circumstances?

## Discussion Guide
## "Traveling Mercies"

1. Barry asks, "How can I be sure I'm going to Heaven when I die?" According to the Bible, how is one saved? (*see Romans 10:8-10, Ephesians 2:8-9 and Acts 3:19*) Are you certain you will go to Heaven when you die? How do you know?

2. Compare Matt's response to Samaria's revelation of who she is with your own. What is the basis for your opinion of who she has been? How do her actions towards Matt challenge or confirm your perspective?

3. Matt says he needs to turn his nasty temper over to God. What about you do you need to bring to God so that He changes it?

4. What in Samaria's life causes her to question God? How does Matt respond to her concerns? What in your experience causes you to question who God is and why He does what He does? Have you searched the Word of God for answers? How does the Bible respond to your questions?

5. What lessons can you learn from the story about who your neighbor is and how to be a neighbor?

## "Traveling Mercies"
## Bible Study/Discussion Guide
## Luke 10:25-37

1. What does it mean to love God with all your heart, with all your soul, and with all your strength? How do you love God in this way? How do you fall short of loving Him like this? How do you know?

2. What does it mean to love your neighbor as yourself? When have you and when have you not loved your neighbor? How do you know?

3. What happened to the man as he traveled from Jerusalem to Jericho? Why was he vulnerable to attack? Have you ever needed someone's help? How did it feel? Did you receive help? If so, did it come from an expected or unexpected source?

4. Who were the Samaritans? (*see 2 Kings 17:24*) What was the relationship between Samaritans and Jews? (*see John 4:9*) Who would be a "Samaritan" to you? Who would consider you to be a "Samaritan?" How do you treat those you consider to be "Samaritans?" How did Jesus treat Samaritans? (*see Luke 17:11-19 and John 4:1-42*)

5. Why did the Samaritan help the man? What lessons can we learn from this about how to love our neighbors?

## Discussion Guide
## "A Sprig of Hope"

1. Compare Spencer and Taylor. How does Spencer break Dianna's trust? How does Taylor keep her trust?
2. Do you think Dianna and her family should have kept the rape quiet? Why? How do you think keeping everything quiet may have affected her healing process?
3. How does Dianna feel about seeing Spencer again? If you were Dianna, would you have gone to the event? Why or why not?
4. How do you think Dianna's relationship with God is affected by the rape? Have you ever suffered something that affected your relationship with God? How have you been able to receive the healing that Christ desires for you?
5. What does Dianna's rose garden symbolize?

## "A Sprig of Hope"
## Bible Study/Discussion Guide
## 2 Samuel 13:1-14:33

1. How was Amnon deceitful? When have you been deceived? How did it feel? When have you deceived someone else? Why?
2. How did the rape affect Tamar? Why? How did she express her feelings? Have you ever been violated in some way? How did you feel? If you were to meet Tamar today, how would you minister to her? What comfort does the Word of God provide those who have been abused? (*see Isaiah 61:1-3, Genesis 50:20 and Romans 8:28*)

3. How did the actions by David's sons reflect his own past deeds? (*see 2 Samuel 11:1-17*) Compare your actions to what your parents have done? Why do these similarities and differences exist? What hope does the Bible give us about our ability to break free from the sins modeled in our families? (*see John 1:12-13 and 2 Corinthians 5:17*)

4. What does the Bible say about the sin that Amnon committed? (*see Leviticus 18:6,9,11,29 and 20:17, 19*)

5. Why did Joab have the wise woman talk to David? Why was this an effective method to get his point across? Had this method been used with David before? If so, when? (*see 2 Samuel 12:1-7*) What lessons about communication can we learn from Joab and the woman?

## Discussion Guide
## "Lust and Lies"

1. How do Samson's choices in life contradict the call that God has given him? How do your choices affirm or contradict God's call on your life?

2. How is Samson trapped by his desire for beautiful women? What desire traps you? How could you safeguard yourself against this temptation?

3. What wisdom does Samson's father share with him regarding barrenness? When have you felt barren? What caused it? How did you respond? What lessons can you learn from this story about how to deal with being barren?

4. What is God trying to birth in you? How are you preparing for this blessing? How do you need to consecrate it, or set it aside, for God's purpose?

5. How is betrayal a theme in Samson's life, both in terms of how others treatment him and how he treats his relationship with God? How does betrayal shape him? Have you experienced betrayal or betrayed someone? How have these experiences changed you?

### "Lust and Lies"
### Bible Study/Discussion Guide
### Judges 13:1-16:31

1. Samson was a Nazirite. What does this mean? (*see Numbers 6:1-21*) How was he faithful and unfaithful to his consecration to God? Why? When have you been faithful and unfaithful to God's call on your life? Why?
2. How does Samson's wife manipulate him into telling her the answer to the riddle? How do you try to manipulate people? How did her manipulation impact their marriage? What have been the results of your manipulation?
3. What did Samson do because he loved Delilah? What have you done in love that was not right? What were the consequences for Samson and for you?
4. How was Samson betrayed in his relationships? How did he respond and why? When have you been betrayed or betrayed someone else? How did it feel? What were the consequences? What lessons can we learn from Samson's experiences of betrayal?

5. Did Samson honor God's investment in him? How do you know? Are you living your life in a way that honors God? How do you know? (*see Romans 12:1-2*)

## Discussion Guide
## "Sword of the Lord"

1. What does Joseph remember about the day of his father's funeral? He says that he remembers it "like it was yesterday." Why is his memory of those events so vivid? Do you have memories of how you been hurt? How do you respond to them? Does your response hurt you or help you? Why? How could you change the impact of these memories on your life?

2. Joseph comments that "sometimes the line is blurred between faith and foolishness." What does this mean? Do you agree? Why?

3. Joseph's mother asks how the fight for the town looks "through the eyes of faith." What does it mean to look through the eyes of faith? Have you ever experienced the difference between looking at a situation from a human perspective and then through faith? What were the differences? Why?

4. Joseph describes himself as a warrior. How does the Bible portray the Christian walk as a battle? What do we battle as Christians? How can we be victorious? What battles are you currently engaged in?

5. Compare the way that Faith, Joseph's wife, prays with how you pray. What is prayer to Faith? What is prayer to you?

What lessons about prayer can you learn from how she prays?

## Sword of the Lord
## Bible Study/Discussion Guide
## Judges 10:6-40

1. What evil did the Israelites do in the eyes of the Lord and what were the consequences? How have Christians today done what is evil in God's eyes? What are the implications of these actions? Have you ever forsaken God? If so, why? What were the results of your actions?

2. What is repentance? (*see Acts 3:19*) How did the people show God that they were repentant? How did the Lord respond? When have you repented? How did you show God your repentance? What is the Lord's response to a contrite heart? (*see Psalm 51:17*)

3. Who was Jephthah's mother, and how did this impact his family's treatment of him? How was God's regard for Jephthah different from his family's? Why was it different? Have you ever been treated poorly because of whom you were associated with? How did this feel? Who is the Jephthah in your family, and how is he or she treated? Why? How might God's regard for this person be different from your family's? How do you know?

4. Because of his background, some may consider Jephthah an unlikely person for God to use. What other examples are recorded in the Bible of God using an unlikely person to accomplish His will? (*see Joshua 2:1-24 and 1 Corinthians 15:9-10*) Has anything happened in your life that has made

you think that God cannot use you? What does the Bible say about this? (*see 1 Corinthians 1:26-31 and Ephesians 2:10*)

5. What qualities made Jephthah a godly leader? How is being a leader in the world different from being a leader according to God's Word? (*see Joshua 1:6-9 and James 3:17*) What prepared Jephthah for his leadership role? What leadership lessons can we learn from Jephthah? Is God preparing you to be a leader? How is He preparing you? What qualities make you a godly leader and what qualities do you still need to develop?

## Discussion Guide
## "The Best of Everything"

1. How does Hannah's unfulfilled desire to become pregnant change her? Why? Have you ever wanted something that you did not have and could not get? How did it feel? How did it change you?

2. How does Hannah's desire affect her relationship with Brandon? With Etta-Marie? With Pastor Ford? Why? How have your unfulfilled desires affected your relationships? Why?

3. Both Brandon and Pastor Ford look to the Bible to find consolation and insights. Have you ever looked to the Bible for answers? Why or why not? If you have, what did you learn? If you haven't, what questions would you like God to answer?

4. Pastor Ford asks Hannah if she truly believes that no matter how her situation turns out that God only wants the best for

her. Do you believe that God only wants the best for you? What does God say in the Bible about this? If you don't believe this, why not? How would believing this change how you understand and approach your current circumstances? (*see John 10:10, Daniel 6:19-24 and Psalm 32:10*)

5. Hannah prays in a number of places, including in her car and in the shower. Where do you pray? Why? What does the Bible teach us about how to pray? (*see Matthew 6:5-15, Luke 18:1-8 and John 14:12-14*)

## The Best of Everything
## Bible Study/Discussion Guide
## 1 Samuel 1:1-20

1. Why did Peninnah provoke Hannah? How did their husband's treatment of them add to their difficulties? When has someone provoked you? How did you react? When have you provoked someone else? Why? Were your actions biblically appropriate? (*see Romans 12:16-18 and Ephesians 5:1-2*)

2. When did Hannah experience ill treatment from Peninnah? When you have seen or suffered from someone's evil behavior while at church? How does the Bible explain the unfortunate reality of wickedness in the church? (*see Job 1:6 and Matthew 13:24-30*) If you were to meet Hannah today, what advice would you give her on how to withstand Satan's attack? (*see Psalm 37:1-4 and Ephesians 6:10-18*)

3. How did Hannah respond to Peninnah's provocation of her? How did this response affect her husband? When has your reaction to something impacted a significant person in your life? What could you do or change to improve the situation?

4. Hannah prayed to God in the midst of her misery. What do you do in the midst of your misery? How does this make you feel? How does the Bible teach us to respond to our troubles? (*see Philippians 4:4-7*)

5. Has God ever answered your prayers and given you what you asked for? When? How long was it before God answered your prayer? What was your attitude while you waited to see God's response? What attitude does the Bible teach us to have? (*see Psalm 27:14 and Isaiah 40:27-31*)